Risky Business

by

Patricia Campbell

Published by
Melange Books, LLC
White Bear Lake, MN 55110
www.melange-books.com

Risky Business ~ Copyright © 2014 by Patricia Campbell

ISBN: 978-1-68046-012-4

Cover Art by Angela Archer

ACKNOWLEGEMENT

Thank you, Ann Moore, for introducing me to your brother, Kenny Thomas.

Thank you, Barbara Bradley, for being the editor who is a dream to work with.

Thank you, Nancy Schumacher and the entire Melange Team, for making the process easy and smooth, and for the great book cover.

Also, I can't forget Molly Jebber, Sonja Gunter, Diana "DJ" Welker and Peg Colyar. You know why you are so important to me--you and all those wonderful and generous writers in SWFRW.

This book is dedicated to Kenny Thomas, for your thoughtful interview responses to my many questions. You are one of so many devoted funeral directors who perform a necessary and noble service, and who are too often the target of thoughtless jokes. Black humor is a natural human response to the fear of death and the unknown. Fortunately, honorable people, like you, help us through the most difficult and painful circumstances of our lives.

Chapter One

Uncle Jack's wake, Simi Valley, California

He was exactly the type of man Mariska was not interested in. Then why couldn't she stop staring at him?

Oh, God.

As if he felt her eyes on his back, he turned. Even from this distance, she could see that his eyes were a clear, deep blue. He acknowledged her with a tilt of his head and an amused smile.

The only reason she came to Jack's funeral and wake was for Bobby and her dad. Ordinarily she could have come up with some excuse to avoid ever being present at one. Funerals gave her the deep down creeps. She clenched her teeth and squeezed her eyes shut at the open casket.

Risky turned her attention back to her father to pick up the threads of their conversation.

"I'm telling you, Mariska, you're asking for more trouble. You can't keep daring the county to come after you for code violations."

"I know, Dad. But what could I do? I'd have to be heartless to leave the poor thing out in the rain, filthy, starving and covered with mud."

"You didn't have to give him a name, did you? You know what happens when you do that." He sighed and shook his head, but it didn't dim the love light shining in his eyes.

"I know. I can't help myself sometimes. Harley needed shelter from the cold rain. He was hungry. You should have seen his big, sad brown eyes. He begged me, Dad." She huffed and cocked a black eyebrow. "Who *is* that guy?" She pointed to the man talking to her cousin, Bobby. "The Viking warrior in the gray suit. He keeps looking at me."

Her father smiled. "He's probably wondering how much gunk you put on your head to make your hair spike up like that. Or maybe it's your overdone eye shadow?"

1

"Come on, Dad, who is he?" Why was she so mesmerized by his platinum blonde hair and big shoulders? Nobody had a right to look that luscious. Risky tingled, picturing how he'd look shirtless.

"His name's Chet Jensen. He goes by the nickname, Digger. He's Bobby's friend. They went to school together."

A nasty little snigger escaped her mouth. "Digger! What does he do, dig graves?"

"Close enough. Bobby asked him to handle the arrangements for Jack's funeral. He's the undertaker, but the name Digger comes from his days as a champion beach volleyball player."

"What! An undertaker?" Risky's vision blurred, her stomach flipped. "Oh, yuck, yuck, and yuck."

The handsomest guy in the room, a ghoul? That's a very good reason not to be attracted to him. So ... why was she?

Her dad reached out and gripped her arm when she gasped. "Are you feeling okay? You're pale. Sit down over here."

Risky brushed off her father's hand. "I'm ... all right. I think I forgot to eat this morning. Yeah, I haven't had anything to eat."

"Well, you stay right there, my girl. I'm going to bring you something from the buffet. It's no wonder you're skinny as a stick. Half the time you forget to eat before you go running." Clucking and shaking his head, he left her.

She wasn't skinny as a stick. At five-foot-eight, a hundred ten pounds was the perfect weight in her opinion. Anyway, she had to run ten miles a day to stay in shape for the L.A. Marathon. She could eat an entire cow and never gain an ounce.

Oh no! Please no!

The blonde ghoul strolled in her direction. She quickly swung around on the chair to face the opposite wall.

A gentle hand rested on her shoulder. A warm hand. A big hand. A hand that smelled so good. A deep, sexy voice that sounded so ... uuhhh. "I couldn't help noticing how pale you look." His touch should've repelled her—so why didn't it?

"I'm fine." She raised her eyes to meet his handsome, square-jawed face. A dimple appeared at the very corner of his mouth when he smiled.

She swallowed. "I ... uh ... I forgot to have breakfast this morning. My dad's bringing me something from the buffet."

"Funerals are often very stressful. May I bring you a soft drink or a club soda?"

Yeah, he'd know about stressful funerals, wouldn't he? He probably rarely crawled out of his coffin before the sun went down. "Yes, thanks, club soda."

At least that would get him to go away. Get his strong, delicious hand off her shoulder. She must be nuts. That was it. Her run-in with the animal control officer this morning before Uncle Jack's funeral had freaked her out.

Where in the heck was her father?

Digger returned with a glass of ice and a small bottle of club soda. "Would you like me to pour it for you?"

Mariska glanced at his eyes. Mistake. "Uh, sure, thanks." She crossed her legs against her tight, black leather skirt, and bounced her foot up and down. Her feet looked huge in her favorite black ankle-strap shoes with the clunky soles. God, were her feet that big? She uncrossed her legs and tucked them under the chair.

"Here you go." He handed her the glass. "Were you close to your Uncle Jack?"

"How did you know he was my uncle?" Heat flared in her neck and cheeks when she accidentally burped like a construction worker after a big swallow of the club soda. Mortified, she said, "Excuse me." Her scalp burned like a forest fire.

"Sure, don't worry about it." He grinned and rocked back on his heels. "Bobby told me Jack was your dad's brother. He claims you're his favorite cousin ... actually his favorite wacko cousin." He chuckled. "His nickname for you is Dog Breath?"

"Good old Bobby, master of tact and diplomacy. I'm his only cousin." Risky pounded her chest with her fist and a discreet burp escaped her lips. "Sorry. I don't always have such bad manners. And if I didn't feel so lousy right now I'd go over there and kick Bobby's behind." Her cheeks heated again.

He raised his eyebrows and grinned. "I see you're getting some color back."

"I didn't mean to say that out loud. It must be low blood sugar. Where the heck did Dad go? He was bringing me some food."

Jensen showed no sign of leaving.

"How're you doing, Dave?" He reached out to shake her father's hand after he handed Mariska a plate. "I've just had the pleasure of meeting your daughter."

"Chet. Nice to see you again, my boy. Too bad it had to be my brother's funeral that got the two of you together."

Together? Had Dad slipped a cog? There was no way they were together. An undertaker? Dad needed a drink. A stiff one. She'd never be in the same room with Digger Jensen again. *Eek!* Risky stuffed a meatball in her mouth to keep from saying something inappropriate. She'd keep her comments to a minimum in front of this guy.

"I was just asking her if she was close to your brother."

Dave chuckled. "I'll let her answer that. Excuse me. I need to speak with some friends before they leave."

Risky nearly choked on the meatball that grew bigger every time she chewed. *Dad, don't leave me with this guy. Please!* There was nothing to do but take a big gulp of club soda and wash the damn thing down.

Digger sat in the chair next to her. "Easy on the club soda. We both know what it does to you." He had a deliciously crooked and sexy smile.

Was he teasing her? There was no other way to account for his wink and twisted lips. She took a deep breath. "If you must know, I hated Uncle Jack, the nasty tempered old tightwad. He said if I didn't change my ways, he'd cut me out of his will. Hah! The old bastard never had me in his will in the first place."

Chet crossed his arms and chuckled.

She crossed her legs again, changed her mind and tucked her feet back under the chair. "Poor Bobby. There are probably so many restrictions and conditions on the old goat's money and property, he'll have to hire an army of lawyers to sort it out. He'll be lucky if he ends up with a dime." What happened to her vow to stop talking?

Digger sat back and laughed. He had a deep, sensuous, rumbling laugh. "You do have a way with words Ms. Williston. Bobby told me I'd like you, and I do. What ways of yours did your uncle object to so strenuously?" He extended his hand. "I'm Chet Jensen, by the way."

She failed at her attempt not to return his smile. "Risky Williston." *Oh, God, the feel of his hand.*

"Risky? Interesting."

"Not really." Her breathing rate increased when Chet eyed her as he would a candy bar. "Uncle Jack was nothing like my dad. Hard to believe they were brothers." She took a dainty swallow of the soda. "Jack thought it was over the top to have seventeen dogs at my small house."

Pleased at the surprise on his face she added, "Now you know why Bobby calls me Dog Breath. Anyway, as of yesterday I have eighteen dogs."

Chet raised his eyebrows. "I'm a dog lover myself, but eighteen? I'm afraid I see Jack's point. I can't imagine what it's like to clean-up after and feed that many dogs."

Tempted to say it couldn't be worse than cleaning up after a corpse, Risky pressed her lips shut and congratulated herself on her unusual restraint. Why did she care what he thought? She didn't plan to see him again once she escaped from the required after-funeral ritual. "My guess is, Chet, you'll never be in a position to find out."

He stood. "One never knows." He extended his hand again. "If you'll excuse me, I'm working today and need to get back to business. It was a pleasure to meet you, Risky."

She took his hand, and her breath caught as tingles went from his fingers straight to her girly plumbing. She needed to get out of there, and fast. Certain her nipples were standing at attention against her sleeveless black turtleneck, she feared drawing his attention there by looking down.

He squeezed her hand, flashed that dimple, and without a word he turned and made his way across the room.

What just happened? Risky's gaze darted around the reception, searching for her father. She gasped with relief when she found him. All she needed to do was tell him and Bobby she was leaving, say a polite good-bye to the grieving widow, five years younger than herself, other relatives, and get the heck out of Dodge.

* * * *

That he found Ms. Mariska Williston so alluring puzzled Chet. She resembled some kooky character on a TV series with her bizarre dress and makeup. Any thought that entered her head came right out of her mouth, uncensored. She had great long legs, but so did a lot of women who were much softer and prettier.

How intelligent could she be if she had eighteen dogs? A psychiatrist would have a field day divining the answer to that question. One thing he did notice—she didn't smell like dog breath, in spite of Bob's pet name. The fragrance of cinnamon surrounded Mariska.

Her scent triggered memories of the day he visited an open-air spice market on a back street in Kowloon.

Searching for herbal blends to use in the public rooms of the funeral home, he brought home pounds of specially mixed potpourri, heavy on cinnamon, made by an old Chinese woman who told him she blended her own herbs with secret ingredients used by ancient Egyptian embalmers.

The blend accomplished exactly what he hoped it would, giving the rooms an exotic freshness. Now he had a standing order with the tiny Hong Kong *doctor*. She shipped product to him every few months.

Chet had always loved the scent of cinnamon, especially that sensual scent surrounding Mariska. It had a hungry, sexy quality to it.

Yes ... Ms. Williston. When he'd placed his hand on her toned, muscular shoulder, an arousal that had long been M.I.A. shot through him. One thing Chet did know—he'd see her again.

Chapter Two

Risky's house on Box Canyon Road

A smile bloomed on Risky's face as the chorus of barks and howls surrounded her the minute she pulled her beat-up SUV into the driveway. Her babies welcomed her home.

Harley grinned at her through the sagging chain-link fence. Somebody must be missing him. Nobody would want to lose a great dog like Harley. First thing tomorrow morning she'd take him with her to the vet to see if he had a chip. Except for being way too skinny, he was a happy, friendly mutt. Risky strolled to the fence, knelt down and pressed her nose against his, dodging back in time to avoid his sloppy tongue. "How's my good boy?"

He wasn't her good boy. She had to keep reminding herself. Harley had somebody, somewhere. She'd go on the lost dog website again after she changed and took the dogs on their daily run. Maybe she had better eat first though. She'd need her strength, especially if she encountered the old curmudgeon living by the big curve down Box Canyon Road.

His daily rants were probably the highlight of the old hermit's life. He spent nearly all day sitting in that beat-up rocker on his front porch, waiting to exchange expletives with Risky. He'd probably sicced Animal Control on her yesterday.

Risky spent so much time pleading for more time with Claire Sandberg from the county that they could possibly end up best friends. If it weren't Sunday, Claire's doggy paddy wagon would most likely have been waiting for her return home. The woman had a soft spot for the dogs, and she'd been very patient up to this point, willing to stretch the rules, wait longer than usual for Risky to find their owners, new homes, or have them placed in a no-kill shelter.

The longer Risky had the dogs, and she really must stop giving them names, the harder it was to let them go. Not for the first time, she had a fleeting concern that she might be a teeny bit tweaked. Thank goodness, Bobby had given her their grandmother's old ramshackle homestead on Box Canyon Road rent-free. The sparse population of odd neighbors, some even weirder than her, was the only reason she dared take in all her strays.

The joyous yips and yaps grew into a welcoming chorus once she had the front door open. The grinning muzzles of Papillion twins, Mickey and Minnie; a miniature poodle, Brutus; a variety of mixed-breed poochies; and Slick, the naked Chinese Crested bounced around Risky's legs, competing for her attention.

Laughter bubbled from her throat. "Hey, cuties, I've only been gone two hours, not two weeks!" She knelt and put herself in range of a variety of excited tongues, all competing for the first kiss. Falling on her back, Risky allowed them to smother her with the kind of bottomless affection only dogs were capable of giving.

Shaken from her joy by loud pounding on the door, Risky sprang up, shushed the dogs and stood frozen.

"Risky, it's Clint, open up." He pounded again.

She yanked open the door while pushing dogs away. "Clint? What's the matter?" Her next-door neighbor's wide-eyed expression alarmed her.

His arm flew to the side. "Look up there!"

Risky's eyes followed Clint's pointing finger. "Oh, my God." Her stomach dropped like a stone at the lateral column of black smoke rolling over the rocky ridge of the Santa Susana Mountains. "I've got to get the dogs out of here."

Clint nodded. "I've already got some of the big ones in the back of my pickup. Let me help you round up the rest of the gang. We need to clear the road for fire trucks."

For a moment, Risky stood glued to the floor. Heart racing, she stared at the smoke.

"Move it, Risk! We don't have much time."

"Yes, okay, you're right. I'll put the little guys in my SUV. How many more can you take?"

"I've got six. A couple of the bigger ones won't let me near them. They haven't been here long enough to know me. Maybe you should just let them loose."

The thought of *her* dogs running free with a fire bearing down on them made Risky sick to her stomach. "I can't do that. If you can take three of the little ones in the cab of your truck, I'll get the others in my car." She scooped up the Papillion twins and Slick. She and Clint ran toward his truck. The now silent dogs stood staring through the screen door and fence.

Clint dropped the dogs onto his front seat then ran around to the driver's side and hopped in. "Are you sure you're okay to get the others?"

Risky waved in the direction of the road. "Yes. Go. I'll round them up. Be right behind you. I'll meet you in the parking lot at Star Market."

She ran around her SUV and flung open the back hatch. Harley had already jumped the fence. He headed right for her and bounced up into the vehicle before she had a chance to get the back fence gate open. The Doberman and the German shepherd obeyed her shouted, "Car!" the instant she let them out. Now, her babies.

* * * *

Risky barreled down the road. Nine dogs of various sizes stared through the back window at the column of smoke. Screaming fire trucks whizzed past. At the last turn before the market, she saw a bedraggled cat at the side of the road, ready to dart into emergency traffic.

Pulling onto the shoulder, Risky leapt from the front seat. The cat backed up, distrusting eyes wide. "Here, baby, I won't hurt you." She stopped for a moment to prevent the cat from bolting. Murmuring quiet reassurances, she approached the scared little thing. "Can I touch you?" Risky reached out. "Can I pet you?"

Just as she thought the cat was calming, another fire truck screamed past. The scraggly feline bolted for the brush and disappeared. Risky watched the flutter of branches as the cat ran farther from the road.

A fire captain's car screeched to a halt. The driver's side window slid down and her old schoolmate, Brad Tucker, stuck his head through the opening. "Did you lose one of your dogs, Risky?"

"No, a stray cat." She pointed in the direction she'd last seen it. "He ran away."

Brad shook his head. "You can't save 'em all, babe. You need to hightail it out of here. That fire is moving fast." He closed the window and drove in the direction of the last fire truck.

Risky jumped into her vehicle. When she slowed in front of Star Market, Clint was nowhere in sight. Yellow emergency tape blocked the entrance of the parking lot. Fire officials directed an evacuation helicopter about to land on the cracked, pot-holed asphalt.

"Is the road open to Simi?" She yelled above the clatter of rotor blades.

A uniformed man ran toward her. "It's still open for now, but you better not waste any time. With this wind, there's no telling which direction the fire will take. Get moving!" He slammed his hand on the top of her car.

Heart pounding, Risky rolled up her window and stepped on the gas. Everything she owned, everything including her purse and cell phone still inside Gramma's old house.

Chapter Three

Mortuary, 11:00 p.m.

Chet Jensen lounged with his feet on the balcony rail, outside his apartment above the funeral home. He stared into his glass of bourbon wondering, not for the first time, if he was in the wrong business.

He loved his work. Had from that first summer when he turned nineteen, and assisted his late Uncle Fred in this very building as a helper. He surprised everybody, and himself, when he switched his major to mortuary science.

His mother, Millie, cringed when he agreed to spend the summer working for Fred. To say she nearly had a fit of apoplexy when he told her he wanted to be an undertaker was a gross under-exaggeration. He could still see her stricken face.

Poor Millie, she still hadn't come to grips with the fact that he'd given up a full sports scholarship to pursue the macabre undertaking profession. She dreaded any social conversation that might prompt her to talk about her son the mortician.

Chet never called himself a mortician. It sounded too much like beautician or esthetician or electrician. He had to admit though, as soon as an attractive woman learned what he did for a living he was morphed into the polar opposite of *babe magnet*.

Today he'd met the first woman he'd been instantly attracted to since his days playing serious beach volleyball. Mariska Williston wouldn't have warranted a second glance then. Not like the bikini beach babes, all sun-bleached hair, bouncy boobs and eager grins, who'd taken very little convincing to a romp between the sheets with him.

At thirty-two, he still had no trouble doing a few sweaty sets of volleyball at Venice or Malibu Beach, and then being invited to accompany an eager young lady home. None of those women held his interest for more than a few days. If they tended to cling, all he had to do was invite them to sleep over in his apartment above Jensen and Jensen Funeral Home.

What was it about Risky, or Dog Breath, as Bobby called her? She was too tall, too skinny, and too odd for his tastes. But when he put his hand on her shoulder at her Uncle's funeral this morning he'd been unexpectedly aroused. To hide possible embarrassment he'd offered to get her a drink so he could distance himself for a couple of minutes.

The sun set at the west end of Simi Valley, nearly obscured by lingering smoke. Hills surrounding the valley still glowed a dull red from the brush fire that nearly got out of hand.

Chet took a long swallow of the bourbon, knowing it wasn't the answer to his heartache. This afternoon he'd received the body of a beautiful little girl. Three years old. Except for a small bruise on her forehead from the auto accident when her family fled the fire, she was the picture of a sleeping angel.

Performing his magic on adults and the elderly had never been a problem for Chet. Death waited for every living soul. Death, our most glaring certainty. His mission in life was to lessen the grief of the living by respecting and caring for their loved ones during a traumatic period in their lives.

But the little kids ... that was something he'd never get used to. Not if he did this job to the last day of his own life, which would be shortened if he didn't come up with something better than getting shit-faced to dull the pain.

A wife and children would be nice.

Beau brought a mellow smile to his face. Old Beau, half blind and deaf, slept most of the day, but always greeted Chet with happy panting and wagging tail.

Beau raised his head and gazed at Chet with his big, soft, brown eyes. Chet was sure the dog could read his mind.

Those brown eyes brought back thoughts of Mariska Williston. Eighteen dogs! Boy, oh, boy, did she need something to fill the gaps in her life, whatever they were. He took another sip of the fragrant, warm, comforting whiskey, and shook his head.

Against his better judgment, he added another blurp to his glass. He'd sit there a while longer and wait for full darkness. Then he'd get in his car and find a likely place for dinner. He didn't feel like eating alone in a public place. Take-out was the ticket tonight. Take-out was the ticket more often than not lately.

He grunted. Enough with the pity party. He stood, went inside, dumped the whiskey in his kitchen sink, and grabbed the car keys. Funerals, wildfires, dead toddlers! *Shape up, Digger. You chose this life.* Damned if he'd turn into a lonely old drunk.

* * * *

Box Canyon

Risky rolled the kink out of her neck from sleeping in her car last night, and surveyed the miraculous sparing of her home. The hills were blackened right up to her back fence. She reminded herself to take a big batch of brownies to the local fire station, and one to the animal shelter where she'd found Clint with her other dogs. They'd put her babies up for the night. Soon as she choked down some food, she'd go retrieve them.

Lord, how she hated to come up with something to eat. A lousy cook, but an aficionado with a can opener, she could rip open a plastic bag in the blink of an eye. Her coach at the runner's club told her she'd never make it through the marathon she trained for if she didn't make an effort to eat better.

From the corner of her eye, she saw a tall, sweaty, runner pound down the road past her house. He stopped, circled back, and headed down her driveway.

Now what the heck did this guy want?

The muscle-man came to a stop right in front of her then bent over and gripped his knees, gasping for breath.

"Risky? Ms. Williston?"

Wary, she took a step back. "Yeah."

He raised his head and aimed deep blue eyes at her. "It's Chet. I met you yesterday." He stared at her face, devoid of makeup, and her wet curly hair.

Wearing jeans and a baggy tee shirt, she'd just showered and changed from the clothes she'd slept in.

Risky leaned closer. "God, you look awful. What happened?"

He grimaced, raised his hands. "I'm ashamed to say I'm running off a hangover." He grinned when her eyebrows went up. He stared at her chest.

Crossing her arms, she gave him a snarky reply, "Too much celebrating at Uncle Jack's funeral?"

"No. I wasn't celebrating. It's a long story I'd rather not go in to."

"Good." She knew her words were clipped, but didn't care.

"You always this cheerful?"

"Look, Digger. My house almost burned down. I barely got out of here with my dogs ahead of fire. If it wasn't for my neighbor down the road, I'd be the one running off a snoot-full. I'm late for my run, and I still have to get my dogs from the animal shelter. So, excuse me if I'm not Miss Sunshine."

Chet leaned back and roared with laughter. Hardly the reaction Risky expected. "What's so funny Bjorn, or is it Sven?"

"Chet will do." He smacked her lightly on the shoulder. "I'm starving. Have you got any coffee?"

"No. The only thing in the house is warm Gatorade and past-dated Yoplait." She returned his grin. "Am I supposed to feed every pathetic drunk who straggles in?"

"No, just this one." He pulled his wallet from his back pocket. "I'll buy you breakfast then help you bring your dogs home. Deal? I could use the company of a gorgeous woman this morning."

Risky snorted. "You came to the wrong place for that."

"I don't think so. Deal or no deal?"

Risky shrugged and raised her hands. "Why not? I'm hungry, you're hungry, and I could use some help with my babies. Where's your car?"

"At the funeral home."

"That's miles from here. How far did you run this morning?"

"Until I barfed, and then I turned around." He winked. "I thought it would never happen."

Risky made a sour face. "You're disgusting, in more ways than one, Digger." What was it about this guy? She should tell him to take a hike. "Okay, get in my car. I'm starving, too."

When they settled in the battered SUV, Chet said, "This car smells like smoke and dogs."

"Yeah? Well you smell like Mrs. Murphy's prize goat."

Chapter Four

Risky nearly doubled with laughter listening to Chet relate stories about his first year at Cincinnati College of Mortuary Science. The last thing she expected was to find anything funny about death.

Chet took a breath. "Even though I'd spent a summer working for my uncle, I almost had a heart attack when the dead old woman's arm few up and grabbed me around the neck." He chuckled. "I was looking for the vein near the clavicle to insert the formalin tube."

Risky polished off the last of her pancakes. "What amazes me, Digger, is that I could eat breakfast while you were telling me this yucky stuff."

"If funeral directors didn't nurture a sense of humor we'd never be able to do our jobs. Every day is a reminder that we'll be lying on the slab ourselves one day."

"Stop. I don't want to think about it."

"It isn't something we need to think about. Once we reconcile ourselves to the fact that life will end, we should live the best we can. Enjoy every day."

"Do you," she paused. "Enjoy every day?"

Chet took a while to answer her. He cut into the last of the big stack of pancakes that accompanied his Grand Slam.

This guy had the appetite of a roustabout.

His blue gaze pierced her. "No, actually. That's why I had a monster hangover this morning."

"Uncle Jack's funeral upset you that much? If you knew what an S.O.B. he was, every day of his miserable life, you wouldn't have cared." She emphasized her words with a firm head shake. "He didn't deserve your sympathy."

Chet set his lips in a straight line. "No, it was something else. I'd just as soon not dwell on it. Sorry to put a damper on the morning."

"Oh, forget about it. Enjoy your pancakes. I never saw anybody eat so much at one sitting." She flashed a teasing grin. Chet wasn't such a bad guy, except for the fact he was so gorgeous and masculine. She couldn't see herself ever wanting to be with a man that much better looking than her. Everybody would assume he'd taken pity.

Why she even had these thoughts, she wasn't sure. True, every time she looked into those eyes of his, she got warm tingles where she squirmed on the chair, but no way was she interested in anything beyond friendship, and not at all sure she wanted that. They were too different. Sheesh, he was probably a Republican.

* * * *

Chet leaned back with a sigh, and patted his stomach. "I feel almost human again. Tell me about your obsession with rescuing dogs."

He didn't miss the offended look in her eyes, and wished he'd phrased his question better. "Sorry. That didn't come out the way I meant. I really am interested. Like I said, I'm a dog lover myself. My old dog, Beau, looks after me every day. He's fourteen now, and he disapproves of bourbon. I can tell by the scowl he gives me."

A smile curved on Mariska's lips. She shook her head, drank some coffee. He sensed a reluctance, and suspected she didn't feel comfortable telling him things about her private life.

She set her cup down. "It goes way back, and it'd take too long to tell you today." She looked at her watch. "They want me to pick up the dogs before noon. I'm going to leave a couple of them there until day after tomorrow. For some reason, more people go to the shelters after a fire or earthquake to find their dog or look for one to adopt."

Chet pushed his plate aside and leaned on his elbows. "That's good, isn't it?"

"Sure. I want them to be adopted, but if nobody does, I have to bring them home. After a few days, they'll be euthanized if they don't find an owner. I'd never forgive myself if one of my rescues got put down."

Her face took on a beautiful glow of determination. It transformed her. The lack of yesterday's bizarre makeup and spiky hair let her natural beauty shine through. Her prominent cheekbones, which tended to present an angular look, now softened with a warm blush, turning her into a big-eyed waif. Someday he'd have to learn what motivated her to go above and beyond the norm when it came to those animals.

Chet puzzled over why he'd had such a powerful physical attraction when they met yesterday. It was a mystery. She was unique and interesting, but certainly not a woman with whom he'd be interested in pursuing a physical relationship. Friends only. If that.

He patted the table. "Okay, let's drive over to my place, and I'll follow you to the pound. I'll take my car and help you get your orphans home."

She stood and tugged her tee shirt. "Where's your place?"

"Jensen and Jensen. The funeral parlor."

Her eyes got bigger. "You live at the funeral home?"

He laughed. "Yes, I do. Don't look so shocked. Beau and I have a nice apartment upstairs on the third floor."

She wrinkled her nose and shrugged. "Whatever floats your boat."

Chet slid out of the booth, picked up the check. "It doesn't float my boat, Risky. It's the free rent and short commute that sold me."

She slung her purse over her shoulder. "Yeah, I guess you couldn't beat the proximity to work."

"You'll have to come and see my place. You can meet Beau, and give me your opinion on my decorating skills. I transformed the former attic into a very functional living space. I've got a nice balcony with a great view of Whiteface and the valley. The only downside is the big beam over my bed. I've knocked my head on it answering calls in the middle of the night." He twisted his lips and rubbed his head.

After he settled the check, she fell in step with him as they crossed the parking lot and pointed at the distinctive mountain. "When Bobby and I were kids we hiked there then climbed all the way to the top of Whiteface. Uncle Jack and my dad grounded us for a month. It was worth it though."

"Why'd they ground you?"

"Oh, some kids got stranded up there once, and one of them got a rattlesnake bite. I think they were pissed because our bikes got stolen. We left them at the bottom of the trail."

"Bobby told me about some of your adventures. He claims you were the instigator most of the time."

"What a wuss. He always tried to lay the blame on me."

* * * *

It was unlikely she'd ever see the inside of Chet's apartment. She bit her bottom lip and imagined he probably designed it after the Addams mansion. As tall as Lurch, it was no wonder he banged his head into the ceiling now and again. Mariska giggled at her bizarre thought process as she pulled into the parking lot behind Jensen and Jensen.

Chet had the door open as soon as she parked. "I'll run upstairs and check on Beau. Shouldn't be more than a couple of minutes."

"Shake a leg, Lurch."

"Very original, Lilith."

"Lilith?"

He jogged toward the back stairs, and hollered over his shoulder, "You figure it out."

She smiled at Chet's Lilith reference. She often watched re-runs of the old *Frasier* series while snuggling on the couch with her babies. A distinct picture of Frasier's morbid wife had her questioning her own preference for somber, morose dress. She looked more like someone who lived in a mortuary than Chet did.

He sprinted up the stairs two at a time then quickly reappeared carrying a medium-sized brown dog. After setting him down by some bushes at the bottom of the steps, he waited while Beau whizzed then took the stairs two at a time up to the third level again.

Impressed by his stamina, Risky understood how he'd run so many miles that morning and ended up passing her house on Box Canyon Road.

Out his door and down the steps in less than a minute, Chet pulled a clean shirt over his shoulders, on his way to a big black Lincoln Continental. He hopped in and fired up the engine.

Definitely a Republican.

Chapter Five

"Grow yourself a pair of balls, boy!"

That statement, and the smack on his shoulder following it, was the last exchange Chet had with his dad before the stiff-necked Marine pilot headed out to his last deployment in Afghanistan. Colonel Chester Nimitz Jensen never returned. He was killed within hours of his arrival at Kabul airport by a roadside bomb.

Sir, as Chet called him since childhood, had been teasing him about overcoming his mother's horror at his decision to study mortuary science. "It's your life, son. Not hers. She'll get over it. Life is too short not to do what you want."

Life proved far too short for Chet's dad that broiling hot day in a godforsaken hellhole in the Middle East. A career officer, Chet's father had lived the life he wanted. His wife complained every time he deployed, but she accepted the fact he did what he loved, what he truly believed his destiny to be. Chet missed Sir more than he ever imagined he would.

Millie Jensen hadn't accepted her son's life choice yet, but Chet figured she'd come around. He was the mirror image of Colonel Chester Jensen. Chet gazed at the tall young Marine in his parent's wedding picture. He could have been looking at himself.

Sir smiled when Chet told him what he wanted to do. He told his son it was about time he thought of something else besides beach volleyball and getting laid. "Not that I disapprove of either pursuit, but it's time for you to settle on something other than practicing to be a playboy."

* * * *

Jensen Chapel

Chet approached the parents of the little girl whose funeral was this afternoon. The young couple, totally devastated, sat in the front row of Jensen's chapel. They held their infant son, their stunned faces and tearstained eyes staring into space.

He went on one knee before them, placed a hand on the father's arm. "It's time to start. We're going to open the doors for your family and friends. Okay?"

They nodded numbly. Then the little girl's mother stood and handed the baby to her husband. "Wait. Please. Wait just a minute. I want to say goodbye to her first."

Chet took her arm and led her to the child-sized, open, white casket. The girl rested against pink satin padding and a ruffled pillow. A beautiful child, without a visible mark on her, small hands folded across her chest, her arms hugged a well-worn lavender walrus. A tiny gold ring with an opal birthstone gleamed on her finger.

The girl's mother kissed her dead child on the cheek. A tear dripped on the girl's collar. "May I have her ring?" the young woman asked after a few moments.

"Of course you may. After the service I'll remove it before we close the casket."

"I'd like to have it now. I need to hold it."

Chet's chest hurt. He didn't want the girl's mother to watch him pry the ring from the child's finger. He placed his arm around her shoulder and turned her toward the bench where her husband and baby waited. "You have a seat. I'll bring it to you."

Once the woman sat, Chet went back to the child and removed the ring. He said a silent apology, gave the little hand a soft pat and rearranged her arms. She looked as peaceful as she had before. He stood there a moment to regain his composure, and then returned to the woman. With gentleness, he lifted her hand and placed the ring on her palm then closed her fingers around it.

"Thank you," the woman whispered. She dropped her head on her husband's shoulder.

Chet stood before them, quietly waiting. Finally, the child's father met his eyes. "You can open the doors now. Thank you for your kindness."

The man's words clogged Chet's throat and nearly brought tears to his eyes. The couple, in their deepest despair, had thanked him. Close to his own age, he guessed, they had suffered an unimaginable loss, yet they had thanked him. His heart and mind roiled with sadness and gratitude. Moments like this reinforced his decision to make this his life's work.

* * * *

Box Canyon Road, 6:00 p.m.

The moment Risky answered the phone she recognized her mother's voice. Anya—drunk. Her usual state. Her mother only called to complain about her current boyfriend, her latest ex-husband, or ex-boyfriend, and to ask for money ... or a place to stay.

Exhausted after hours of cleaning her house and yard, airing the house of the stench of smoke, and caring for her dogs, Risky was in no mood to talk to her. "I'm busy. What do you want?"

"Is that any way to talk to your mother? After I nearly died bringing you into this world, and then spent the best years of my life caring for you?"

Risky's head fell back. She stared at the peeling paint on the ceiling of her old-fashioned kitchen. Lips pinched in a straight line, she wouldn't answer that unanswerable question. The question she'd heard all her life.

"Mariska? Are you there?"

The note of desperation in her mother's voice failed to touch Risky's heart. "Yes, Anya, I'm here. What do you want?"

"I wish you wouldn't call me by my first name. You sound so distant and unloving when you do that."

"I'm busy, Anya," she repeated through clenched teeth. "What do you want?"

A long-suffering sigh groaned through the phone. "I need to stay at your place tonight, sweetheart."

Risky sighed in return and clenched her teeth harder. After a lifetime in the U.S., her mother still spoke with a distinct Russian accent. It became more noticeable when she was drunk. Like now. "No."

"But why, *myah sladkaya?*"

"Because you're drunk. Because I have a lot of dogs. Because you hate dogs. The only time you call me your 'loved one' is when you're wasted. It's been a long day. I'm tired. I'm going to bed. Call somebody else."

She was sure the next call Anya made would be to Risky's dad, Dave. Always Anya's last resort, Dad never failed to help her even though she'd married him for one reason only—permanent residence in the U.S. It took him years to come to grips with that truth, and Risky knew he still loved Anya in some secret place in his heart.

So sad. Risky saw that love in his eyes when she asked him years ago how he could love a woman who'd treated him so badly.

"Your mother is a damaged, fragile woman, Mariska." He took her hand, lifted it to rub against his cheek. "I fooled myself into believing that if I just loved her enough, if we had a child, if she felt safe for the first time in her life, she'd be happy. I was wrong. She'll never change. She can't."

Maybe her father could forgive Anya, but Risky would always despise her mother for what she'd done to her.

Chapter Six

Twenty Years Ago

Mariska sobbed, she held her palms together in front of her trembling mouth. "Please, mama, please don't hurt the puppy." She shrieked and fell to her knees on the hard tile floor.

Anya held the whining puppy by the scruff of his neck. "How many times have I told you not to drag one of these filthy creatures home?" She held the fat, yellow pup over the kitchen sink. "I told you the next time you brought home an animal I would push it down the garbage disposal. Didn't I, Mariska? Didn't I warn you?"

Mariska reached forward and grabbed her mother's leg. She dropped her head and screamed, "Mama, please! Please, I'll never do it again, I promise. Please don't hurt the puppy. It's not his fault."

"Mariska, I have to teach you a lesson once and for all." Anya held the puppy above the churning garbage disposal while her six-year-old daughter stared, screamed and pleaded.

The back screen door flew open then slammed shut with a loud bang. "What the hell is going on in here?"

Mariska raised her tear streaked face. "Daddy, Daddy, please don't let Mama hurt the puppy. Please, Daddy."

Dave took two long strides across the kitchen and lunged for the pup just as Anya moved her arm down. He snatched the terrified animal from her hand and dropped it on the floor next to Mariska.

She pressed the dog to her heaving chest, snuggled it against her cheek. The pup whimpered and trembled against her, dribbled pee down the front of her shirt.

Anya yelled as Dave snapped off the garbage disposal. "I told her. I told her before not to bring those filthy beasts into my house." She raised her arm as if to strike her husband.

Dave grabbed her wrists and pushed her hard against the sink. "You're drunk! Goddammit, Anya, you're drunk." She struggled and kicked. "Where's the bottle, Anya? Where did you hide it this time?"

Anya screamed obscene curses at her husband. She yanked and pulled at her arms, trying to free herself from his grip. She threw up her knee and stomped on Dave's foot, hissing and spitting like a feral cat.

Frightened and nauseated, Mariska scooted backward until she'd moved as far away from her parents as she could, her bony back pressed against the bottom cupboard doors. She pulled up her skinny legs and rested her chin between scabby knees, and peeked through her lowered lashes as the all too familiar scene between her parents played out.

"Mariska," her dad said through bared teeth, "Go to Bobby's house. Don't come home until I call."

Anya screeched and kicked. "I hate you, David! Do you hear me? I hate you! You're *govno* on the bottom of my shoes! Govno!"

Mariska scrambled to her feet, stumbled, and then regained her balance. The frightened pup struggled against her arms. She raced through the screen door and ran across the large back yard, through the hedge, and into the pasture behind the big house where Bobby, his dad, and new stepmother lived.

Mariska didn't like Uncle Jack. He never smiled. She wasn't welcome in Bobby's house when Jack was home. Her daddy and Uncle Jack worked together. They left for the warehouse in the same car this morning. If Daddy was home, Uncle Jack was home, too.

Instead of going to Bobby's house, she stopped at the far edge of the back lawn, climbed the ladder to the tree house and crawled into a far corner. She shivered in the cold autumn air. "It's okay puppy. My daddy won't let Mama hurt you." The soft puppy warmed her chest and stomach. She stroked his tiny body and hummed in his floppy little ear, "Good boy, good boy."

It had been dark a long time when she heard the creak of the ladder. Her back stiffened when a scary shadow loomed in the hatch. She sighed when a gravelly voice whispered, "Risky? Are you up here?"

"Uh huh."

Bobby crawled through the low opening leading to the interior of the tree house. The weak beam of his flashlight bounced off the walls when he tossed a quilt inside. "Uncle Dave is looking for you. How long have you been out here?"

"I'm never going home again. Never," Mariska whispered, her lips against the puppy's neck. "I hate her."

Bobby sat beside her, pulled up the blanket and flung his arm across her shoulders. "It's okay. She's not there, Risky. Uncle Dave took her back to the place." Bobby petted the pup. "He wants you to come home. Can I hold the dog?"

"Uh huh." Mariska held it toward her cousin. "He's so little. He's afraid and hungry."

Bobby set the flashlight on the floor with the beam pointed to the ceiling. An eerie light filled the small space. "I can keep him for you. Your dad asked my dad if it'd be okay. Marsha doesn't like it, but she doesn't like anything. Dad told her to shut up. He gave her some money, and she went to the mall to shop."

Bobby was talking about his latest stepmother. Risky couldn't remember how many he'd had. His real mother died when he was born. Bobby was her very best friend in the whole world. He was a lot older than she was. He was nine, and he always looked out for her. She'd been so disappointed when her daddy told her she couldn't marry Bobby when she grew up because he was her first cousin.

Bobby bumped his shoulder against hers. "Let's give him a name." He held the pup up and gazed into its big glossy eyes.

Mariska shook her head. "No. Daddy says I shouldn't ever give them names because I can't keep them. Mama won't let me keep them."

"Ah, come on," Bobby said. "I told you I'd keep him for you." He rubbed the pup's nose against his. "How about Buster?"

"That's a dumb name."

"Well, you come up with a better one then."

"I like Galahad."

Bobby snorted. "Now that's a dumb name for a dog, if I ever heard one." The puppy whimpered. "See, he doesn't like it either."

"It's a good name. I saw a movie about King Arthur and his knights. Galahad was a good knight."

"He was not. He stole the king's wife."

"He did not."

"He did too."

"Did not."

"Did too."

"That's all you know, Bobby. Lancelot stole the queen. So there." She punched his shoulder and raised her chin. "Boys are so dumb."

"Are not."

"Are too"

"Are ..."

"You kids get down from there," her dad's voice called from the bottom of the ladder. "Mariska, it's late and you haven't had supper."

Risky and Bobby crawled to the low doorway. Bobby backed down the ladder, clutching the pup in one arm. She followed him with the flashlight.

Dave plucked her off the ladder before she reached the bottom. "Come here, my beautiful girl." He wrapped her in a hard hug. "Let's go home." Daddy ruffled Bobby's hair. "Bob, you take real good care of that pup." He set Mariska on her feet.

With her small hand in his big one, they crossed the pasture. Once they were through the hedge and beyond Bobby's hearing range, she asked, "Is Mama sick again?"

Chapter Seven

She was eleven when her mother came home from *the place*. Mariska feared the happy years with her daddy were over. Daddy had visited Anya every week during the entire five years. He reassured her that her mother was completely well and ready to come home. She wasn't so sure. The memory of the puppy and the garbage disposal glared bright in her mind.

An adult dog now, Galahad had boundless energy and an unquenchable appetite to fill his sturdy, rust colored body. Risky and her dad worked together to construct a comfortable backyard doghouse. Gally had free rein over their yard and Bobby's yard because even though fences surrounded three sides, no fence stood between the two homes. He'd never been allowed inside either house.

Dave told his little girl she could keep her pet as long as he lived outdoors. Someday her Mama would come home from *the place*. Risky knew Anya couldn't abide pets of any kind in her house.

Risky often wondered why her mother hated animals. Her daddy tried to bring up the subject with his wife, but it sent her into a downward spiral of drunken hysterics. They never talked about it again.

* * * *

Bobby pumped the pedals on his bike, riding hard to get past his cousin, but Mariska had strong legs and wouldn't be left behind.

She screamed, "You can't beat me, Bobby! I'll get there a half a block before you do."

He laughed between huffs for air. "Not this time, squirt."

"I'll bet you five dollars, zit face." She knew the hated nickname would push him to catch her. But he'd fade right at the end, and she'd have another five dollars in her dog treat budget.

He was hot in her wake. "I hate you, you skinny butt brat."

She giggled as she worked her never-fail race strategy on him, allowing him to catch her, and even get a little ahead. Then she put on a burst of energy and sprinted ahead, screeching to a halt in front of Burger King.

Head down, gasping, Bobby pulled up beside her. "Here's your five bucks. Now I'll have to sit and watch you stuff your face with a Whopper while I starve to death."

Risky smacked him on the shoulder. She hopped off her bike and handed him the chain and lock. They padlocked the two bikes together against the wrought iron fence and went inside. "That's okay, Bobby, I'll let you owe me. Again." She laughed and dodged his punch. "Come on, slowpoke."

They ordered then took a booth by the window where they could watch their bikes. Bobby carried the tray to the table, and slid it across the shiny plastic surface.

Risky looked up. "Mama's coming home today."

"I know. Are you scared?"

Lips pressed together she unwrapped her burger. "I don't know. She's my mom, but I wish Daddy would leave her at *the place* forever."

Bobby took a long draw on his cola. "My dad says she's crazy. He doesn't know why Uncle Dave ever married her, besides the fact she was knocked up."

"What?"

"Knocked up. You know, pregnant."

"She was not."

He snorted. "Oh yeah? You're the math whiz. You figure it out. They got married in January and you were born in August. How many months is that?"

She gave him a superior glance. "That's seven months. I was premature, smarty."

"Like hell."

"I'm going to tell Uncle Jack you're swearing again."

"Go ahead, snitch, then I'll tell Uncle Dave you mooned half the soccer team with your skinny ass." He nearly choked on a mouthful of fries.

Risky slapped the table. "That was an accident, Bobby, and you know it. I told coach I needed a safety pin."

"If you had some meat on your bones you wouldn't rattle so much when you ran."

"Yeah? If you'd quit doing that with your *thing* you might not have zits all over your chin."

Bobby paled, and she regretted her words the minute they left her mouth. This was something she wasn't supposed to know. She'd come upon him accidentally when climbing the stairs to the tree house. Eyes wide with shock she stared, swallowed, and slowly climbed down the rickety ladder, afraid she'd make a noise and he'd see her.

It wasn't as if she'd never seen his *thing*. They'd skinny dipped in the above-ground pool every summer since they were toddlers. It's just that she never saw him do what he was doing to it before that day.

Bobby swallowed and put down his half-eaten burger. "You did see me last week, didn't you? You called from the bottom of the tree, but I heard you on the ladder. You're not going to tell my dad are you?"

She clamped her mouth shut and stared at the table, shaking her head. "No. I didn't mean to say anything. I'm sorry, I ... what were you doing?"

"I'll tell you when you get older."

"Tell me now."

"No. I'll get in trouble if I do."

"I won't tell anybody, I promise."

Risky sat wide-eyed with shock as Bobby leaned across the table to whisper an explanation about what boys sometimes do. She asked him if all boys did it, or just some?

Bobby said that as far as he knew all boys did it, and it felt really good when you were all finished. Sometimes he couldn't wait to get home from school so he could run out to the tree house and do it again. Sometimes he did it in the shower. His face took on a deep red glow when he explained to her what happened.

She leaned in and whispered, "Can I watch you next time?"

Eyes big, Bobby shook his crimson face. "Not unless you want your dad to kill me—after my dad kills me."

"Why? Is it a bad thing to do?"

"I don't think so, but I'm not sure." He flopped against the back of the booth bench and sipped the dregs of his cola. "I don't want to talk about it anymore."

Risky played with the last few fries.

They carried their trays to the trash bin, dumped the wrappings and leftover food, and then headed out to their bikes.

Halfway home Risky speculated, "I bet big boys do it too, Bobby. I bet even dads do it, if it feels so good."

She thought how unfair life was. Boys got all the good body parts and stuff.

"I don't think my dad does. He spends half of his life in the bedroom with Lannie. He doesn't have time for anything else except eating and going to work."

"Maybe he does do it, and he lets her watch."

"Nah. She probably does it for him. At least sometimes it sounds like it to me."

Shocked, Risky peddled in silence for a couple of blocks.

Bobby glanced at her. "Are you mad at me?"

She shrugged and shook her head. "No. I'm worried about my mama coming home today."

"You can come to the tree house later and tell me what happens. Okay?" He turned on his street and waved.

* * * *

Mariska took a bath, dressed in clean cutoffs and a new tee shirt. Then she straightened the living room and waited for her dad to bring her mother home. Mama would only be there for the weekend this time. If she did okay, the people at *the place* would let her visit longer until she could stay all the time.

She'd refused to visit with her mother the past five years, and only spoke to her on the phone a few times. She wondered if Mama looked the same. Anya used to be beautiful, with her black hair and big brown eyes.

Dismayed when she studied herself in the mirror, Risky saw that she looked more and more like Anya every day. Daddy told her she was beautiful, and should be proud of her dark, gypsy looks. Why couldn't she have blonde hair and blue eyes like the popular girls?

The car pulled into the driveway, and the motor to the overhead garage door groaned. Risky's heart pounded. She sat on the couch, her hands clamped between her shaking knees.

The door to the kitchen opened. "Mariska? Are you here?" Daddy's voice called.

"I'm in here," She answered with a trembling croak. She jumped up as her dad entered the room. "I gotta go to the bathroom. I'll be right back." She raced to the hall, afraid she'd fall before she got inside the small powder room next to her bedroom. She leaned against the door and swallowed the raw fear that overcame her the minute the screen door squeaked. Her mother was home.

Chapter Eight

Simi Veterinary Clinic

Mariska pushed the rolling mop bucket down the hall toward the kennels. She glanced through an open exam room door and stopped short when she recognized Chet. He leaned over a dog on the examination table, petting and speaking in a soothing voice.

"Digger?"

He straightened and turned to face her. His blue eyes red-rimmed and devastation covered his handsome face. For a moment, he stared blankly, as if he didn't recognize her. He nodded, swallowed, and tears slid down his cheeks.

Risky dropped the mop handle and rushed into the room. "Is that Beau?"

Chet cleared his throat and nodded, his attempt to speak failed.

"Chet, what happened?" She tentatively reached to touch the unmoving dog. "Is he sick?"

He dropped his head and pulled a couple of tissues from the box on the end of the table. "No, he ..." Chet mopped his eyes and blew his nose. "He fell down the balcony stairs. I turned to close the door, and he fell. It's my fault. I should have been holding him."

Overwhelmed with sadness and compassion, Risky turned and squeezed his arm. "Oh, I'm so sorry, is he ...?"

Chet embraced her before she had a chance to ask if Beau would be okay. Her ear pressed to his chest, his gasping sobs gave her the answer. Her own eyes burned with threatening tears. Mariska had never seen a man cry. "Chet?" She hugged him.

The vet entered the room. He stopped short at the sight of Mariska comforting Chet. He cleared his throat. "Do you want me to give you a few more minutes, Mr. Jensen?"

Chet straightened, released Mariska, and shook his head. "No."

Mariska wiped her eyes and turned to face her boss. "Are you going to ...?" The syringe in his hand stopped her question.

Chet placed his hand tenderly on Beau's head. The old dog's milky blind eyes rolled in the direction of his master's voice. "It's okay, old boy. You don't have to feel the pain anymore. I'll stay right here with you." He kissed Beau's gray muzzle. Chet's tears dripped on his beloved companion.

Risky's hand flew to her mouth to stifle her gasp. She reached for Chet's hand, grasped it and squeezed. Then she moved closer and put her arm about his waist.

A voice from outside the door called, "Who left this mop bucket in the middle of the hall?" A woman's head appeared through the open door. She paused, backed out, and closed the door while murmuring a soft apology.

Mariska stayed by Chet's side while he said goodbye to his faithful old dog. Her heart a frozen lump behind her ribs, her ability to breathe seemed to shut down.

Finally, Beau was at peace. Chet drew in a sharp breath and slumped onto a bench next to the table. Risky sat next to him, never letting go of his hand. The vet left, quietly closing the door to the inner clinic.

After several moments, Chet turned his ravaged gaze to the woman next to him, seeing her clearly for the first time. "What are you doing here?"

"I work here."

"Oh." He looked at their joined hands. "Thanks, for ... uh ... thanks." He let her hand go and rubbed his face. "Wow, I really lost it. I've had him for almost fifteen years. I wasn't prepared for this."

Tears brimmed on her lashes. She glanced at the lifeless form of Beau and rubbed Chet's arm. "It's okay. I know how you feel."

Chet blew a deep breath between tight lips. "What happens now?"

"We can wrap him in a blanket, and you can take him home, or if you prefer, leave him here and we'll send him to the crematorium."

An ironic chuckle escaped Chet's mouth. "My god, I didn't cry this bad when Sir was killed in Afghanistan."

"Sir?"

"My dad. He was a colonel in the Marines, killed by a roadside bomb. I was just twenty at the time." He rested his head on the wall behind his chair, rolled it slowly from side to side. "I guess it was because I always expected it might happen. It's something you think about a lot, if you're in a military family."

Risky had no answer or comment on his revelation. She didn't know anyone in the military, even though it was impossible not to be aware that many

American soldiers were in harm's way. "I'm sorry."

"I'd take Beau home, but I have no place to bury him. I guess I'll have to leave him here."

"You could pick up his ashes later, or I'll bring them to you." She stood, drew in a shaky breath, and rubbed her palms on her jeans. "Would you like me to tell Dr. Larry?"

Chet stared at Beau. "Yeah, I'd appreciate it."

Risky touched his shoulder. "I'll be right back." She crossed the small room and opened the door to the clinic.

After a short time, she returned. "My shift is over. Why not come home with me? I'll fix something for dinner, and you can help me with my babies. Maybe later we can take them for a run."

Chet sighed and stood. "I don't want to leave Beau here alone."

"I'll carry him to the back, and Dr. Larry will take care of everything. He won't be alone." She opened the door to the clinic then stepped to the exam table.

Chet lifted Beau and placed him in her arms. "Should I wait here?"

She noticed for the first time that he was dressed in a business suit. "You live close by. Why don't you go home and change into your running clothes? I'll follow you, and then we'll go to my place."

* * * *

Risky's house on Box Canyon Road.

Chet stepped from the car right into the happy commotion of dogs jumping, bouncing off one another, and barking to greet Risky's return home. He watched her jog to the fence and reach for them as they jostled for her attention. An involuntary smile tilted his lips. Ms. Williston had a house and a yard full of dogs, and she worked in a veterinary clinic!

Chet required order in his life. He could never live in the middle of such a circus of noise and disarray. Mariska obviously thrived on it. He studied her slender back and bottom as she leaned over the fence talking to her dogs. She didn't have a spare ounce of flesh on her bones, but still managed to look feminine and sexy.

She turned at his approach. "Do you think they might be happy to see me?" Her eyes sparkled then dimmed. "I'm sorry. I didn't mean ..."

He rubbed Harley's big head. "Hey, they're crazy about you. That's nothing to be sorry for. I'll bet you come home to this joyful greeting every day."

Risky grinned and nodded. "Yep."

"I envy you."

She pulled him in the direction of her front door. Her strong, slender fingers sent a relaxed, warm sensation through him. "Come on in. The little guys in the house need to get outside before they pee on the floor. They know what's going on out here."

From all the excited scratching sounds, there couldn't possibly be a speck of paint left on the inside of the door. He'd only had a brief glimpse in her house the day he'd help her transport the dogs home after the fire. He had no idea what her living conditions were.

Risky opened the door. Four little dogs danced on their hind legs yapping and vying for her attention. She knelt and gathered them close. Her spontaneous laughter excited them even more.

Chet grinned at the sight. "You must feel like a million bucks every time you open that door." He reached out to touch Slick, the hairless Chinese Crested. "You are one funny looking dog."

Risky stood and glared. "They understand English, you know. His name is Slick. You hurt his feelings."

He winked and directed his comment to Slick, "I beg your pardon, Slick. I had no idea I was in the company of such an educated fellow." He picked up the little guy and allowed him to lick his face.

Risky grinned. "That's more like it." She stepped back so the dogs could make a beeline for her scrap of lawn. Once they were done she stepped inside, and they bolted past her.

She pointed to the sofa. "Have a seat. How about a glass of wine? I picked up a bottle of Shiraz at Star Market the other day."

Chet headed toward the sofa. The cluster of dogs followed his every step. "Nothing ever sounded so good, Mariska. Thanks." He looked at the well-worn couch and hesitated for a moment. Once seated the skin on his back prickled as he imagined all the dog hair coating the butt of his sweats.

His bottom had barely reached the cushions when all four dogs were shoving for space on his lap. He laughed aloud for the first time all day.

Mariska returned with two beautiful crystal wine glasses of ruby liquid winking in the afternoon light.

She stopped and grinned. "Hey, you fickle little traitors. The first good-looking guy shows up here and you're all over him? I'm heartbroken."

Chet reached above the crowd on his lap for the glass she extended in his direction. "Beautiful glasses." He raised his elbow high and took a sip. "Very nice wine, too." Was he really the first 'good looking guy' to show up in her house? He doubted it. In spite of her bizarre hair-do and coal black eyebrows, he found Mariska very attractive.

Risky Business

"The glasses belonged to my dad's mother. She left me a bunch of old stuff. Bobby's still green with envy. I have her complete set of Royal Bireley crystal and Royal Doulton china. I rarely have an excuse to use them."

"Whoa, take good care of that stuff, it's worth a fortune. The plates alone probably cost three hundred dollars each."

Her eyebrows flew up. "Gee, thanks. Now I'll be afraid to touch it. How do you know so much about it anyway?"

"My mother's a collector. She loves to browse antique stores, and used to drag me with her until I got too big to drag." He chuckled.

"Chet? Are you a mama's boy?"

"Guilty. I'm Mama's only boy."

Risky pressed her lips together and smirked. "I'd never have guessed." She raised her glass. "To Beau."

"Beau." Chet smiled sadly. "Never a better dog lived." His eyes dampened.

Risky sat at the other end of the couch and all the dogs except Slick hopped to her side. "You found a new friend, I see." She nodded at the Chinese Crested.

"So it would seem." Chet ran his hand over Slick's soft hairless back, and flashed him a smile. "You are very handsome, my man. How could I have been so insensitive?"

Risky laughed. "Yes, he is. As for dinner, the only things I know how to cook are spaghetti and meatballs or a cheese omelet. You pick."

Chet set Slick on the couch cushion next to him and stood. "An omelet sounds just right. I'll help with dinner?"

"Great. Follow me." She led him to her old-fashioned kitchen.

"Holy smokes! I haven't seen a stove like that since I was a kid. In Italy, we rented an old villa near the base. My mom loved all the old appliances in the kitchen." He strolled to the antique Weir gas stove and ran his finger along the enamel-warming shelf. "It's a treasure."

"This used to be Gramma's house. Uncle Jack and my dad were born here. They played on that old set of monkey bars by the dog run out back." She walked across the room and pointed to a drawer that she opened with a downward tilt. "Do you know what this is?"

"A flour bin?"

"That's right. And this?" She opened a cupboard with wire shelves.

"No. Other than a cupboard, what is it?"

"It's a cooler. The shelves are chicken wire, and cool air circulates up from the area beneath the house. She also had an ice box, but since the iceman no longer cometh, I had to buy a refrigerator."

Chet grimaced. "Eugene O'Neill. That was one grim play."

She brightened. "Hey, I have an idea. If you want to help me, why don't you feed the dogs? My kids out back eat dog chow. You'll find some twenty-five pound bags on the back porch. Their dishes are lined up outside the screen door. Just fill them to the top."

"Sure. What about water?"

"The hose bib has one of those dog licker thingamabobs on it. They can get themselves a drink anytime they're thirsty."

"Sounds like a plan. What about these little guys?"

"They're very fussy. I'll take care of them, and then I'll fix a cheese omelet for us, okay?"

"Sounds great."

Mariska set dog dishes against the far kitchen wall as Chet came back inside. "Here you go, babies."

"All taken care of. What do you want me to do?" He proceeded to the sink and washed his hands.

"I have some bagels in the fridge. Pick the kind you like and put a couple of them in the toaster oven. This will go fast. We can eat at the little table in here."

Chet stepped around the noshing dogs, wiped down the table with a wet paper towel then placed their wine glasses on the battered wooden surface. He washed his hands again before getting to work on the bagels. By the time the bell on the toaster oven dinged Mariska was dishing up their omelets. During their simple dinner, he got up and toasted himself a second bagel.

Risky poured the rest of the wine into their glasses. They finished eating in companionable silence.

Chet grinned. "That hit the spot. Thanks for feeding me and cheering me up."

"You're welcome. Now I'm putting you to work. I usually take the dogs out in two groups for their evening run, but with you here we can run all of them together. Harley's the only big guy who needs to be leashed. The others will stay right with me, but those four dozing over there all have to be on the leash." She pointed to the little dogs that'd flopped on the floor to sleep in front of their empty dishes.

"By my count, you're down to ten dogs. Four in the house and six out back. How'd you manage that?"

"I'm friends with the animal control officer, Claire Sandberg. After the fire a couple of months ago, she helped me find new homes for some of them, and the vet clinic placed the rest."

"Are the others up for adoption?"

"Yes, but not many people want big dogs. The cute little ones are easier to place." She pointed to the four across the room. "Those are *my* babies. They're not going anywhere."

Chet carried their plates to the sink. "I'm ready whenever you are." He turned on the tap, lowered the stopper and squirted liquid soap in the sink.

"What are you doing?"

"Washing dishes."

"Don't do that, Chet."

He caught an edge in her voice, turned off the water and wiped his hands on a paper towel. "Don't you want to do the dishes first?"

She frowned. "No, let's go before it gets dark. I'll take care of the dishes later." Risky brought their empty glasses to the sink.

"I hate leaving the kitchen in a mess."

"Hey, Lurch, it's my kitchen, okay?"

He pursed his lips at her outburst. "Okay."

"I have to change my shoes." She left the room.

Chet scratched his head and shrugged. He'd done something to annoy her. Damned if he knew what.

By the time they had all the dogs rounded up and out on the road, the sunrays lowered on the hilltops. Risky ran with the four small canines on leashes, and Chet held Harley's lead. The other big dogs fell into line without being told.

A half mile along the road, they neared the bend. Risky told him the Old Grouch's house was at the turn. Sure enough, the elderly man rocked on his front porch glaring and grumbling as they got closer.

He shouted and raised his fist. "You keep them damn dogs off my lawn!" He picked up an ancient shotgun and held it aloft.

Risky made a face at him. "Put a sock in it, Oscar!"

"I'm calling the sheriff on you goldurn hippies right now!" He stood and waved his cell phone.

"Go ahead, you old skunk!" She laughed and kept running.

Chet jogged alongside her. "You know that guy?"

She chuckled. "I don't know his name. I call him Oscar. His reason for living is to wait for the dogs and me so he can wave his gun and yell at us. He called Animal Control once when one of the big boys raised a leg on his oleander."

Chet didn't like the menacing threat in the old man's warning. "You're the one who should call the sheriff."

She flapped her free hand. "He's harmless. Once, before dawn, I saw him sneak up the driveway and drop a big bag of kibble on my front porch. The dogs went nuts, and he high-tailed it in his old truck. It solved a mystery as to who was leaving dog food at my door."

"You live in a very interesting neighborhood, Ms. Williston."

She shot ahead of him, and he enjoyed the involuntary tightening in his groin when he stared at her tidy bottom and muscular calves in the lowering light.

"Yes I do, Mr. Jensen. Great, isn't it?"

He grinned. "Yes, better than great."

Chapter Nine

Jensen and Jensen Funeral Home

Mariska approached the front door of the mortuary, stopped, took a breath, waited for the jitter in her stomach to go away then reached for the ornate handle. She pulled it open and tiptoed inside. Eerily quiet except for soft elevator music, the place looked, well, dead. A nervous giggle escaped her mouth before she could stop it.

She was about to leave when a voice asked, "May I help you, young lady?" She pressed a hand to her thumping heart, and turned to see a kind looking elderly man with an abundance of snow-white hair approach from a side room.

An unwelcome memory threatened her fragile composure. She'd been here before. She'd seen this man before. No! No, she didn't want to remember that day.

"No, Mama, please, I don't want to." Risky dug in her heels and tugged against Anya's painful grip on her arm. She yelped when her mother's hand tightened. It hurt.

"Anya, please," Her father whispered.

"You listen to me, you ungrateful, spoiled brat. Madame Petrovska did her best to make a ballerina of you, you clumsy child. She deserves your respect." Anya yanked her arm and pulled her toward the open casket.

Forced by her mother to take ballet lessons at the age of four, when all she wanted to do was run and play with Bobby, Risky had hated every minute of her exhausting, dogmatic, and often painful ballet exercises. She'd pleaded with her daddy to allow her to quit, but he'd taken her mother's side, saying that if she took the lessons it would make Anya happy, and might bring them closer together. Risky didn't want to be close to her mother.

"Anya, perhaps we should leave," her father said. "The long funeral is over, and it's been an ordeal for everyone, especially a young child. Let's go

home now."

"She will do as I say, David! You've spoiled her since the day she was born." Anya dragged Risky to the edge of the casket. *"Look at her! Look at this beautiful, old woman who devoted so many fruitless hours to make a dancer of you."*

Risky squeezed her eyes closed and struggled against the steel grip of her mother's hand at the back of her neck. She would not look at the hateful old crone no matter how long her mother forced her to stand there. Suddenly, she felt herself being lifted and tilted toward the corpse.

"Kiss Madame goodbye. Do it now, Mariska!"

Risky's eyes flew open. Terror stricken, she gagged then urinated on the floor and the front of her mother's dress. Anya set her on her feet and slapped her face.

"You monster!"

"That's enough." Her father pushed Anya aside and lifted Risky into his arms while his wife sputtered and protested. *"We're leaving."* He hurried from the room and offered a murmured apology to the solicitous funeral director.

The kindly man said, "It's quite all right. Please don't concern yourself."

That had been over twenty years ago, and now she was staring into the face of the same man.

"Oh ... I ... uh ... is Chet Jensen in?"

His beneficent smile put her at ease. Here was a man who actually looked the part of an undertaker. Not at all like Digger who looked like some mythical Viking god.

"Mr. Jensen is off today. May I be of assistance?"

"I told him I'd stop by this afternoon. He didn't say he wouldn't be here. Maybe I misunderstood."

"Oh, no, he's at home. His apartment is upstairs in the back. Would you like me to ring him?"

"You don't have to do that." She pointed at the small box she held. "I have a package for him. I'll just take it to his, uh, place." She started to leave by the front door when the nice man pointed to the hallway.

"You can go right through that way, Miss."

No way was she going any further into the funeral home than necessary. "No, that's okay. My car's out front. I'll drive around to the back. Thank you."

He clasped his hands at his waistline and bowed slightly. "You're most welcome. Have a nice evening." Unexpectedly, his smile broadened and he winked.

What was that all about? "Uh, thanks. You, too."

Risky returned to her car, set the box on the passenger seat and drove around the Spanish style building to the back lot. Chet's apartment door was open at the top of the stairs.

She carried the box with Beau's ashes to the bottom of the steps then paused to look up when she heard voices.

A shapely redhead stepped through the doorway. "Okay, honey, I'll see you Saturday. Don't be late. You know I hate greeting guests without a handsome man at my side." Her hand rested familiarly on his bare chest.

Chet laughed. He nearly filled the doorway. Shirtless and barefoot, he wore snug fitting bicycle shorts. "Millie, darling, have I ever disappointed you?" He kissed her cheek.

She smiled and turned. "There's always a first time, sweetheart."

Risky stood on the bottom step, unable to move. The redhead approached. She could barely lift her feet enough to step out of her way.

The woman was movie star stunning. "Oh, hi there. You here to see Chet?"

If Digger was into cougars, he'd picked a good one.

The woman's form fitting tank top and stretch jeans emphasized a perfect figure. Flawless skin glowed as if she'd just had a vigorous workout.

That let Risky out of the picture—not that she was in the picture—not that she wanted to be in the picture.

Her face heated. She fought to erase unwelcome visions of wild sex from her brain. Speechless, she glanced from the woman to Chet and back again. "Um ..."

"Go right on up. I'm finished with him for today. He's all yours. I'm Millie, and you're ...?"

"Ri ... Ri ...," She cleared her throat. "Mariska Williston. I was just ..."

She laid bejeweled fingers on Risky's shoulder. "Go right on up, honey. Chet mentioned he was expecting you." Millie turned and waved at a grinning Chet. "Bye, sweetheart. You be nice to this young lady."

"Bye, Mil. See you Saturday." He motioned for Risky to come up.

She almost expected him to say, "Next!"

Eyes glued to the stairs under her feet, Risky climbed. Her legs leaden, the steps felt spongy under her meager hundred-plus pounds. Embarrassed at her intrusion on the intimate scene, she swallowed a lump the size of Slick, and plodded upward.

"Hey, Dog Breath. Glad you're here early."

What? No shower between rounds? Hop right to it?

"I ... uh ... got off early. Sorry, I didn't know you had company." She thrust the box toward him. "I gotta go."

"Wait. I'd like you to come in for a few minutes. I'll shower and take you for dinner." He tucked the box under one arm and extended a hand to her.

Risky shook her head with conviction. "Oh, no, I ..."

"Oh, come on, Mariska. I promise I don't bite."

A bite from Chet didn't sound so bad, but she never liked seconds. Planning to go back down the stairs, her body took over control of her brain, and she stepped inside. "Okay then. I'm sorry I disturbed you and—"

"—Millie? She's my ..."

Like a crossing guard, she thrust her hand forward. "That's okay. None of my business." She dragged her gaze from the front of his shorts, cursing her disobedient eyes.

Chet cocked his head for a moment of confusion then his blue eyes danced, and a big sexy smile lit up his face. The dimple at the corner of his mouth twitched. "Have a seat. I'll just be a couple of minutes."

Her mouth watered at the sight of his departing back. He had a small half-moon of sweat below the waistband of his bike shorts. The stretch fabric emphasized a perfect butt to complete the picture of male perfection.

Warmth flooded her insides from her hips to her ribs.

Risky looked at her chest in horror. She pressed her palms against her tingling nipples. What was going on with her? Whatever it was, it wasn't welcome.

Her gaze darted around the small living room. Not a single thing out of place. In fact, it didn't seem like anyone actually lived here. The magazines on the glass-topped coffee table were arranged into a precise fan shape. Coasters protected the surface of end tables that didn't show a single speck of dust.

The only thing juxtaposed in this room was Beau's empty dog bed in the corner. She swallowed remembering Chet's tears shed over Beau. At the very least, it proved him human. That could be good—or bad.

The sound of the shower conjured visions of water running down Chet's naked chest and legs. And running down ... Stop, Mariska, don't go there! No! No! No!

She slapped her leg hard enough to hurt, stood, and paced.

Oh, God.

Risky halted in front of his bedroom door. It stood slightly ajar. She listened, made sure the water was still running, and then pressed one finger to the edge very cautiously. She snatched her hand away. What was she doing? She just wanted a peek. That was all. What harm could come from a quick peek into his bedroom?

She took a deep breath and pushed open the door. As orderly as the living room—she couldn't even detect the sparkle of a dust mote in the sunray slanting past his drapery. The bed was made. Not a wrinkle. Hmmm. Was she wrong about Millie, the vah-voom cougar? She jumped when the shower went off and hurried back to the couch.

Chapter Ten

Chet grinned into the shower spray. He was pretty sure he knew, from Mariska's blush and unease, what she imagined when she saw him with his mother. Millie was nineteen years older than he was, but she looked a good dozen years younger than her actual age. She'd always been gorgeous. Sir had been crazy for her and loved having her on his arm at any occasion, private or military.

He rubbed himself dry, stepped into clean shorts and went to his bedroom. A pair of jeans and a New York Jets tee shirt completed his outfit for the evening.

Risky looked about as relaxed as a stone carving on his couch. He'd let her stew a while before telling her the babe she caught him with was his mom. He welcomed her discomfort. It could only mean one thing—she was attracted to him. Great. The feeling was mutual.

She looked up. "That was quick."

"I said I'd just be a couple of minutes." He shoved his wallet in his back pocket. "Have you ever been to the Korean Barbeque on L.A. Avenue? It's really good."

She stood and stuck her hands into her pants pockets. "No. Is that where we're going?" She backed up a step as he approached and stopped so close she had to tilt her chin to see his face.

He placed his hands on her shoulders. "You look great, Mariska."

"I do?"

"Never doubt me." He put an arm around her shoulders and walked toward the door. "And thanks for bringing Beau's ashes. I'm going to take them to the beach tomorrow and scatter them along the water's edge. Beau loved the beach before he lost his sight. He tried to horn in on every volleyball game."

"He did?"

"Yep." He opened the door. "Want to go with me?"

Her head went up and down like a bobble-head doll. "Yes."

He reached out to straighten a picture, a fraction of an inch, hanging on the wall next to the door. Then he held her hand and walked beside her all the way to the bottom of the stairs. "Let's take my car."

"Okay."

Chet opened the passenger door and invited her inside. She slid across the soft leather seat. "Nice."

He caught her staring at his flat belly when he put the keys in the ignition. The powerful engine purred to life. Her hands glided over the burl-wood panel on the dash. "Are you a republican?"

He barked a short laugh. "What?"

She flashed a sappy smile. "Never mind."

Chet chuckled at Risky's question. Glancing sideways, he noticed her hands clenched in her lap. She stared out the window as if in a trance.

He often had that effect on women, but for Mariska to react that way was a happy surprise. She was no flighty Valley Girl, but a grown woman. A woman he was very interested in getting to know better.

He ran a finger down her arm, and she nearly jumped off her seat. Uh huh, a lot better.

Chapter Eleven

Korean Barbeque

Risky watched Chet turn the strips of meat on the grill in the center of their table, the chopsticks in his hand as efficient as a pair of tongs. He'd done this before. Probably with that Millie person. She would not ask him about the redhead. No, never, ever.

A diminutive waitress in ethnic Korean dress set a tray of butter lettuce leaves on the table. She raised her eyes to Mariska's. "You know how make lettuce wraps? Mr. Jensen show you. He here many times."

Chet smiled at the pretty girl. "Thank you, Min Cho. I'll take it from here." He took Risky's plate, lifted a lettuce leaf with his chopsticks and laid a couple of strips of meat on top of it. "You can wrap the lettuce around the meat as it is, or add one of these sauces."

Mariska reached for one of the sauce dishes. Chet's hand shot out. "Maybe you'd better dip your chopstick in it first and put a drop on your tongue. That one's pretty hot." He pointed at the various dishes. "This one's on the sweet side, and they get hotter and hotter until you get to that one."

She shrugged. "I like spicy food."

"Okay." He cocked an eyebrow. "It's up to you, but that one's more hot than spicy." He took a spoon and drizzled a small amount of sauce on his meat from the dish in the center.

* * * *

Risky pursed her lips and sniffed. She didn't need Chet to warn her about what to eat. One of her favorite dishes was Jamaican Jerk Chicken, and that rated pretty high on the heat scale. She poured a generous spoonful of the sauce on her meat, rolled it up in the lettuce, and took a healthy bite.

44

Her teeth closed over the mouthful. She didn't know which was worse—the shock or the tightening of her throat. She couldn't swallow it, and she couldn't breathe. Her nose burned and began running, tears formed in her eyes. She glanced quickly at Chet to see if he was watching.

He glimpsed then raised his hand to signal the waitress. Risky prayed he was summoning her to bring more cold beer.

"Min Cho," he said when she hurried to the table, "I'd like a side order of kimchee and some of my favorite pickles."

She dipped a quick nod and left.

Chet took a long swig of his beer. "Have you tried kimchee? Most Americans don't care for it. It took me a year or so to get past the smell of it when we were stationed in South Korea, but now I really like it. I'll put a dab on your plate."

If Risky swallowed the boiling fire from hell in her mouth, it would burn a hole right through her stomach, all the way to a place she didn't want to think about. Heart pounding, she clenched her teeth, raised a finger, and pointed to the restroom sign. She slid from the booth.

Shoving through the swinging doors, desperately looking for the sign to the women's room, she turned the nearest door handle to discover it was the men's. She didn't care at this point. She ran to the nearest stall, gagged and spit into the toilet. Gasping, Risky fell back against the side wall and nearly cried with gratitude as she sucked stale bathroom air into her screaming throat and lungs. By now, she would have welcomed the hideous fragrance of skunk.

She flushed, opened the door with caution, peeked into the short hallway then made a beeline to the other door. It had to be the women's restroom. Please, God. At the sink, she splashed water in her mouth and on her lips. They felt twice their normal size. Afraid to look in the mirror, she grabbed a couple of paper towels from a basket between the bowls, saturated them with water and held them to her mouth then her eyes.

A fresh, frosty bottle of Korean beer stood in front of her plate when she slid back into her side of the booth.

Chet constructed another lettuce wrap for himself. "You okay?" He twisted his lips as if trying to prevent a smile.

Boy-oh-boy was she tempted to throw a fist in his smug face. "I'm great. Thanks for ordering me a new beer."

He took a bite of his wrap, dished up what looked like garbage from a bowl in the center of the table, and dropped some on his plate. "Like to try the kimchee?"

"I don't know. What is it?"

"The Korean national dish—spiced fermented cabbage. You could call it extreme sauerkraut."

She wrinkled her nose at the smell. "I'll pass." She pointed to the other serving dish. "What's that?"

He smiled. "Ah, yes. These are really good pickled cucumbers. They're sweet and salty. A good taste contrast to the spicy dishes."

Risky spooned up a generous portion of the pickles, took a healthy mouthful, chewed, and chased them down with cold beer. She'd never tasted anything so good. Her mucous membranes cheered as the wonderful combination rolled down her throat. "Um, good."

She'd punch him in the face some other time.

He lifted a lettuce leaf. "That first wrap was probably a little too spicy. Why not make another one?"

She chewed some more of the cooling cucumber. "Okay. I'll give it another shot." Using her fork, she took a couple of beef strips from the gas grill and dropped them on lettuce. Wisely avoiding the hot end of the sauce line-up, she chose the one Chet said was the sweetest.

He leaned against the back of the booth, picked up his beer and raised his eyebrows. "Good?"

Risky swallowed. "Very. Maybe I'll try a bite of the kimchee. Just so you don't think I'm chicken."

He grinned. "Mariska and chicken—that's an oxymoron." He put a small spoonful of kimchee on her plate. "Go ahead, I dare ya."

She took a nibble. Made a face, and swallowed some beer. "Yuck. It tastes as bad as it smells."

"Like I said, it takes some getting used to."

In a lighter mood, Risky and Chet made plans for the next day. They'd meet at his car by eight in the morning. She needed to be back in time for her afternoon shift at the vet clinic. He assured her she wouldn't be late.

They parted in the back parking lot of the mortuary. She'd half-expected Digger to invite her to his apartment, but he smiled and walked her to her car. He waved as she backed out then took the stairs two at a time.

* * * *

On the way to Malibu the next morning

Chet pointed to the small, insulated bag on the floor next to Risky's feet. "There's a thermos of hot coffee in there if you want some."

"I'm fine for now. I've been up since before six. It takes me an hour to get the dogs fed and settled every morning. I drank at least three cups of coffee already."

"I also brought chilled juice and a couple of muffins."

She reached for the bag. "The muffins are calling to me. As usual, I had breakfast hours ago, and that was only a bowl of Cheerios. The minute you said 'muffin' my stomach growled."

Chet smiled to himself and remembered the day of Bobby's dad Jack's funeral. Risky had come without having breakfast or lunch. He'd confused starvation with grief when he saw her pale face. Her milky complexion contrasted sharply with her jet-black hair and dark eyes, making her appear perpetually wan.

"Help yourself. On the way back we'll grab a quick lunch. You'll have plenty of time to get to work."

Her skin was luminous and beautiful, flawless in texture, and drawn tightly over prominent cheekbones. She artfully accented her dark eyes with shadow, but her generous mouth lacked lipstick. Naturally pink, and sensuous, when she smiled his heart made a little blip.

"Thanks for coming with me, Mariska."

She faced him, and mumbled through a mouthful of muffin, "Happy to." A few crumbs flew from her lips on the 'to.' She blushed, put her hand over her mouth and swallowed.

Chet laughed at her embarrassment. "Sorry, I shouldn't laugh, but you're cute when you blush."

"Yeah, I'm a real eye-catcher." She snorted and stared out the side window.

He briefly touched her shoulder, and she turned. "You are, you know."

She squinted as if confused. "I'm what?"

"An eye-catcher."

"Hah, so is Camilla Parker-Bowles."

He gave the steering wheel a light smack. "Knock it off."

"Knock what off?"

"Putting yourself down. It's the same as calling me a liar, or worse, a shallow flatterer with an ulterior motive."

"I ... didn't mean ..." Her cheeks glowed bright red.

Chet shook his head and squeezed her shoulder. "Forget about it. I must be touchy because of our mission today."

They drove in silence for some time. "Let's stop there on the way back." Risky pointed ahead to a small country store tucked into a wide spot on the twisty road. "Every time I drive Topanga Canyon Road I plan to stop there, but I never have."

"Okay. Their sign on the front says they have sandwiches and cold drinks." He pressed his lips together then said, "Look, Mariska, I'm sorry I bit your head off back there."

"I already forgot about it. You should, too."

Chet sighed and rocked back and forth in his seat. "Yeah, thanks."

Not long after, they spotted the gleam of the Pacific in the distance. It promised to be a perfect, cloudless morning. When they got to the beach, Chet found a good parking spot. They stepped out of his car, took off their shoes and rolled up their pant legs. Chet picked up the box with Beau's ashes. They trudged across the warming sand.

Risky took his hand and they exchanged melancholy smiles. Chet's heart squeezed at her kindness. She was the most interesting, complex woman he'd ever met.

They sat for a while near the water's edge. The tide was coming in, and got closer with each wave until it touched their bare toes. Chet stood and held his hand out to haul Mariska to her feet. He opened the box and took a handful of the contents, stepped forward and let the small grains fall slowly from his hand. He held the box out to Risky.

She took a handful. "They're really not ashes, are they? It feels more like sand." She stepped close to an approaching wave and let them drift into the water as it receded.

"It's almost entirely bone. There may even be a recognizable piece in here. They have to be crushed after cremation so they can be put in urns or scattered."

"I never knew that."

"Most people don't. They're usually sealed in an urn, when you receive them, and you never actually see or touch them." He winked surreptitiously and spoke from the side of his mouth, "We're breaking the law here, so let's stroll up and down the beach while we do this."

"It's illegal? But, people scatter ashes all the time, in lots of places."

"They rarely enforce the law. I suppose if we were on private property, and didn't have the owner's permission, we could get cited for it." He trailed a handful in the water as they walked.

"Why is it illegal?"

"It goes way back. People think it's bad for the environment, or that the ashes are somehow contaminated. In fact, they're sterile."

Risky reached for some more of the vastly dwindling cremains in the small box. "I have a few dogs buried around my yard. That seems worse than scattered ashes, but it's legal."

Chet tipped the remainder of the box into the breeze, and let the last of Beau blow along the sand. "Laws often don't make sense. Once they're on the books they tend to stick like ticks."

Risky and Chet stared out to sea. A faint gray shadow on the distant horizon revealed one of the many Channel Islands.

Chet put an arm around her shoulder and turned her in the direction of the parking area. They strolled slowly across the sand, each lost in their own private reverie.

* * * *

Risky found the sandwich from the Canyon Market tasty and filling. Chet took the cold juice from his bag, and they ate at a rustic redwood picnic table under the shade of a gnarled live oak tree. When they were finished, Chet picked up their trash and dropped it along with Beau's empty box, into a large waste can next to the store.

At the funeral home, Chet parked next to Risky's car. When she got behind the wheel, he waited until she was seated and belted-in then leaned into her window. He brushed a soft kiss on her temple. "See ya, Dog Breath."

Her pulse pounded, but she masked her reaction by wrinkling her nose. "See ya, Digger." She backed out of her space and waved as she headed for the street on her way to work at the veterinary hospital.

She wondered about Saturday. Chet was to escort the Magnificent Millie someplace. It wasn't likely she'd ever know. In fact, she didn't want to know.

Chapter Twelve

Lost Canyons Golf Club, Simi Valley

Chet stood in the reception line next to his mother. He wore a white tuxedo jacket, white shirt, and black pants. The annual gala fundraiser provided scholarships for children of wounded veterans.

Millie worked tirelessly for various military causes. Her swept-up red hair revealed an elegant neck. A green sequined cocktail gown showcased her youthful body. She and Chet made a striking couple.

A grizzled soldier in full military dress shook hands with Chet. "My God, boy, you're the image of your father."

Chet had heard similar comments several times that evening. "Thank you, General. I take that as a high compliment."

"What business are you in, son?"

"I'm a fu ..."

Millie reached for the man's hand. "General Wayne! How very nice to see you. Is Mrs. Wayne here this evening?" Her gaze scanned the room. "I haven't seen her for some time."

The old general lifted Millie's hand and brushed a gallant kiss across her knuckles. "She couldn't make it this evening. I'll tell her you asked after her."

Chet now chatted with the next guests in the line, so the old man moved on. When a brief lull gave them a breather, he whispered in his mother's ear, "Millie, darling, my occupation isn't a state secret. Sooner or later you'll have to accept it."

She slapped his arm. "Oh, I know, but I can't seem to help myself." She looked into his eyes and sighed. "Such a waste of so much masculine potential."

He grinned and spoke the name he rarely said aloud. "Mother."

"Shush!"

"Talk about denial. Most of the people in this room know I'm your son."

"Most—not all. Be a good boy and snag one of those glasses of champagne over there for me. The auction will start soon." She pulled his sleeve and gave him a little shove toward the buffet.

Chet loved the little game he and his mother played. She seemed not to care about the sideways glances and whispered comments from people who didn't know them.

He returned with two glasses. Handed her one then touched his glass to hers. "Here's to raising lots and lots of dough tonight."

She leaned close and whispered, "I think we're on track to break all previous records. That new Focus Simi Valley Ford donated has already exceeded fifty thousand in twenty dollar raffle tickets."

With feigned innocence he said, "I offered to donate a free funeral, but you turned me down."

"What am I going to do about you, Chester?" She turned on her heel then looked over her shoulder. "Go charm some of those lonely young ladies over by the orchestra. Make yourself useful for a change."

Chet chuckled and slowly cruised the room, stopping to chat with several acquaintances along the way. When he reached the other side of the dance floor, he bowed before General Wayne's granddaughter, Rose. "May I have this dance, beautiful?"

"Following General Mom's orders, Digger?"

"Yes, but she told me I could ask whoever I chose. I choose you, brat."

"So charming. How can I resist?" She set her glass down and took his hand.

He pulled her close and growled. "Don't even try."

As adolescents, Chet and Rose had been classmates in the middle school at Ramstein Air Force Base in Germany for over two years. A required part of the curriculum was ballroom dancing. Military men, and the sons of military men, were expected to be skilled and gentlemanly dancers.

"You still dance like a dream, Rosie." He gave her a little hug.

"That's not what you always thought."

"I was twelve. Give me some slack. Anyway you were taller than me then."

Rose pulled away and twirled. Back in his arms, she said, "It's a shame we always felt like siblings, isn't it?"

"Yeah—It's a shame we still do. We make a great couple on the dance floor though. I've noticed several envious glances from the sidelines. Randy is giving me the evil eye."

The music morphed into a soft tango. "Doesn't hurt to keep a husband on his toes. Let's give him something to think about. You game?"

He grabbed her by the waist and yanked her against his body. She threw back her head, locked her right knee to his hip then dragged her left leg seductively behind, ran her hand down his chest, and nestled her face against his shoulder. They commenced a steamy and dramatic performance that had all the couples drifting off the floor, leaving it to them alone.

When the orchestra leader saw what they were up to, he ramped up the volume and the heat, to the delight of the watching crowd. At the conclusion of the dance, Chet and Rose bowed and accepted the applause. He grinned, picked her up and carried her back to her table.

"Your wife, I presume?" He set her on Randy's lap.

Randy put his arm around Rosie's waist. "Just keep remembering that, pal," he said with a warning grin.

Millie approached them, kissed Rose, and then took Chet's hand. "One dance and I'll leave you alone the rest of the evening. You'll be free to break hearts to the wee hours."

"I'd rather dance with you, ma'am. You're the most gorgeous woman in the room, you know."

* * * *

The evening wound down. Chet and Millie thanked each guest as they left the country club. The orchestra packed up their instruments and sound equipment. Waiters began clearing in earnest.

Millie fell into a chair and kicked off her four inch heels. "Oh, God, my feet are killing me."

Chet sat opposite her and lifted her foot to his knee. He began a gentle massage. She sighed with relief and pleasure.

"Why in hell aren't you married yet, honey? You'd make the perfect husband. Someday, not too soon mind you, I want a grandchild or two."

The love in his mother's face warmed Chet to the core. "Same old cliché — I haven't found the right girl."

Millie lifted her other foot to Chet's knee. "What about that bizarre little number I bumped into on the stairs the other day?"

Chet laughed softly. "Mariska Williston."

"How do you know her?"

"She's Bobby's cousin. Her nickname is Risky. It suits her perfectly. Bobby calls her Dog Breath."

"Whatever for?"

"Sexy little Ms. Williston lives in a quaint old house on Box Canyon road with ten dogs and an absolute fortune in antique appliances and rare tableware. She had no idea of its worth."

"Ten dogs? I can't imagine."

He grinned. "She actually had eighteen the day I met her at Jack Williston's funeral. She's compelled to rescue dogs, and she works for a veterinarian. For relaxation, she runs marathons. I'm very attracted to her. She's unlike any woman I've ever met, and she smells like cinnamon." He returned Millie's stare.

"Oh dear. Cinnamon—Kryptonite to my baby boy."

"At thirty-two I'm hardly a baby."

She wiggled her fingers. "Tell me more."

"Well, she actually gave you a very nice compliment. She thinks you're my girlfriend."

A smile lit Millie's face. "She said that?"

"She didn't have to. It was all over her face and demeanor."

"Did you set her straight?"

"No. I think I'll have a little fun with it for now."

She withdrew her feet and slipped them back in her shoes. "I'd love to see that house of hers."

"It's total Bizzarro World. If Sir did a white-glove inspection, she'd be on latrine duty forever." He laughed. "I'm afraid I'm doomed to love in vain. There's no way I could ever live with those conditions. She dislikes what I do for a living, and thinks I'm a total square."

"You ... a square?" She bit her bottom lip. "Why do you suppose she thinks that?"

"She asked me if I was a Republican then withdrew the question." He grinned at Millie's amused expression. "Risky Williston is one complex woman. The relationship isn't going anywhere, but I'd sure love to get her in my bed."

She slapped his knee. "I'm your mother, remember? I don't need to know everything."

"True, but you're also a friend. You've helped me out of some difficult corners."

"Like Noreen Perillo?" Millie sighed. "The last thing you needed was to end up in the middle of a couple divorcing."

He nodded his face sober. "I was in love with Nori. The most beautiful woman, with the biggest heart I've ever known. I still have a soft spot for her. I wonder if she and Steve ever got back together."

"Who knows? A lot can happen in four years. Come on, your old mother needs to get home and to bed. It's a lot of work to hold back the sands of time."

He put his arm around her shoulders, and they left the club. "You'll be beautiful when you're ninety."

She rested her head on his shoulder. "Oh, Chester, I miss your father so much. Do you ever think of him?"

"Every day."

Chapter Thirteen

Risky pinned Harley's picture on the Found Dogs bulletin board in the lobby of the vet clinic. She'd put it there before, but you never knew when someone might recognize him. Just last week the owners of the Airedale came to claim her after she'd lived with Risky for over four months.

A co-worker called to her, "Risky, you've got a phone call."

"Who is it?"

"Some woman, she wouldn't give her name."

Risky sighed. "Rats! Take a message or a callback number. I'm about half an hour late taking the boarding dogs for their afternoon romp on the grass out back."

The woman murmured into the phone, shook her head then rolled her eyes at Risky. "She wants to talk to you now, and still won't give her name. Sorry."

"Yeah, well I'm sorry too. Tell her I can't come to the phone." She quick-walked back to the rear of the clinic, approached the entrance to the boarding kennel, and opened the door to a choir of excited barks and howls.

Mariska slipped leashes over the heads of six of the happy canines, and led them out the back door to a large grassy area. They pulled, wagged their tails, and fidgeted as she slid the leashes off their heads. The dogs tore across the big lawn, romped and rolled in the grass. The smallest one yipped and chased the big dogs around the fence perimeter.

Risky laughed and stood with hands on her hips. Why was it always the littlest dog making the most noise?

She picked up the pooper-scooper and a handful of plastic bags, keeping an alert eye on them for the inevitable.

The receptionist peered through the back door. "She called back. She says she's your mother. It's an emergency."

Risky dropped her head back and rolled her eyes. The last person in the world she wanted to talk to, except maybe for Chet's girlfriend, Marvelous Millie, was Anya. "I'm busy, Margie. I doubt it's an emergency. Take her number."

"She's calling from Simi Valley Hospital. She just took your dad there." Margie raised her hands helplessly, a pained look in her eyes.

"Dad!" Risky put her hands on her temples and squeezed her eyes shut for a moment. "Here ... take this." She thrust the bags into the woman's hands, pointed to the scooper on the ground, and rushed past her into the clinic.

In the employee lounge, she opened her locker to retrieve her jacket and backpack.

"What should I tell her?" Margie was right behind her. "Where are you going?"

"To the hospital."

* * * *

Risky parked at the side nearest the emergency entrance. Slinging her backpack over her shoulder, she rushed through the swinging doors to the nurse's station. "My dad's here. David Williston. Which room?"

The attendant reacted to her desperate tone, and pointed to the end of the curtained enclosures. "He's in the last one on the right." To Risky's retreating back he called, "He's okay, miss."

She heard her parent's voices before she slid back the curtain. They looked up. Anya opened her arms to her daughter. Risky brushed past her mother and went straight to her dad.

Her stomach twisted at the blood on his shirt. "Dad, what happened?" Without waiting for an answer, she threw her arms around his shoulders.

"I'm okay. It was an accident." He patted her back then raised his hand to her cheek. "Take a breath. It's not serious." Dave smiled and nodded. "Here, sit." He tapped the exam table where he was seated.

Risky ignored her mother's extended hand after she boosted herself onto the table next to Dave.

"Mariska, why are you being so angry with me, *kokhana*?"

Risky's chest squeezed until she was sure her heart would be crushed. Anger, so deep it threatened to drown her, flushed hot on her cheeks. "I have nothing to say to you, Anya."

"Is it because I call you at work?"

Risky emitted a sad, ironic chuckle. She stared at her mother a moment then shook her head. "No."

"What then?"

Anya's big dark eyes bored into Risky until she almost looked away, but

56

that would mean her mother won again, wouldn't it? "I don't want to have this conversation, Anya. I came because of Dad. Not to talk to you, okay?"

The curtain flew back as a young doctor stepped into the small space. He pushed a stainless steel cart next to the exam table. His badge identified him as Dr. Terry Redmond. He cast a curious smile at Mariska as she hopped off the exam table.

He reached for the gauze pad Dave was holding to his forehead. "Okay, Mr. Williston, let me have another look." Dave dropped his hand and the doctor gently lifted the pad and palpated the area around the jagged cut. "Doesn't look too bad. You won't need stitches. I'll just glue it and apply a non-stick dressing. Should take about a week to heal. You might experience some bruising around your eye here." He brushed his fingers across Dave's eyebrow.

Dave winced and reached toward his eye.

Dr. Redmond grasped his wrist. "No, don't touch it until I have it bandaged. Lie back." He urged Dave to lie down then turned to Anya and Mariska. "Would you ladies step into the waiting lounge? I'll let you know as soon as I'm finished here."

Risky brushed past Anya on her way to the nurse's station. She sat on a plastic chair then pulled her cell phone from the backpack and punched in the number for the veterinary clinic. As soon as Margie answered she told her she'd be back to hose down the lawn when her Dad was released. "He got a cut over his eye. It doesn't look serious. Yeah, my mother totally freaks when she sees blood." She nodded and um-hummed into the phone. "Yes, I'll be there. If the front office is closed, I'll go around back and knock on the kennel door. Okay. See ya."

Anya took the chair next to her and rested her hand on Risky's knee.

Risky jerked, jumped up and moved over to the next chair. "Don't touch me." She was acting childish and she knew it, but couldn't help herself. Anya's touch always sent a chill through her body like a walk through a cold graveyard.

As a child, Risky had done her best to give Anya the benefit of the doubt, but by the time she was thirteen she recognized that it was a lost cause. Her mother was too damaged. Too needy. Too weak. Like a vampire, she sucked Mariska dry of any residual feelings of love, of hope, of obligation.

"I don't understand you, Mariska."

Risky snorted. What a useless exercise it would be to respond with an answer. She'd never understand. In the whole world, there wasn't enough explaining. Anya lived in her own twisted sphere. A world where nobody's needs but her own were paramount.

Whirling on her, Risky didn't mask the venom in her eyes. "What happened to Dad?" She threw out her arm, palm directly in front of her mother's face. "Don't tell me some lie about an accident. I can smell booze on your breath. What did you do this time?"

Anya's expression crumpled. "Mariska, it *was* an acci ..."

Jumping to her feet, Risky grabbed her backpack. "Tell Dad I went back to work. I'll call him later. In the meantime you can go straight to hell!"

Risky knew her mother was already in hell. She'd been living in that special hell since she was fourteen, when she and her little sister, Nadia, had been kidnapped by the flesh peddler on their way home from ballet school on a busy street in Kiev. But, God help her, Mariska just didn't care anymore.

No amount of love, devotion and patience her father had doled out over the years had made as much as a dent in Anya's damaged soul. He'd nearly bankrupted them many times in the pursuit of special hospitals, treatment centers and doctors in his dogged attempt to help his wife.

Dave tried to explain to Mariska when she was a teenager, why he fell in love with the beautiful, melancholy Russian girl. The girl with flawless ivory skin, large dark eyes, and ballerina's body. Risky understood how he could have fallen in love with her, but she would never understand why he still loved and protected her.

Anya had left them so many times. Sometimes it was involuntary, like when she had to be hospitalized. Sometimes it was because of another man, but mostly she'd just disappear. For days, weeks, or months.

Once her mother was gone for over a year, and offered no explanation of where she'd been, or with who. Risky got home from school and discovered her standing in the kitchen preparing dinner. Anya turned and smiled as if she'd been there to wave goodbye when the school bus pulled away that morning.

That was when Risky began to hate her mother more than fear her. She never addressed her as Mother after that day. The loathing was as alive in her gut today as it was fifteen years ago.

* * * *

As Risky was about to drive out of the hospital parking lot she noticed Dr. Redmond wave to her from the doors at the Emergency entrance. Panicked, she slammed on the brakes and opened her door.

She shouted as they walked toward each other, "What's wrong? Is something wrong with Dad?"

Dr. Redmond shook his head and waved his hands. "No, Mr. Williston is just fine. I didn't mean to scare you."

She shielded her eyes from the sun. "What is it? Why did you stop me?" It could have been a trick of the bright daylight, but she'd swear he blushed.

His smile was crooked and looked uncomfortable on his rugged face. "I'm sorry, Miss Williston. I didn't want to frighten you. I hoped to catch you before you left, but when I got to the waiting room your mother said you'd already gone."

Risky scrunched up her face and shook her head in confusion. "If Dad's okay, what?"

He reached for her elbow. "Let's move over here, out of the middle of the parking lot."

She followed his lead to two park benches in the shade of a large oak tree.

"Here." He pointed to the nearest bench. "Let's sit down."

She sat and pulled away her elbow. "You're still scaring me, doctor. What the heck is going on?"

He smiled that crooked smile again. This time she saw something else on his face, in his eyes. "This is rather awkward. I, uh, I've seen you at the vet's. I recognized you the minute I saw you with Mr. Williston in the exam room."

Still clueless, Risky shook her head and raised her eyebrows. "And?"

The blush deepened and he cleared his throat. "I, uh, was hoping we could have coffee sometime." His hands balled into nervous fists.

"You scared the living daylights out of me so you could hit on me?" In spite of herself, she choked out a laugh.

"Yes, I can see how you would think that, but ..."

"What then? You want advice about a pet?" She perversely enjoyed the discomfort of Terry Redmond. So good looking with dark brown curly hair and deep brown eyes, he'd be some woman's dream date. If she was interested. Which she wasn't.

He chuckled. "Can we start over?"

"I don't have all day. I have to get back to work."

"Yeah, me too." He placed his hands on his knees. "Okay, here it is. I've noticed you before, and I find you very attractive. I'd like to get to know you. Could I please have your phone number?"

Instead of answering him, Risky crossed her arms and gave him an appraising once-over. His question intrigued her, tempted her. He seemed very nice, and definitely sexy, in a very masculine, very un-doctorly way. Hmm. He didn't give her that involuntary clenching sensation between her legs like Chet did though.

She thought about Chet Jensen. Yes, she would be more interested in Chet if he wasn't a neat freak, and if he didn't already have a beautiful cougar girlfriend who was too old for him and who she couldn't compete with. But Chet was an *undertaker,* for crying out loud! She couldn't get her mind away from visions of Chet looming over corpses, and he was way too deep in the category of mouth-watering male model. By comparison to Millie, Risky looked like a ... a what?

Chet's teasing eyes had a way of making her feel as if her blouse was unbuttoned, or she forgot to put on her pants. That look caused her mouth to water, her lips to hunger for a taste of his chest. What she saw in Chet's eyes was the question: How about a hop in the sack with me? Uh, nope, not gonna happen.

"Here's the deal, Terry. You go in there and tell my dad that I said *he* could give you my phone number if he thought you were a man he'd want me to go out with. If Dad says okay, you can call me." She stood and headed back to her car. "I gotta go to work."

Dr. Redmond stood next to the bench with a gleaming smile on his face. He waved and turned back toward the hospital.

That night he called her.

Chapter Fourteen

Malibu Beach

Chet gulped down the entire bottle of water Bobby offered him. "Whew. That was some workout. I must be getting old." His shoulders shook with a rueful chuckle.

Bobby wiped sweat from his forehead with a towel. "We're both too old to play with these Pepperdine kids, my friend." He slapped a straw hat on his head.

Chet surveyed the disbursing crowd of spectators. He caught the eye of a bumptious brunette who'd been giving him come-hither glances throughout the match.

Sorry, sugar, not interested.

"Yeah, well maybe we're too old to play with these kids, but we beat 'em, Bob."

"Hah. Barely." Bobby's arms flopped to his sides and he dropped his head on the back of the sand chair.

Chet put his shades back on and turned his head in the direction of his best friend to discourage the girl-woman who looked as if she was planning join them. "Go away, please," he mumbled.

Bobby snorted. "Must be nice."

"What?"

Bobby lowered his sunglasses and stared at Chet. "To have so many women interested that you have to wish them away."

Chet stood. "She's all yours, buddy. I'm going to get something from the car."

"Oh no, don't do this to me, pal. I'm engaged."

Chet whirled around. "You're what!"

"Engaged. It's official. Anita and I are getting married. I planned to tell you on the drive home."

Chet grabbed his gear bag and folded the chair. "Fine. Pick up your stuff and let's get out of here." He rolled his eyes to the left. "She'll get the message." From the edge of his vision, the woman's nicely rounded backside bounced as she turned to her friends. He knew why he'd deliberately avoided her. Mariska.

On the road home through the mountains, Bobby told Chet he and his girlfriend of two years had finally decided to make it official. "Anita more or less told me to piss off if there was no permanent future for us. She wants to have kids. Mine—or somebody else's if I can't decide to make an honest woman of her."

Chet glanced away from the road for a second. "You lucky S.O.B. Anita's one in a million, and I have no idea what a gorgeous babe like her she sees in you."

"Yeah, well, I'm the world's greatest lover."

A guffaw rose from deep in Chet's gut. It was a joke between them going back to college days. "Second greatest."

Bobby and Anita finally tying the knot. That left Chet the last singleton in their old crowd.

"Congratulations, Bob, I mean it, but it brands me an unwelcome outsider. When I show up alone, the married men don't like me around their wives, and when I bring a woman, the wives don't want them around their husbands."

Bobby brushed sand off his feet onto the floor mat of Chet's car. "It's not like you haven't had your pick of any woman you wanted for the past several years, you know? What's your problem, other than the fact that all you're looking for is a quick lay?"

"God, that makes me sound like a complete bastard."

"If the shoe fits."

"That's not it." Chet sighed deeply. "I don't deny I enjoy a fun tumble now and then. I just never found a woman I wanted to spend the rest of my life with. To have kids with."

"You poor bastard. If you're looking to duplicate the never-ending love affair your parents had, you're shit out of luck. That's the stuff of fairy tales."

"You're wrong. It *is* possible, and that's exactly what I want." He paused as he navigated a long curve on the narrow road. "I recently met a woman who really fires me up, but her lifestyle is so bizarre it could never work out between us."

Bobby shifted in this seat. "Please, tell me you're not talking about Dog Breath."

"Yup."

Bob dropped his head on top the headrest. "You've got to be kidding me. I love Mariska like a sister, but she's a flat-chested stick of a tomboy, and unmanageable to boot."

A chuckle rumbled in Chet's throat. "You grew up with her. You're too close to the situation. She's a sexy little package, and she's far from flat-chested. Big tits are a nice bonus, but don't rank high in my criteria." He laughed again.

"Careful, you're talking about my cousin."

"It's all academic. There's zero chance of anything long term."

Bobby slapped more sand from his knees. "You blind-sided me with this, man. You and Risky. Who would have guessed? How does she feel about you?"

"Mostly I annoy her. We've only spent a couple of days together. She's turned off by my profession. That much I can sense. I'm a compulsive neatnik, and that bugs her too. She made that clear when I had dinner at her place."

"Spaghetti or an omelet, right?"

Chet grinned. "Cooking isn't high on my list either. The thing is she smells good enough to eat, and all I can think about is getting my hands on her ass. But that's not all. There's a lot going on in her pretty little head. I have a sense she's deep. She's interesting in a mysterious way."

"You picked up on that, I see." He gave Chet a light punch in the shoulder. "As for how she smells, I know her secret. She boils cinnamon sticks in water, stores it in a jar in the bathroom, and uses it to rinse her hair. I forgot how you drool over cinnamon. Where did that come from?"

Chet pressed his lips together and shook his head. "No clue." Visions of his big hands holding Risky's tight rear end sent a jolt through his libido.

Bobby tossed his hat on the back seat. "Most guys shy away from women with children. Last time I checked, Dog Breath had about a dozen of the four-legged variety living at her house. You'd be better off to set your sights elsewhere, pal. That's stiff competition."

"I'm sure I'll have her out of my system by the time I get back from Germany. Millie and I'll be there two months."

"Does my cuz know you're leaving town?"

"No, but I suspect she might not care one way or the other." He shrugged. "She won't miss me."

* * * *

Later that afternoon Chet called Risky to tell her about his upcoming trip and ask her to have dinner with him before he left. He liked her. They could be friends. He held faint hope that he'd ever get a taste of her in his bed.

He punched in her number.

"Hello, I'm kind of busy, who is it?"

Just like her. No beating around the bush. "It's Chet Jensen, Mariska."

An uncomfortable few seconds passed. Maybe the call had dropped. "Risky?"

"I'm here, I just, what do you want?"

"Look, if you're in the middle of something, I'll call later."

"No it's ... okay. The pipe under the sink is leaking. I just put a bucket there. I'm trying to figure out if I can fix it, or if I have to call a plumber. Was I rude?"

"Uh, yeah." He smiled picturing the look on her expressive face. She'd be an easy mark in a poker game.

She sniffed. "No wonder I'm an old maid, huh?"

He laughed. "I'd never call you one."

He paused. Here was an opportunity. "Why don't I come over and have a look? Sir taught me to fix just about everything around the house. He was gone a lot."

She cleared her throat. "Great, you might save me a plumbing bill. Are you sure Millie won't mind?"

Chet's broad smile covered his face. She was jealous of his mother. A good sign. He'd keep her in the dark for a while longer. "Why would she?"

"I got the impression the two of you are pretty close."

"We are. Very close, but we have an understanding."

"Oh."

He enjoyed this misconception of hers.

"While I'm on the phone, get under the sink with a flashlight and tell me if you can see where the leak is coming from."

"I did that already. It only leaks when I have standing water, so it's probably right at the drain."

"Okay. I'll be there in about an hour. Sounds like a quick fix."

"Uh, Chet?"

"Yeah?"

"Thank you."

"My pleasure, Ms. Williston."

Chapter Fifteen

Risky mopped the water on her kitchen floor then went through the living room to rearrange her clutter. She ran the sticky roller over the furniture to catch dog hair. No sense in turning Neat Freak Chet off the minute he showed up. She had work to do on loosening him up on that front.

Even when she tried not to, she spent a lot of time thinking about Chet. She could see no way they'd ever be a couple, but he sure got her hormones raging. She pictured Millie. Curves in all the right places, a lush head of hair, and her rosy coloring made Risky grit her teeth with envy. Millie was a dead ringer for that faded old movie poster of Rita Hayworth that her dad had over his tool bench.

He and Millie were "very close," Chet had said.

The engine in his big Lincoln purred when he pulled into her front yard about a half hour later. She hurried to the bathroom, looked in the mirror, grabbed a brush and whipped it through her hair. "Oh, to heck with it!" She tossed the brush in the drawer. It was hopeless.

Chet's knock got all her babies yapping. Risky waded through them on her way to the door. Her insides buzzed when she saw him standing there in all his blonde magnificence, a sexy smile on his face, a tool belt low on his hips. She nearly swooned, and tightened her traitorous knees. A tool belt!

Oh, God.

Slick startled both of them when he took a flying leap right up into Chet's arms without an invitation.

Chet instinctively grabbed him and pulled him close. "Whoa, big boy. You nearly knocked me down." He nuzzled the homely, hairless dog, ran his hands over Slick's soft skin, and then set him on the floor.

Risky puzzled over the tilt of Chet's head and his questioning grin. His eyes sparkled, and he waggled his eyebrows.

"What?"

He opened his arms. "I'm waiting for you to leap into my arms like Slick just did."

She pursed her lips and sniffed. "You wish."

Chet chuckled and stepped over the sash. Once the door closed, he knelt and patted the four small canines competing for his attention.

Every time Chet touched one of her dogs, Risky shivered as if he'd touched her. Each pat and stroke sent a thrill from her throat to her feet. She swallowed the urge to thread her fingers through his thick blond hair.

He raised his head. "Show me your plumbing problem, lady. I work by the hour."

Her plumbing problem at the moment scorched its way through her lower torso. She swallowed again, and pointed. "The kitchen."

Chet stood, shifted the tool belt lower on his hips and ambled into her kitchen.

Risky shoved her trembling hands into the back pockets of her shorts. What the heck was wrong with her? He's Chester Jensen, the undertaker, for crying out loud. A total turn off, right? Well then, why was she turned on?

Chet peered under the sink with a flashlight. He knelt with his bum in the air.

Risky squeezed her eyes shut for a second and gritted her teeth against naughty, erotic visions.

Chet rolled, sat down then lay back so he could look up under the sink. He bent his knees and relaxed his legs, forming a triangle that pointed directly to his ... his ...

Oh, God.

Risky moaned.

"It's nothing serious."

A lot he knew.

Chet pushed himself forward and sat up. "Looks to me like you've got more than one problem here."

No kidding! "I'll have to call a plumber then?"

"No, I can fix it, but I'll have to make a run to the hardware store for a gasket and some plumber's tape."

She didn't want him to leave. "Before you do that you should check the shed out back. There's all kinds of tools and stuff out there. Bobby did some work in here before I moved in." She pointed to the back door. "Come on, I'll show you."

Mariska led the way across the yard to a small shed off to one side. She felt Chet's gaze heating her rear end. Too bad she couldn't click a re-wind button and reverse the walking order.

"Where are all the dogs?" He glanced around. "I only see Harley and the old shepherd."

"Three were adopted, and the Airedale's owner claimed her."

"Really? Good for them." He grinned. "You're down to six."

"Yeah, kind of lonely around here lately." Risky returned his smile then continued across the yard. Inside the door of the shed, she stopped and waved her hand above her head, searching for the string to the overhead light bulb.

Chet slammed into her.

"Oof."

He grabbed her and pulled her against his chest. "Sorry, Mariska, I didn't mean to run into you. Are you okay?"

Was she okay? With Chet's arms around her? With her back pressed against his chest? Her bottom pressed against his ... tools? How could she be okay? Her legs gave way, and he tightened his hold.

"I'm fine. You kinda knocked the wind out of me."

He held on.

Visions in her head ran rampant. She imagined his nose in her hair, his breath on her neck.

"God, you do smell good, Mariska. I could swallow you whole."

His nose *was* in her hair!

She poked his muscular forearm. "Uh, you can let go now, Chet." Not that she wanted him to let go. She hadn't felt so deliciously cuddled by a man since she last sat on her daddy's lap. This wasn't the same though. Not the same at all.

He slowly loosened his arms and slid her down his body until she was steady on her feet. "Okay?"

"Yeah." She stepped away, found the pull string and yanked it. A sudden wash of bright white light had the same sobering effect as a cold squirt from a garden hose.

Risky raised her eyes to Chet's.

He stared at her. A slow smile built on his lips and his gaze oozed testosterone. "That was fun. For me anyway." He winked. "Where's the stuff?"

"The stuff?"

"We came out here to look through the plumbing supplies Bob left behind."

She gasped and pointed. "Oh, it's over there, next to the lawnmower, that shelf there." She straightened her back and brushed non-existent dust from her shirt. What a brilliant move. It drew Chet's gaze right to her tingling boobs.

She crossed her arms. "I'll, uh, I'll go back inside and get some old towels and empty the drip bucket."

Chet grinned. "Take your time. It'll take me a while to dig through those boxes."

He didn't move out of her way, so she sucked in her breath and inched past, careful not to touch any part of him. Once out the door she streaked to the house as if the Prince of Darkness chased her.

Inside the kitchen, she slumped back against the door. "Breathe, Risky, breathe." She took a few deep breaths and shook herself. "It's Chet the *undertaker*, remember? The ghoul? The guy who handles dead bodies for a living?"

She stomped to the short hallway between the kitchen and bathroom, yanked open the linen closet, and grabbed an armload of old beach towels. Back in the kitchen, she dropped them next to the open cabinet doors under the sink.

Bending at the waist, her nose in the refrigerator, she reached to the back of the bottom shelf and pulled out a bottle of beer, stood, twisted the cap and guzzled like a sailor on shore leave.

"You got another one of those?"

She jumped and choked. Beer spurted from her nose. "Chet! Dammit, you scared me!" She pulled up the hem of her tee shirt and wiped her face.

He grinned at her bare stomach. "Sorry—again. Seems like I just said that."

She thrust a bottle of beer into his hand and glared. "You're one big blonde pain in the butt, Jensen."

He merely smiled then took a long pull on the cold beer. "I better get to work. Don't want to be here all night, do I?"

Maybe he didn't want to be there all night, but she could think of more boring ways to spend her time. "Did you find what you needed?"

"Yep. I should have that leak fixed in about a half hour."

Her head bobbed. "Good. Okay. While you do that, I'll take Harley and Shep for an abbreviated run. The little kids were out earlier."

Leaning low over the old-fashioned deep sink, Chet's voice echoed when he called, "Okay. See you when you get back."

* * * *

Risky had been gone about fifteen minutes when the phone rang. He recognized Terry Redmond's voice leaving a voicemail on the device in the living room. Striding across the kitchen he reached for the wall mounted phone. "Hey, Terry, I heard you leaving a message. It's Chet Jensen here."

"Chet? Did I call the wrong number?"

"I don't know. Who were you calling?"

"Not you."

"Who?"

"Ms. Williston. Mariska."

Chet bit the inside of his cheek. "This is her house."

"What are *you* doing there?"

"At the moment I'm finishing up a small plumbing repair on Risky's kitchen sink."

"Who's Risky?"

"That's Mariska's nickname."

"Um ... can I talk to her?"

He leaned his shoulder against the wall. "No."

"No? Why not?"

"She's out running with a couple of her dogs right now. I'll be glad to tell her you called. You want to leave your number? No, wait, my hands are dirty, and I don't see anything to write on." He stared at the note pad hanging on a nail next to the phone, and the pencil dangling on a string.

"No, that's okay. I'm working tonight. I thought I might catch her before I started my shift. Just tell her I'll call back later, when I take a break."

"Ten-four."

"Are *you* going to be there later?"

"I doubt it. I'm just finishing up."

"Okay then. I'll see you around."

"No doubt." Chet lowered the old-style handset on its hook, the curly stretch cord impossibly twisted. He stopped himself from reaching out to untangle it. Good, Chet, that's a step in the right direction.

Why was Terry Redmond calling Mariska? How did he know her? Perhaps they were a couple. He saw Terry at the health club three mornings a week. He never mentioned having a girlfriend.

The back gate squeaked open. Through the window over the sink, he watched as she roughhoused with the two dogs, removed their leashes and secured them behind the fence. He ducked his head and finished installing the new gasket ring at the drain.

The screen door squeaked closed behind her. "Wow, it's really beautiful out there this evening. The sky is so clear, and I could see the crescent moon and Venus rising. She's so close to him it looks like they're going to bump into each other."

He glanced over his shoulder. "Have a good run?"

She took a deep breath. "Those two always give me a workout."

"Did the old codger down the road have something to say?"

"Oscar, the grouch?" She chuckled. "Of course. He's as predictable as the sunset." She gestured to the sink. "How's it going?"

"Just finishing up." He straightened, took a handful of paper towels and wiped down the sink and countertop. "Good as new." He turned and enjoyed the vision of her flushed face and heaving chest. He tossed her one of the beach towels.

She rubbed her face and neck. "Thanks, Chet. I really appreciate it. The last thing I need right now is a plumbing bill."

He watched her mop away the enticing trickle of sweat snaking its way between her breasts. His lips twisted in an effort to suppress his grin.

"What?"

He cocked his head and raised his eyebrows. "You mean I'm not getting paid?"

She smirked and shook her head. "You'll have to settle for another cold beer. I'll even throw in a sincere handshake when you leave."

"I'll take it." He removed his tool belt, took another paper towel and wiped his face and hands. "In here?" He pointed to the kitchen table. "Or in there?" He pointed to the living room.

She opened the refrigerator and pulled out a beer and a bottle of water. "If you want your lap free of dogs, in here is better."

He took a seat at the small table, and reached for the beer she held. "In here it is." He took a satisfying swallow of the cold, malty brew. "This is good stuff. I've never heard of the brand."

"It's from a small family brewery in Baja. Star Market carries it." She sat across from him and twisted off the cap of her water bottle.

The last thing he wanted to tell her after the brief conversation with Terry Redmond was that he'd be out of town for two months. He had to tell her Terry called, of course. It would be churlish of him not to, but dammit! He hated to leave town for several weeks with Redmond sniffing around her.

He set his bottle down then lifted it and made a series of sweat rings on the worn wooden table. "You had a phone call while you were out."

"Oh, thanks, I'll check the message later."

"I answered it because I recognized the caller. It was Terry Redmond." He looked directly into her dark brown irises, trying to discern her reaction.

Her eyes wide, she said, "You know Terry?"

Chet took a pull on the beer before answering. "Yeah, we work out at the same health club. Nice guy. How do you know him?"

"I met him at the hospital yesterday. My dad had a small accident, and Terry was the attending physician in the ER. He asked for my phone number."

A ridiculous wave of relief washed through Chet's gut.

She and Terry weren't a couple. They just met. They hadn't even had a date. Yet. Maybe they wouldn't like each other once they spent some time together. "You gonna go out with him?"

"Not that it's any of your business, Digger, but he hasn't asked me. I will if he does though. That's probably why he called. Did he leave a number?"

"No, he, uh, he's at work tonight. He said he'd call you later when he takes a break." What timing. His leaving town at the same time Redmond planned to make a move on her. Shit!

"Mariska, I'm leaving town day after tomorrow. I'm going to be in Germany for a couple of months." As if she cared.

"Germany? Two months?" She set her bottle on the table and gripped it with both hands.

He grasped at a ray of hope when her chocolaty eyes flashed with regret. It looked like regret. He was certain it was regret. "Yes, my mother and I have several friends there, from the time Sir was stationed at Ramstein. And I'm going to put in a little volunteer time at the base mortuary. We finally caught a window when we could both get away."

"How does Millie feel about it?" Her lips pinched as if saying his mother's name left a sour taste. Definitely a good sign.

"She's all for it. In fact, she's looking forward to us leaving. Chet smiled inwardly at Mariska's perplexed scowl.

She picked up her water and sipped. He imagined he heard the synapses firing in her brain. Her forehead wrinkled, pulling her black eyebrows close together.

He set down the empty bottle. "I should take off. I'm technically working tonight, so I'd better get back home and relieve my helper." He stood. "Thanks for the beer. I'll call you when I get back in town, okay?"

She nodded and stood. "Yes. Call me." She rounded the table and moved toward the living room. Near the door, she turned and stuck out her hand. "Have a good trip."

Chet stood with his hands on his hips, the tool belt dangling off one shoulder. "What? No kiss goodbye?"

Instead of answering, she shocked him by standing on tiptoe and puckering her lips.

He grasped her shoulders, lowered his head and planted a chaste kiss on her mouth. To his happy surprise, Risky put her hands at the nape of his neck, and kissed him back with lips as soft and warm as a good French brandy.

She withdrew slightly. "Chet, I ..."

No way was he going to let this opportunity go to waste. The tool belt slid from his shoulder and landed on the floor with a loud clunk, setting off the dogs. Chet put his arms around her and kissed her again. This time there was nothing chaste about it.

He wasn't sure how it happened, but her arms were entwined around his neck. Mariska leaned into him so hard that he fell back against the door. The next thing he knew her legs were wrapped around his hips, and she held handfuls of his hair. His response was instant and strong.

He teased her mouth open with his tongue. She welcomed his intrusion and tangled her tongue with his. Floored, Chet wondered where all this came from?

He spoke through their kiss, "My God, Mariska. You smell so good, and taste so good, I could eat you up." He planted his hands firmly on her bottom, held her tight against him.

Risky slanted her lips against his. "Chet, what are we doing?" Her grip on his hair tightened. She nipped his bottom lip.

"I don't know, baby, but don't stop. This is good, very good." He held her small butt with one arm and slid a hand up her back to her hairline, slowly bent his knees and slid down the door until they were on the floor.

That's all it took for four dogs to be all over them. They pulled apart, stared into each other's eyes. Risky ducked her chin and pressed her forehead against his shoulder. His pulse thundered in his ears despite the commotion.

She mumbled through a deep exhale, "You should go."

He burrowed his nose in her hair, sucked in her scent. His erection throbbed against her bottom. "Really?"

She pushed back and scooted off his lap. "Yes, really. I think this was a mistake. You'd better go home."

Her eyes contradicted her words. She was as much into the passion of the moment as he was. She glanced away, her cheeks bright pink.

Chet pulled up his legs and dropped his head between his knees. She was probably right. The timing was all wrong. "Give me a minute." He glanced at Risky.

Her blush deepened with her sudden recognition of the reason why he needed the minute. "Okay, sure. I need a minute too." Her breath skittered.

Slick wriggled between Chet's legs and licked his chin. He took a deep breath then huffed a chuckle as his heartbeat slowed to a more normal speed. "Thanks, bud, I needed that." He scratched Slick's chin and ears.

Risky stood. "Chet?"

"What, doll?" He extended a hand so she could help him to his feet.

She pulled his arm with both hands, held on for a beat longer than necessary. "I'll miss you while you're gone."

He ran a hand over her head, marveling at the springiness of her silky black hair. "I'll miss you too." He brushed a soft kiss on her hair, picked up his tool belt and left.

Chapter Sixteen

Risky stood rooted to the floor. She stared blankly at her front door. Chet's headlights flashed across the room as he backed up, turned, and pulled away from her house.

Clutching her upper arms, she gasped. What had just happened? She shuffled to her couch and flopped onto her back. Mickey, Minnie, Slick, and Brutus sprang up after her and vied for comfortable places to snuggle, like her stomach, chest, neck and head. Idly, she rubbed each of them and mumbled nonsensical baby talk.

This wasn't good. Not good at all. She told Chet the truth when she said she'd miss him. On the other hand, she was glad he was leaving. They needed some breathing room. At least *she* needed some breathing room. He told her he'd be gone a couple of months. That should be plenty of time for her to get him out of her system.

And for Chet to get Millie out of *his* system.

Now where in the heck did that come from? Why should she care whether or not Chet got Millie out of his system? He meant nothing to her, right? The thing was she did care. Darn it! Darn it! Darn it!

Her thoughts churned in six different directions. She needed a distraction. That was it! When Terry Redmond called back, she'd ask him for a date. She needed to get the show on the road. What better way to get her mind off Digger than to spend time with another man?

Terry Redmond, nice, good looking, smart, a doctor. Every parent wanted their daughter to marry a doctor, didn't they? She'd bet on her dad's enthusiastic approval if she dated Dr. Redmond. Dave wouldn't say anything, but she knew he was anxious for her to get her life in some kind of order, some kind of direction.

Order and direction. The words immediately generated thoughts of Chet.

Great. He was all about order and direction. He lived in an orderly, clean apartment. He'd settled into a profession he loved. *Ick.* He had friends. He took care of his body. He liked strenuous physical activity. *Stop it, Risky. Physical exercise, as in sports, you gutter minded doofus!*

A shiver of speculation streaked across her shoulders and arms when she remembered The Kiss. Hands down, the best kiss of her entire life. She'd been completely unprepared for the flame of hungry passion that engulfed her when Chet put his wonderful, long, strong arms around her. And especially when she tried to conjure the feel of his big hands on her bottom.

Oh, God.

Her palms itched with the memory of the texture of his hair. The hair she'd grabbed fistfuls of and held onto for dear life. She just knew that if she hadn't been holding on to his hair so tight, he would have swallowed her whole. Just like he said he wanted to do when they were in the shed.

Oh, God.

She'd begun rinsing her hair with cinnamon water when she realized how much her babies liked the smell of it. Whenever she washed her hair, which was every day, sometimes twice, she'd sit down, and they'd climb up in her lap and sniff around her hair and ears. Just like Chet had.

Oh, God.

When she and Chet landed on the floor in front of the door, with her sitting on his lap, with her legs clamped around his waist and his ...

The phone rang. *Thank God.*

Risky struggled up under the weight of her babies. She pushed them out of the way and reached for the phone. "Hello?"

"Mariska? This is Terry Redmond. How are you?"

"I'm good. How are you?"

He chuckled on a soft sigh. "I'd be a lot better if I had tonight off. I'd love to have dinner, spend an evening with you."

"I'd like that too, Terry."

"You would?"

"Yes. I know what. Let's meet at Chi Chi's tomorrow night. Their eggplant parmesan is the best. After, we can go to the batting cages and hit some home runs. I really want to hit some balls. How does that sound?"

He laughed. "It wasn't exactly what I had in mind, but yeah, sounds good."

"What did you have in mind?" Had she screwed up already?

"I don't know. I thought you might like miniature golf. You surprised me with the batting cages suggestion, that's all."

"Oh. I'm not into miniature golf, but we could go to the driving range if you'd rather. We could hit a couple buckets of golf balls there." She needed to hit something, baseballs, golf balls, whatever.

"Uh, is Chet Jensen still there?"

"No. Why?"

"He took me by surprise when he answered your phone. I was wondering if the two of you, if you and he were ...?"

"No! Me and Chet?" She choked out a laugh. "We know each other because he's my cousin ... no he's not my cousin. Bobby's my cousin. He's Bobby's friend. They're friends." *For heaven's sake, stop blabbing.*

"He said he was there to fix your sink."

"Yes! He fixed my sink. That's all. The sink." Why in Gods' name didn't she shut her trap?

"It's really none of my business, Mariska. I was just wary of asking you out if you and he were ..."

"We're not." She clamped her lips together.

"Good. So, tomorrow evening at Chi Chi's, right? What time is good for you?"

"Six? No wait, better make it seven. I have six dogs, and I don't get home from work until around five-forty-five. They need to be fed, and walked, and ..."

"Seven works for me."

"Okay. I'll see you at seven then."

"I look forward to it."

"Me too."

"So long."

"Bye, Terry."

She'd come off like a complete and total moron. It's a wonder Terry didn't hang up on her and run for the hills. She barely said two words to him at the hospital yesterday, and tonight her mouth gushed like a fire hose.

She bounced off the couch, went to the floor and did a dozen push-ups, and then a dozen sit-ups, and then a dozen squats, then she ran in place for a while, and then she hit the shower.

Chet. Oh, God.

Chapter Seventeen

Los Angeles International Airport

Millie Jensen held out her coffee cup. "Would you mind refreshing my coffee, sweetheart?"

"Not at all." Chet stood. "I could use some myself." He made his way across the Delta VIP lounge to the complimentary coffee and beverages area.

They'd been through security, were checked in, had boarding passes, and about an hour to kill before their Lufthansa boarding call.

He perused the snacks then put together a plate of nuts, cheese and crackers. Using a small tray, he carried the coffee cups and plate to where his mother had moved to sit by the window overlooking the aircraft parking gates.

"Here you go, Mom." He winked when she gave him a sour look.

"Don't call me that. I'm trying to discourage that attendant from coming over here and slipping you her phone number." She tilted her head in the direction of the reception counter. "I can't accomplish that if she knows I'm your mother."

Chet chuckled. "I wouldn't mind having her phone number. Maybe I'll stroll over there and ask for it."

She picked up one of the crackers. "What about that slender little marathon runner? The dog lover."

Chet sighed. "That relationship ended before it ever got off the ground. I don't expect to be seeing her again."

"That's unfortunate. I thought she had potential."

"Yeah, me too. I even pulled the old tool-belt-trick on her a couple of days ago."

"She didn't fall victim to your masculine charm?" Millie sat back and blew on her coffee, an amused twist at the corners of her mouth.

"Yeah, she did. It never fails." Chet shook his head regretfully. "God, I'm such a bastard."

Millie smiled and nodded. "Not your fault, honey. It runs rampant in the Jensen male line."

Chet snorted. "The bad news is I didn't get her in bed. The good news is she had sense enough to put a stop to it before we progressed beyond a kiss." He shook his head and smiled at the memory of their hungry clutching and pawing.

"Smart girl. Is that why you've been so blue all day?"

He gave her a sad smile. "Yeah, that, and the fact that I recalled one of the main reasons why I could never get away for more than a few days at a stretch—Beau."

"Poor, dear old Beau. Do you miss him that much?"

He nodded. "It's pretty damn quiet in my apartment. I haven't been able to bring myself to get rid of his bed yet. It's sits so empty in the corner of the living room."

"Oh, sweetheart, I'm sorry." She patted his arm. "You've had him with you since your nineteenth birthday."

"The best present you and Sir ever gave me."

They sat in silence for a few minutes, drank coffee and picked at the cheese and crackers. Chet stood abruptly and strode to the reception desk. He smiled, leaned on his elbows, and had a brief conversation with the attendant. She handed him a piece of paper. He tucked it in his jacket pocket, and returned to sit next to Millie.

"Hmm, I see she gave you her phone number. Did you have to confess that I wasn't your significant other?"

"I told her I worked for the CIA. That you were a German double agent, and I was returning you to Berlin for trial and imprisonment."

She sat back, her eyes wide with shock. "You did not!"

He grinned. "No, I didn't. I asked her if I could call her when we got back to the States. She agreed, and complimented me on having such a beautiful, young mother."

Millie's pleased grin warmed Chet's heart. He set his cup down and leaned back against the couch with his arms spread across the back, his long legs crossed. "You are beautiful, you know. I love you, Mom."

Her eyes sparkled, full of affection. "I love you too, Chester. But, I would like to know why you won't be seeing the little brunette again. You don't have to tell me if you don't want to."

"Thanks, Mil. Maybe later."

* * * *

He and Millie arrived in Munich the next evening. They took a taxi to a downtown hotel. They planned to rest away some of the jet lag, and sightsee for a couple of days. Chet had fond memories of Sir taking him to the Munich technology museum when he was a boy. He particularly remembered the bridge construction exhibit, and wanted to spend a few hours there while Millie shopped for gifts for their friends at Ramstein Air Base.

On the third day, Chet picked up a rental car, and they left for a leisurely drive south to Kaiserslautern, in the heart of wine country known as the Palatinate. Throughout the journey, thoughts of Mariska intruded into the memories of his adolescence in Germany.

"Chester, you've been awfully quiet this past hour. What's on your mind?" Millie opened a packet of *keks* and handed one to Chet.

Chet put the whole cookie in his mouth and pointed to his cheek while he chewed. After taking a swig from his water bottle he said, "Sorry to be such lousy company. I've been remembering some of the good times we had here. I drank my first glass of Riesling on one of our winery outings."

Millie chuckled at the recollection. "I wasn't at all happy with your father that day. I don't know what got into him, pouring a big glass of wine for a fourteen year-old then grinning at your silly face while you drank it."

Chet smiled, and his shoulders bounced. "I'm pretty sure 'what got into him' was a big bottle of wine. You were the designated driver, remember?"

"Yes, I remember. I didn't speak to him for hours after that. The two of you behaved like complete jackasses the rest of the afternoon."

"God, he was a great dad! I always knew exactly where I stood with him, what he expected of me." He pointed for another kek. "The absolute worst was when I knew I'd disappointed him. All he had to do was look at me with those steely blue eyes, and I knew I was in deep shit. I'd rather have had a beating than be on the receiving end of Sir's special look."

Millie put her hand on Chet's forearm. "Someday you'll be a good father, too."

"Not at the rate I'm going. For the last five years, my business has dominated everything. I'm beginning to have visions of myself lying on one of those slabs as an old man who kicked off with nothing *but* his business—no wife, no kids, just work."

"Good heavens! Where are these morbid thoughts coming from all of a sudden?"

Chet downshifted and pulled into the right lane. "Mariska Williston has an old geezer neighbor she calls Oscar."

"Oscar, as in Oscar the Grouch?"

"Yep."

"His entire life seems to revolve around sitting on his front porch waiting for a chance to yell at her and the dogs when they go by."

"The poor man, but to be fair, you don't know anything about him, about his life. Do you?"

"No, you're right. If I were planning to see her again, I'd be tempted to walk up to his porch and start a conversation, just to satisfy my curiosity."

"But you're not planning to see her again?" Millie shifted in her seat. "Why, honey? Did the two of you have a falling out?"

Chet took a breath and thought about his answer. "No, that's just it. There's no basis for a falling out. We like each other, but there's got to be more than physical attraction. I thought that maybe I could get her out of my system if we slept together. But she had the good sense to stop it before we passed the point of no return. I like her too much to treat her as a casual encounter."

She patted his arm. "You're a good man, in spite of your lady-killer reputation."

"Those days are past. I'm a straight arrow, a respected business man, and a credit to my profession." He squeezed his lips together and nodded. "My pal, Bobby, is finally going to tie the knot. He's asked me to be his best man. I'm the last domino to fall."

"What's this, number three? Always the best man, never the groom?"

"Jeez, Mom, don't rub it in. I'm only thirty-two."

"Exactly the age your father was when we married. Ripe for the picking, I'd say."

She stopped teasing when Chet turned off the highway. "Where are you going?"

"That winery where Sir supervised the loss of my alcohol virginity is just down this road. I thought we'd pick up a few bottles for the big reunion dinner tomorrow."

"What a convenient way to change the subject."

Chet grinned.

* * * *

Ramstein Airbase one week later

A young airman caught up with Chet as he left the base mortuary. "Mr. Jensen! Wait!" Breathless, he handed Chet a note. "I took this message while you conducted your seminar. The caller said not to interrupt you."

Chet reached for the note. "Thanks, corporal." He stuffed the note in the pocket of his chinos then proceeded to the lot for his car. Once inside he unfolded the note and read it.

Risky Business

Chet,

I know you're busy, but I need to see you while you're here. It's important. I'm at the same number.

Noreen Perillo

Chet stared at the brief, handwritten message with jumbled gut reactions. He hadn't seen beautiful, gentle Noreen for years. Their parting had been full of pain. He fell in love with her, but she was married. Her husband, Steve, had been temporarily stationed at the Aviano NATO airbase in Italy. Separated, they'd started divorce proceedings.

Chet and Nori returned from an idyllic week in Switzerland where they explored the beauty of the country during the day, and made explosive, white-hot love every night. Chet planned his future with her.

When they got back to her house in Kaiserslautern, a letter from Steve Perillo awaited Noreen. Scheduled to return to Ramstein in ten days, he begged for a reconciliation. He didn't want the divorce. Being separated from her for four months made him realize how much he loved her and wanted their marriage to work.

Chet had reached a crossroads in his career, ready to assume full responsibility for the management and operation of Jensen and Jensen. His uncle wanted to retire.

There could only be one solution. He had to leave Nori. Had to break it off. Had to return home to California. She wanted to give Steve and their marriage a chance. His heart breaking, Chet wouldn't stand in their way.

Noreen never called after that day. A week later Chet and Millie left Germany on schedule. His mother supported his decision, and kept her comments to a minimum. A grown man, he would ask for her advice if he wanted it.

In too much pain to pretend otherwise, their trip home was a long and sad one.

Now Noreen wanted to see him, after all this time. Not a single communication had passed between them since the day he left her. It was important, she said.

He drove to the home just outside the military installation, where he and Millie were guests of friends. They had plans to attend a large dinner party with old acquaintances that evening.

Noreen wouldn't say it was important unless it was true. He'd call her before they went to dinner.

Chapter Eighteen

Chi Chi's restaurant, Simi Valley

Mariska stepped inside the crowded Italian eatery, and glanced around the dining room.

The hostess smiled. "May I help you?"

"I'm meeting someone, but I don't see him."

A gust of wind ruffled her hair as the doors opened behind her. She turned as Terry entered. "Here he is."

Dr. Terry Redmond grinned. "Mariska, you beat me here." He wore faded jeans, a black tee shirt, and a high-school letterman jacket, looking more like a soccer coach than an emergency room physician. He ran his hands over his head to smooth down his dark, windblown hair. "I hope you haven't been waiting long."

She returned his smile. "Nope." She ran her hands over her own head. "Just walked in the door. I thought I'd be the late one."

The hostess selected two menus. "Do you prefer a booth or table?"

Terry deferred to Risky with raised eyebrows.

Risky pointed. "Is that booth by the window open?"

"Follow me, it's all yours." She led them toward the back of the room, and placed the menus on the table.

"Jeremy will be your waiter. Have a nice evening."

Terry waited until Risky took her seat then slid in across from her. "This place smells great. I feel like I haven't eaten all day." He made a show of sniffing the air like a hungry dog. His brown eyes sparkled.

She smiled and picked up her menu. "Me too, only in my case it's true. I get involved in something and forget to eat. It's a life-long bad habit."

Terry studied the wine menu. "Would you like a glass of wine? Or we could share a bottle." He raised his hands. "But I don't even know if you drink alcohol."

"The house red is good by the glass or carafe. I'm an easy-to-please, cheap date."

He signaled the waiter. "We'll see about that."

Mariska relaxed during dinner. Charming, funny, and sexy in a non-threatening way, Terry talked and laughed with her as if they were old friends. She'd never felt so at ease with any man other than her dad or Bobby. Appearing interested in everything she had to say, he laughed in all the right places. By the time they finished dinner she was mellow and happy. Thoughts of Chet briefly came to mind, but she'd pushed them to the back of her consciousness. Tonight she wouldn't shortchange Terry by thinking of another man. Even Digger.

He held the door for her as they left the restaurant. "My ride is right over there. I'll drive to the batting cages then bring you back for your car later. Okay?"

"Sure, that works for me."

He led the way across the parking lot, and stopped next to a pimped-up, antique, muscle car.

Astonished, Risky stared. "This is your car?"

He patted the roof with a loving grin. "Yeah. You like her?"

She ran a hand across the glossy blue paint. "Wow. She's great. What make and model year?"

Terry unlocked the door and held it open. "This hotrod is a 1966 Pontiac GTO. My dad gave her to me when I graduated medical school. This baby's my pride and joy."

Risky ignored the open door. "Show me the engine."

Terry's eyes went wide with delight. "You really want to see?"

"Sure. I love classic cars. Open her up." She paused at the back wheel, and bent down. "Are those Crager Mag wheels?"

"Yes. I'm impressed, Mariska. How do you know that?"

She stroked her fingers over the aluminum wheels. "My cousin Bobby and I loved going to classic car rallies. We'd hang around all day talking to the geezers about their cars."

Terry chuckled and popped open the hood. "Well, let this geezer show you what this baby has." He leaned on his elbows and pointed. "461 V-8 engine, Kauffman racing aluminum heads, Holley carburetor, Kauffman exhaust manifolds, 3.55:1 positraction rear end, and five speed manual transmission, for starters."

Risky made a big O of admiration with her mouth, and ooh-ed and aah-ed as he named the features. "Wow. I'd love to drive it sometime."

Terry stood up and lowered the hood. "How about now?"

Risky wrinkled her nose. "Don't tease me. I'm in love with your car, and I'm very vulnerable."

He handed her the keys. "Not kidding. She's all yours. Let's take her for a spin."

Risky squeezed the keys in a fist against her chest. Bouncing up and down on her toes, she squealed with anticipation, and threw her arms around Terry for a quick, impulsive hug. "Oh boy, oh boy, oh boy. Let's go."

She pulled out of the parking lot and drove the short distance to the onramp of the Ronald Reagan Freeway. Heading west, she accelerated, careful not to exceed the speed limit. The powerful thrum of the engine echoed through her body. She glanced at Terry and laughed aloud at the pleased grin on his face.

Wind thumped through the open windows, and pounded their ears, making conversation impractical. Her grip on the steering wheel sent vibrations coursing through her arms and shoulders.

No doubt about it. Once she got home, she'd have to set fire to her old junker.

She took the 23 ramp, exited the freeway at Madera Road and headed back to the center of Simi Valley. They rolled up the windows and she slowed to a city pace. "Terry, this is one great car."

He caressed the custom dashboard with his fingertips. "I won't argue the point. How do you like driving her?"

Risky relaxed her shoulders and glanced at him. "I could keep going for hours." Yes, she could get used to Terry and his car real easy.

He winked. "Say the word."

"I wish."

"What's stopping you?"

"Six dogs."

Chapter Nineteen

Kaiserslautern, Germany

Chet stood across the street and stared at Noreen's small house. His heart squeezed painfully when he remembered the last time he walked out that door some four years ago. Now here he stood again, and she still had the power to hurt him.

She wouldn't tell him what was so crucial, but she promised it was something as important to him as to her. Her voice broke over the phone, and she could barely get the words out. She begged him to come in person, alone.

Where was Steve? She said she'd tell him everything when he got there then begged him to trust her.

He rang the old doorbell. The buzz echoed through the entry hall. He held his breath when the door opened, and there she stood, his beautiful Nori.

But she'd changed.

Her glossy sable hair lay dull and lifeless; cut short—a boyish shag. The memory of her long hair sliding through his fingers punched him in the gut.

Dark circles smudged beneath her light brown, almost golden, cat's eyes. The unnaturally pale skin of her face stretched tight across her elegant cheekbones. If they'd passed on the street, he wouldn't have recognized her.

Tears sprang to her eyes. "Chet, you came." Her hands flew to her mouth.

He clenched his teeth, his throat clogged with anguish. Instead of speaking, he opened his arms, and she stepped into his embrace. He caressed her back. The sharp definition of her shoulder blades startled him. She'd lost a good deal of weight. "Noreen, what's happened to you?"

She lifted her forehead from his chest. "Come inside." She took his hand and led him to the living room. A room so familiar. Little had changed. The same furniture, in the same arrangement. Noreen always put fresh flowers in her living room, but not today.

She pulled him toward the loveseat, and he sat next to her, still holding her hand. "Nori, what's happened? Are you ill?"

She swallowed, nodded, but couldn't speak.

He touched the side of her face, flicked away a tear with his thumb. "Is Steve on deployment?"

She clamped a hand over her mouth to still her trembling lips. After a deep breath, she composed herself and choked out the words, "Steve's dead."

"What! When ... how ...?"

"A long time ago." She took a breath. "Years."

"Why didn't you tell me?" She should have told him. She owed him that much. "Why didn't you contact me?"

With her elbows on her knees, Noreen dropped her head into her hands and sobbed. "Because ... because I'd already done enough damage to your life."

He placed an arm around her shoulders. "Noreen, don't talk nonsense. We were adults. We walked into our love affair with our eyes wide open, and we suffered the consequences for our mistake." He hugged her to his side.

She raised tearstained eyes and gazed directly into his face. "You weren't a mistake, Chet. Don't ever think that. You were the best thing that ever happened to me."

He kissed the top of her head. "If only I'd known, if only you'd told me I would ha ..." A small cry sounded from the back of the house. He straightened. "Is that a child? Do you have a kid?"

She stood. "Yes, it's my little boy, Christian." She pointed to the bedrooms. "Wait here, I'll be right back."

Noreen had a child, a son. How had he not known this? His stomach clenched. When she made the decision to give her marriage another chance, Chet thought his life was over. He'd walked out, never once bothering to inquire about her.

He'd consciously, deliberately avoided looking back. They'd been so in love, how could he have slammed that door so firmly and walked away with such finality?

Seeing her today, it seemed impossible.

Her frailty was obvious when she went for the child. Her bony elbows and wrists seemed oversized on her thin arms. Her graceful neck didn't appear sturdy enough to hold up her head. What had happened to her?

She spoke gently to the child as they walked slowly from the back of the house. The little boy rubbed sleepy eyes, looked up at her and whispered a question. She nodded and patted his head.

They stopped in front of Chet. He stared at the child, struggled to breathe, his chest crushed under painful tightening chains. He raised his eyes to her.

"Is he ...?"

A soft feminine hand stroked the boy's blond curls. "This is your daddy, Chris. Remember I told you that someday you'd see your daddy?"

The boy stared at Chet with sober sapphire eyes mirroring his own. He stared at his mother again then back at Chet. "My daddy?" His rosy little face twisted with that hope-filled question, and a spark of wonder shone in his eyes.

Chet extended trembling hands. Unable to speak, he nodded, reached for the child, and swallowed the huge lump in his throat. His gaze went to Noreen. Tears streamed down her cheeks.

Christian looked to his mother. She smiled and nodded, so his chubby arms went around his father's neck as Chet embraced him. "Hello, Daddy."

A wrenching sob escaped Chet's throat. He buried his face in the mop of blond hair. "Hello, son. I'm so glad to meet you."

The child giggled and held up three fingers. "I'm three and a half. I can read, and I know all my numbers. When Mama goes to her job at the school, I go with her every day. She told me to be good so you would love me." He placed his small hands on Chet's damp cheeks, gazed solemnly, "Do you love me?"

Chet's head spun, he laughed. "Absolutely. I do love you, Chris." He lifted the boy to his lap, reached for Noreen's hand, and pulled her down to sit with them.

Christian sighed with drama and wagged his head. "That's a relief." He smacked his hands against Chet's cheeks. "I was pretty tired of waiting."

Despite the gravity of the moment, Chet and Noreen laughed. And cried.

The boy giggled along with them. "Are we a happy family now?"

Chet nodded. "My God, Nori, he's wonderful, he's beautiful, and he's wise."

Noreen stroked her son's grinning cheek. "My little Christian is an old soul. Aren't you, love?"

The boy nodded and wriggled off Chet's lap. "I gonna show you my soldiers." He ran from the living room then turned back, "Don't go away, okay?" His footsteps pounded down the hall.

Chet laughed through his confounding breadth of emotions. "I'll stay right here."

Noreen gripped his hand. "Chet, we have so much to talk about. I don't know where to begin. I know I blindsided you. I'm sorry."

He shook his head against dizziness. "Did Steve accept Christian as his son?"

"Steve was killed in a traffic accident on the base a month after he got home from Aviano. He flew hundreds of NATO missions then ended up getting killed in a senseless car wreck. He didn't know I was pregnant."

Chet sighed and leaned forward, elbows on his knees. "I don't know what to say, Nori, except I'm disappointed and angry that you never told me. You kept him from me. He's my son, for chrissakes! How could you?" He turned to stare at her. "And why now?"

Her eyes pleaded with him. "Don't be angry with me, Chet."

He glared, his hands clenched into tight fists. "Don't tell me what to feel, Noreen. This is my kid. I've missed all of his life so far. You didn't answer me. Why now?"

She pressed her lips together, swallowed, and said, "I have pancreatic cancer. I'm dying. I don't have much time."

Horrified at his angry words, Chet gasped and reached for her. "My God, I'm sorry, Nori. I'm so sorry."

Christian appeared in front of them, his arms full of plastic soldiers and jet planes. "Why are you crying, Mama?"

Noreen cleared her throat and pasted a smile on her face. She brushed her fingers through the boy's hair. "Remember I told you I might have to go away, honey?"

Eyes wide, he nodded. "Uh huh, I 'member."

"Well, I will go away soon. I don't want to leave you, but I have to, sweetheart."

His forehead creased as he stared at her with huge eyes. "Who will take care of me?"

Noreen gazed steadily into Chet's eyes. "Your daddy will take care of you. You'll go to live in America with your daddy and your grandma."

His little face brightened. "I have a gramma?"

Chet lifted him to his knee. The child clutched his toys against his small chest. "Yes, son, you have a beautiful grandma. She's going to love you so much. She'll be very happy to meet you, just like I am."

Christian hopped off Chet's lap. "Okay then. Do you want to see my soldiers?" He grabbed Chet's hand. "Come on, Daddy. I know how to share. I'll let you play with my soldiers."

Hours later Noreen tucked Christian into his trundle bed. They'd spent all afternoon at the park then had supper at a local German restaurant. The boy fell asleep on Chet's lap before they'd finished eating.

Noreen took an envelope from her desk drawer, and joined Chet. "You'll need this." She handed him the official-looking documents. "It's his birth certificate and his passport."

Chet unfolded the paper and read. He was named as the father of Chester

Christian Jensen. Noreen Louise Perillo as Chris's mother. The boy's birthday was seven months after Chet had returned to the U.S.

He held up the paper. "You were two months pregnant when I left?" He didn't know what to feel. Happiness? Betrayal? Emotions warred in his soul. "Noreen, you should have told me."

Her lips in a grim line, she shook her head. "I didn't know, at least I'd ignored the signs. I was so crazy in love with you my brain was numb. I existed on sheer emotion, and went from the heights of joy to the depths of despair when Steve said he wanted to start over."

Chet scoffed. "You weren't the only one."

She slumped in the chair across from him. "I didn't know what to do. I was twenty-three years old, blinded by happiness, and then paralyzed by pain. You were the love of my life, Chet. I love you now."

Chet sank back in his chair. He pressed his fingers against his temples in a useless exercise to tamp down a burgeoning headache. "I never stopped loving you, Nori, but I moved on with my life. After a year or so it was possible for me to enjoy the company of women again without comparing every one of them to you."

She leaned forward and gripped his arm. "Now I have a bigger favor to ask of you."

"Bigger than dropping a kid in my lap?" He snorted. "I doubt it."

"You have to marry me. It's important. It's the only way."

Chet gasped. She couldn't have possibly said what he just heard. "Marry you? You want me to marry you now? Why, in God's name? Chris hasn't had a father all this time."

Noreen pulled up the corner of her shirt and wiped her eyes. "Steve's parents have demanded custody of Christian when I die. They choose to believe he's Steve's son, even after I told them about you. You're his biological father. Chris should be with you. They've told me they'll fight for him, Chet. If you marry me, they won't have legal standing."

Groaning, Chet dropped his head back. "Jesus H. Christ, Noreen. What are you doing to me?" He got to his feet and paced the small room. "I already told you I'll take him. I want him. Is there anything else I should know?" He threw up his hand in a wild gesture then raked his fingers through his hair.

She shook her head and curled forward until her forehead rested on her knees. Sobs wracked her body.

Chet knelt beside her, took her in his arms. "I'm sorry. That was uncalled for." He gripped her fists in his hands. "I'm having trouble taking it all in, that's all."

Long silent minutes passed. Chet lifted Noreen in his arms and carried her to the bedroom. After making her comfortable, he removed her shoes and covered her with a hand crocheted shawl. He remembered the shawl. Her grandmother had made it for a wedding gift when Nori'd announced her engagement to Steve.

He sat next to her and stroked her emaciated arm.

She brushed her fingers across his chin. "Lie down with me, Chet. I need to rest. I'm so tired. We have so much to plan, but I can't I ..."

"Shhh, shhh. No more talking." He pulled off his shoes, and lay next to her with his arm across her frail body. "We'll talk later."

Chapter Twenty

The next morning

Chet breathed with relief when his mother answered the phone instead of her friend, Gloria. "Mom, I'm checking in. I didn't want you to worry about me."

"I gave up worrying about you long ago, Chester. What you do isn't my business. Anyway, I didn't realize until I got up this morning that you hadn't come in last night."

Chet took a deep breath. "What I'm calling about is very much your business. I hope you're not getting ready to go somewhere. I'd like you to meet me at the Starbucks just outside the base. It's important."

"Why so mysterious? Don't tell me you got secretly married or something." A soft chuckle followed her question.

His stomach clenched at her innocent tease. "You always were perceptive, Millie, but no, I didn't get married. Can you meet me there in an hour?"

"Give me a hint?"

"Gotta go. See you in an hour."

* * * *

Chet spotted Millie sipping coffee and perusing a menu card when he entered the coffee bar.

She looked up and waved. Her expression changed when Chet bent his knees and spoke to the little boy with him. They approached the table.

The child stepped forward and solemnly said, "Hello, Gramma."

Millie gasped. Raising her gaze to her son, she glared and hissed, "How dare you do this in a public place. How dare you!"

Chet's heart sank. He opened his mouth to say something as the little boy ducked back, hid behind Chet's leg, and clung tightly to his pants.

"She doesn't like me, Daddy."

Millie's face crumpled, and she extended her arms. "Oh, honey, of course I like you. I'm mad at your Daddy, not you. Come here." She flashed a warning glower at Chet.

The child, chin tucked against his chest, shuffled forward.

Millie reached for him, and put her arm around his shoulders. "You're a very handsome boy. What's your name, sweetheart?"

"Chester Christian Jensen. I'm three and a half." He held up four fingers. "I can read and I know all my numbers and my mama told me that if I was good my daddy would love me." He raised his eyes and looked at Chet. "You do love me, don't you Daddy?"

Chet clenched his jaw, flexed his hands, and took the chair across the small bistro table. "Yes, Chris, I do."

Millie stifled a sob. Her eyes were awash with unshed tears. She hugged the boy. "You're my very first grandson, Christian. I love you, too." She hugged him to her chest.

"Can I have some chocolate milk, Daddy?"

Chet reached for his wallet and pulled out a couple of bills. He pointed. "See that case over there?"

Chris nodded.

"The chocolate milk is on the bottom shelf. Take one and pay the lady at the cash register, okay?"

Grinning from ear to ear, the child grabbed the money. "I know how to do it myself. I'm big."

Chet's chest flooded with pride. He ruffled Chris's hair before he dashed across the room toward the cold case.

Millie gave him a cold stare. "I'm so angry with you, Chester. I can't even get coherent thoughts together. How could you have kept this child from me?" She smacked her hand on the table. "He's three years old!"

Chet reached to cover his mother's hand. He gripped it hard when she attempted to pull away from him. "Mom, I didn't know anything about him until yesterday."

Astonishment covered her face. She shook her head. "What are you saying? You had a son, and you didn't know about him?"

"That's exactly what I'm saying. Noreen sent me a message night before last. She begged me to come to her place. I went to see her yesterday."

"My, God, Chet. Are you still in the middle of that troubled marriage? I thought that was all in the past." Millie put her elbow on the table and lowered her forehead into her hand. She sighed and rolled her head from side to side.

"Mom, Steve died before Christian was born. Noreen didn't know she was pregnant when I left Germany. By the time she knew, Steve had returned home, and she really wanted to give their marriage a chance. A month later Steve was killed in a car wreck on the base."

Millie's eyes sparked anger. She pressed her lips in a disapproving line. "She should have told you, Chester. You had a right to know, she ..."

Christian set his box of chocolate milk on the table then opened his small hand and dropped the change in front of Chet. He grinned at Millie. "Daddy gave me too much money, Gramma."

Chet's heart clenched. "Come here and sit on my lap while you drink your milk."

"Why?"

"Because I love it when you sit on my lap."

Chris shrugged. "Okay, but don't squeeze me." He turned his back to Chet and raised his arms.

A couple of tears escaped Millie. She put her palm over her mouth then reached for Chet's hand. After a sharp inhale on a sob, she gazed at her son, her grandson, and then her son again.

Chet watched her take in their resemblance. Same blond hair, same blue eyes, same dimple at the corner of the mouth, one eyebrow slightly higher than the other.

"Your father's chest would be out to here, Chester."

He squeezed her hand, and tipped his head toward his son. "There's more. We'll talk later."

* * * *

Ten days later Chet and Noreen were married at the local *Standesamt* office in Kaiserslautern. Friends and acquaintances of Millie and Chet went to extraordinary lengths to help them obtain the paperwork and permissions. The registrar had finally received all the documents necessary to perform a marriage between two American citizens.

Immediately after the private ceremony, Chet took Noreen to the hospital. "Chet, please don't stay. I want you to take Christian to California with you as soon as you can."

Chet could barely breathe from the tightness in his lungs. "Nori, please don't ask me to leave you here alone."

She squeezed his hand. "You don't have to see me like this. There's nothing you can do, and the doctors have exhausted all treatment. All they can do now is keep me comfortable."

"Nori ..."

"I'm not afraid. You'll be a good father to Chris. I love you, and I'm so happy to be your wife."

So choked he couldn't speak, Chet held Noreen's hand until she fell asleep.

She died that night.

Chapter Twenty-One

Simi Hills Golf Course, Simi Valley, California

Mariska yelled, "Look out!" when a duck waddled in front of Terry as he teed off. He lost his balance and fell on his butt.

Risky bent over and roared with laughter. "That's one lucky duck. I thought for sure he was a goner when you went into your backswing."

Terry shook his head and grinned at the nonchalantly retreating bird. "I should get a mulligan for that stroke. That damn bird's lucky to be alive." He struggled to his feet and brushed off the seat of his pants.

Risky shook her head. "Oh, no you don't. You've already got me beat by five strokes and there's only one more hole to play."

Terry grumbled and took his stance behind the ball. "You're a mean, spiteful, unforgiving opponent, if I've ever met one."

"Cry baby."

He took his shot, laughed and pointed when it flew long and straight. "I think you're going to owe me dinner, Ms. Williston."

Risky made a sour face at his great shot. "Only if you let me drive your car to the restaurant, Dr. Redmond." She planted her feet, took a swing, and sent her ball down the fairway almost as far as Terry's. A satisfied grin broke across her face. She raised her hand, held it like a gun, and blew on her finger.

Terry dropped the driver in his bag and slung it over his shoulder. "You've got a deal, hotshot."

Risky and Terry and been going out a couple of times a week for the past two and a half months. They hadn't progressed much beyond kissing. She had the feeling he'd be expecting more than kisses, and soon. She really liked him, they had a lot of fun together, but she wasn't ready to go the extra step.

They finished the round. Terry followed her home so she could take care of the dogs before they drove to Sherman Oaks for dinner. She'd never heard of the restaurant, but it was one of his favorites.

She was game to try anything with him—well, almost anything.

Once she had her babies and the big boys settled she locked up the house and slid behind the wheel of Terry's car. She berated herself for thinking that maybe she liked his car better than she liked him. No, she liked him fine. He wasn't Digger Jensen, but he was one super guy.

Now where did that thought about Chet come from? She'd been determined not to compare Terry to Chet. It wasn't fair to Terry, or to her. Who wouldn't prefer the company of a handsome and charming doctor over that of an undertaker?

It was just that Terry's kisses and his hands, while super nice, didn't get her heart pounding and her legs trembling like Chet's had. She took a deep breath to clear her head.

"Something wrong?"

"No, my mind wandered. I was thinking about Bobby's wedding tomorrow, that's all."

"What time do you want me to pick you up? I have an early shift tomorrow. I'll be off by three."

"We don't need to be at the church until six. Five-thirty will be plenty early. Anita let me off the hook from being a bridesmaid. She knew I'd go screaming from the church in one of those puffy pink dresses."

Terry chuckled. "I think you'd look great in one of those puffy pink dresses—or out of one for that matter."

"Pay attention to where I'm driving. Give me plenty of time to change lanes when I have to."

"You're good at changing the subject. Move to the middle lane after we pass the next light."

His cell phone rang. "Dammit! Not now." He looked at the screen. "It's the hospital. Redmond here. What's up? Okay, I'll get there as soon as I can."

Risky glanced at him. "You have to go to work?"

He pointed at the next intersection. "Yeah, I'm on call, sorry, make a U-turn at the corner. There was a big pile-up on the Simi Freeway. Multiple cars. They're calling in all the E.R. staff."

Mariska got in the left lane, executed a smooth turn and headed back the way they'd come. "Darn it. That's too bad, Terry. I was looking forward to the rest of the evening."

He squeezed her shoulder. "Me too, I packed my toothbrush."

Her breath stuttered, she swallowed, gripped the wheel and stared straight ahead. He'd packed his toothbrush? He was planning to spend the night? How had she missed the signs? There must have been signs.

He chuckled, "You don't have to look so relieved."

She shook her head, still staring straight ahead. "I'm ... uh ... not ... relieved, I just ... you were planning to spend the night at my place? With me?"

He tugged on her ear. "I was hoping to, but it doesn't look like you were planning to invite me."

Risky's face burned hot, and she was glad it was dark. She was no inexperienced teenager, so why was she so unsettled when she realized what Terry wanted? She struggled to find something to say to him, but no words came.

"Relax, Mariska. If you're not ready, I'm cool with it. There's no rush."

"I'm so embarrassed. I like you a lot, Terry. I'm acting like a naïve kid. Did I mess up everything?"

"I'm a patient man. If you want slow, we'll take it slow."

She stifled a sigh of relief. "Do you want to drop me off at my house?"

"No, we don't have time to back-track. Take me to the hospital. Drive my car home, and I'll get somebody to give me a lift to your place after we get through the crisis. It'll be late, so leave the keys under the seat."

Her shoulders relaxed. "I'm really sorry about dinner. Looks like it'll be a can of soup for me tonight." She moved into the right lane as they got close to the off-ramp for the hospital.

"At least you get soup. Pity your poor trauma doctor. My mouth was watering for those ribs."

She pulled into the parking lot near the emergency entrance and put the car in park.

Terry leaned in for a quick kiss then reached for the door handle. "See you at five thirty tomorrow, gorgeous."

She grabbed for his arm, but missed. "Terry, wait!"

He turned and ducked his head back in the car. "What?"

"Bring your toothbrush. Just in case, okay?"

His grin dazzled. He closed the door and jogged to the emergency entrance. Before going inside he turned and waved. His handsome face glowing, he gave her a thumbs-up.

Oh, boy. Would she ever learn not to say the first thing that came to her head?

* * * *

Bobby's wedding and reception

The usher seated Mariska and Terry on the groom's side, second row. Her parents were seated in the row behind them.

Terry leaned forward and whispered, "Your mother and father are here."

"I know. I saw them when we came in."

"Your mother is beautiful. You look a lot like her."

She rolled her eyes and smirked. "Lucky me."

Risky surveyed the packed church, smiled, and waved at acquaintances. Bobby had always done a good job staying in touch with their childhood friends. If she didn't see somebody she knew in her normal daily routine she rarely thought to call, to keep in touch. Shame on her.

Bobby told her more than once that she couldn't whine about her meager social life if she didn't put in some effort to nurture friendships. Blah, blah, blah. Bobby always preached.

She did a double take when she spotted Millie several rows behind, mountains of gleaming red hair, diamonds in her ears. Millie smiled and wiggled her fingers. Risky whipped her head around and stared forward.

Oh, God.

The wedding singer concluded a very decent interpretation of Whitney Houston's big hit, I Will Always Love You. Bobby's and Anita's favorite song. They'd been known to drive friends screaming from the room by singing it endlessly at parties.

Soft music filled the large chapel. Bobby and Chet entered and took their places in front next to the minister.

Her heart thudded. Chet.

Oh, God.

Risky couldn't exhale, her chest so full of air it was a wonder she didn't float right off the pew. She grabbed Terry's hand to keep herself from becoming airborne. He squeezed back and moved closer so their knees pressed together. She wiggled her bottom on the hard bench, but not because of Terry's leg, because she tingled from her navel to her knees at the sight of Chet.

Oh, God.

When she wiggled closer, Terry misinterpreted her move, dropped his arm over her shoulder, and leaned in to kiss her cheek. She blushed so hot she must have looked like a selection on the menu at Red Lobster. Terry moved closer.

The Wedding March rang through the chapel. Bobby and Chet turned to face the center aisle. A huge, happy smile lit her cousin's face. The audience rose to welcome the bride. Chet winked at her.

Risky's libido purred then roared, the rest of the ceremony a blur. How they got out of the church, to Terry's car, and then the country club for the reception fuzzed in her brain. Here she was, seated next to Terry, across the table from her parents with a glass of champagne in her hand.

A younger couple, friends of the bride, joined them for the lavish, break-the-bank dinner banquet.

Anya and her father declined champagne, to Risky's audible sigh of relief, opting for the non-alcoholic punch. Her dad nodded his reassurance.

Serenely beautiful, Anya remained exotic and charming all during dinner.

Risky breathed easier and relaxed.

Chet, as best man, offered a heartfelt and hilarious toast, immediately followed by many others. Anita's father escorted her to the dance floor. Bobby cut in, and they danced their first dance as husband and wife.

Mariska swallowed weepiness when her parents rose, and Dave took Anya's hand. Anyone who didn't know the details of their tragic marriage would assume they were a happy couple without a care in the world.

She coughed and excused herself from the table. In the ladies room she repaired her mascara, studied herself in the mirror, disgusted that she'd chosen to wear a subtle gray suit with silver earrings her only accessory. She composed herself and returned to the reception.

Terry stood and grinned. "May I have this dance?"

Risky nodded and took his hand. She would enjoy this wonderful party, celebrate with her cousin and his bride, and push the troubled past from her mind.

Terry embraced her in warm, comfortable arms, intimate and relaxed. She moved closer and enjoyed the closeness of him, the gentleness and patience he was so generous with. It didn't hurt at all that he smelled masculine, fresh and sexy. He gave truth to the expression — eye candy.

Chet and Millie danced several couples away, Risky gawked and stumbled.

Terry followed her gaze. "Jensen's mother is a looker, isn't she?"

"Is she here tonight?"

"Yes, that's who he's dancing with, his mother, Millie Jensen. I see her at the health club. She's a sweetheart."

Terry danced Risky in their direction.

"What are you doing?"

"I'm moving close to them so I can ask her for a dance." He twirled her closer. "Hey, Jensen. How do you always rate the most beautiful woman in the room?" He smiled at Chet's mother. "Hi, Millie. How about a dance later?"

Millie grinned. "Hello, you sweet thing. You're doing all right in the beautiful woman category." She pointed at Mariska. "I'm tired of dancing with Chester. Let's switch partners."

Terry faced Risky. "Are you okay with that, Mariska?"

Change partners? Was he kidding? Her inner voice screamed, no, no, no.

"Uh ... sure. Go ahead. I'll just—"

Chet took her in his arms. "—dance with me." He leaned close to her ear. "How you doin', Dog Breath? Haven't seen you since I got back. I see you've got old Terry under your spell." He inhaled through his nose. "Probably because you smell so damn good."

She wasn't sure who was under whose spell because her knees went weak and her insides jittered.

Tilting her face so she could stare into his eyes, she hissed, "You jerk! How long were you planning to let me think she was your girlfriend?" She gave him a sharp punch in the chest.

Chet grabbed the offending fist. "Easy there, doll, I planned to tell you as soon as I returned from Germany. This is the first time we've both been in the same vicinity." He held firm when she tugged her hand. "No, I'm not letting go until you promise not to hit me again." He dimpled with the world's sexiest grin.

Oh, God.

Might as well throw in the towel. How would she ever make it through this dance without slobbering like a teenage groupie?

He almost accomplished the *coup de grace* when he raised her fist to his lips and kissed the back of her hand.

She whimpered. "Please don't do that, Digger."

"Why not, doll?" He sniffed her hair and groaned.

"I'm here with Terry Redmond, not you. He's a super nice guy and I'm leaving with the man who brought me to the party, okay?"

"I wouldn't have it any other way. I never did like women who played games." His right hand drifted dangerously close to her bottom. "How about tomorrow?" He whispered.

She reached back and shoved his hand up. "Stop it!"

He stepped back a few inches and put on a no-nonsense face. "Okay, you win. I'll be good. But I do have a favor to ask of you."

Risky snorted. "This should be good."

"No, seriously, there's this little boy whose mother died recently. He's in a deep blue funk, and nothing seems to raise his spirits. I think if he had a dog it might cheer him up."

She frowned and pushed out her lips. "Maybe."

"The thing is he hasn't been around dogs much. I was hoping I could bring him to your place tomorrow, and see how he reacts to them. How about it?"

What harm could come if Chet brought over a little boy to play with her dogs? It's not like he asked her for a sexual favor.

"Okay." She gave a long-suffering sigh. "I have to work in the morning, but I'll be home about one."

"Great. I'll pick up a pizza and we'll have a picnic. He loves to romp outdoors."

"What's his name?"

"Christian. I call him Chris."

The music ended, and Terry escorted Millie back to Chet and Mariska. The men shook hands, and Risky blushed when Millie spoke.

"Nice to see you again, Mariska. This wedding has been a fairytale. Chester tells me you and Bobby grew up together, and that you're close."

"Close enough to kill sometimes. He's been like a big brother to me ever since I was this high." She held her hand at knee level. "I was broken-hearted for an entire week when at seven, I found out I couldn't marry my cousin when I grew up. I'm crazy about him, but don't let that get around."

Chet and Millie smiled at Risky's confession.

Terry reached in his breast pocket for his cell phone. He placed a hand on Risky's shoulder. "Would you excuse me for a minute? I hope it's not the hospital, but I'm on call."

"Sure, go ahead."

Millie took her arm. "Why don't you sit with Chester and me for a minute? I've never had a chance to talk with you."

What could she do? Just because Chet was a jerk didn't mean Millie had any part in his deception. "Okay, that'd be nice."

They moved between the tables toward the raised seating for the bridal party, and took an adjacent table. Chet pulled out his mother's chair then indicated where Risky should sit. He signaled the waiter and asked for a clean champagne glass for Risky.

Millie patted her hand. "Honey, I want to apologize right up front for that nasty little trick Chester pulled on you. While I'm flattered you thought me young enough to be his girlfriend, it was mean of him to lead you to believe it." She reached over and smacked her son's arm. He didn't look the least bit apologetic. He twisted his lips and winked instead.

Warmth rose in Risky's neck and cheeks. "I wanted to kick him when Terry told me you were his mother."

"His childish attempt to make you jealous. I told him it was silly because if you couldn't stomach the idea of getting cozy with an undertaker, jealousy wouldn't do the trick."

Embarrassed that Chet and Millie somehow knew she had that hang-up, she longed to deny it, but the words wouldn't come.

Millie sipped champagne and smiled. "Don't you worry, honey, I can't reconcile myself to it either." She smiled into Chet's eyes. "Right, sweetheart?"

"How many more years is it going to take, Mom? I've been at it over a decade." He pressed his lips together and shook his head. "I'm not likely to give it up now."

Terry reached their table and interrupted them. "Sorry, it was the hospital. I have to go in." He gave a resigned shake of his head.

At their groans, he continued, "You probably don't want to leave this early, Mariska. I'll arrange for a cab to take you home."

Millie flipped her hand. "Don't be silly, Terry. Chester and I will take her home when we leave."

"That's great, thanks." He kissed Millie's cheek. "Would you step outside with me for a minute, Mariska?"

Risky jumped to her feet and nodded.

Terry took her hand and they made their way through the crowded ballroom and out the front entrance. He tugged her to the side, away from the doors.

"I'm so damn sorry. I was looking forward to tonight. That toothbrush is never going to find its way into your medicine cabinet." He chuckled ruefully as he took her in his arms. His warm, sweet kiss had the taste of regret.

Risky hated herself for her sense of relief. She must be a truly rotten person. Here was a wonderful man who longed to be with her. A man whose arms were strong. A man whose arms were gentle and kind. A man whose arms absolutely did not ignite the flames that flared when Chet held her.

She stayed on the steps until the valet brought Terry's car then waved as he drove away.

Chapter Twenty-Two

Risky's house, next afternoon

Risky peeked out the window when she heard Chet's car stop in front of her house. He got out then opened the back door on the passenger side and lifted the little boy out. They followed her front path to the door.

Risky pushed it open before Chet had a chance to knock. "Hey." She looked at the little blondie standing beside him. "You must be Chris. Come in and I'll introduce you to my dogs."

He gazed at her with serious blue eyes. "How many dogs do you got?"

"Right now, I have six."

"That's a lotta dogs."

Chet put his hand on the boy's head. "When I first met Ms. Williston she had eighteen dogs living here." Chet led him inside. "Isn't that amazing?"

Chris raised his eyes to meet Chet's. "I think that's silly."

Risky chuckled and tousled his hair. "I agree with you, Chris. That's why I only have six now." She shared a grin with Chet.

Chris's gaze swept the room. "Where are they?"

"Out back, I'll let them in. They've been waiting all morning to meet you."

His small face showed a flash of pleased surprise. "They have?"

"Yes. Wait here. I'll be right back." She left them standing in the living room while she went through the kitchen to the back door. Eager whining and scratching greeted her footsteps. Once the door opened, they streaked past her legs in a race to the living room.

By the time Risky caught up with them, Chet and Chris were on the floor surrounded by a whirlwind of excited canines. Chris's squeal of excitement tickled her.

Chet raised his eyes and smiled. "Looks like this boy is a natural dog lover."

"Looks like."

Mickey, Minnie and Brutus pushed and shoved against one another to be the center of the boy's attention. Slick concentrated completely on Chet, standing on his skinny hind legs, his tongue lapping at Chet's dodging chin.

Risky figured that Slick, in his own doggy way, was as enthralled by Chet as she. Some kind of mysterious chemistry thing going on?

She giggled. "Slick can't get enough of you."

Chet laughed and raised an eyebrow. "Unlike somebody else in this room."

The heat of a blush burned through her chest, neck and cheeks. The significance of his words made her thighs tingle. Glad for Chris's presence, she pictured herself grabbing Chet, throwing him down, and then crawling all over him, just like Slick.

Oh, God.

"I have no idea what you're talking about."

"No?"

Chris squealed with delight. "Can I have this dog, Daddy?" The little boy hugged Brutus, the toy poodle, to his narrow chest.

Some invisible marching band member slammed his big, brass cymbals against the sides of Risky's head, because she lost her hearing and blackness swirled in her vision.

Daddy? Did he say Daddy? Yes, he did, because Chet answered, "No, son, these are Ms. Williston's pets, but I'll bet she knows where we can find just the right one for you."

Her hearing returned, and her vision cleared a bit.

Chris's bottom lip pushed out. "But, I want this one."

She glared into Chet's eyes, with tight lips and a slight shake of her head. "Why don't I let you borrow Brutus for a few days? Then you and your *daddy* can decide if you really want a dog for a pet."

Chris smiled, wide-eyed with happiness. "Could we borrow him, Daddy? Or could I live here with the dog lady instead of your house?"

Risky touched Chris's head. "I have an idea. You and the dogs come with me. We'll go to the back yard and I'll introduce you to Harley and Shep, my big dogs. They live outside because they're too big for the house. The little ones will come with us, and you can play with them on the grass. Okay?"

Chris sprang to his feet, and bounced with excitement. He tugged Chet's pant leg. "Come on, Daddy."

Chet got to his feet. "Mariska, let me explain. I brought him to meet you because ..."

Risky cut him off. "Here we go, Chris." She turned her back on Chet, took the boy's hand and led him from the room.

* * * *

Chet stood at the screen door and watched. Risky led Chris to the chain-link fence. Shep and Harley paced and wagged their tails when she picked the boy up and let him reach over the top of the dog run to pat their heads. Chris said something to her. She opened the gate and carried him inside, admonishing the big dogs, "Down!" She pointed. "Stay!"

Tails whipping with excitement they obeyed her command, waiting patiently while she set Chris on his feet. She leaned down and spoke quietly in the boy's ear.

He nodded, and extended his hand to Harley.

Risky gave Harley a silent hand signal, and the big dog held up his paw. She repeated the signal with Shep, and he mimicked Harley, his big paw dangling in front of him. Chris shook Harley's paw first then Shep's.

Chet's heart melted when his boy's face lit with a huge, happy smile. Those smiles had been scarce ever since they left Germany. In spite of Nori's meticulous preparation, Chris wanted his mother every waking minute. Chet or Millie could do little to console him.

Risky led Chris from the dog run and closed the gate. They sat on the grass, and the four small dogs yapped and bounced, ready to play and romp. She pulled a red ball from her pocket and tossed it across the yard. The dogs streaked after it. Mickey got there first and ran back to her. She handed the ball to Chris.

While she played with the boy, Chet looked on. He sighed, relaxing hands he'd balled into tight fists when he'd followed them to the door.

After a few minutes, she left Chris with her babies. Chet stepped back when she opened the door.

An angry glare darkened her face. "Anything else you want to spring on me, you world-class liar?"

He raised his hands helplessly and began to speak.

She threw up a hand and silenced him. "No, let me guess." Bitterness oozed from her words. "You've been married all along. In addition to letting me think Millie was your girlfriend, you had a wife and a kid stashed away. Millie knew. What kind of people are you?"

Chet held his hands out. "Look ..."

She beetled her brow and pushed her face close to his. "Look my ass!"

"Mariska, think about it. If I were married, Bobby would have told you. I'm not married."

Scowling, she jabbed a finger toward the back yard. "How do you explain him?"

He shrugged. "You don't have to be married to have a kid."

"Maybe you don't, but I sure as heck do. Why do you have him now? Where is his mother?"

"Noreen died two weeks ago. I brought Chris home from Germany with me." He recognized a flash of regret in her eyes. "Mariska, I want to explain everything to you. Will you let me do that?"

"This better be good." She pulled a chair from the kitchen table and positioned it so she could see Chris and the dogs. "Start talking."

He put his hand on her shoulder. She jerked away.

"Talk, Digger, and make it good because I'm ready to hit you with something."

He dragged a chair from the table and sat. "I met Chris's mother in Germany, through mutual friends, around four years ago. She and her husband, an air force pilot, were separated. A group of pals took a day trip to Lake Constance. It was all very innocent. It wasn't a date or a set-up."

Risky gazed steadily into his eyes. She nodded in the direction of the back yard. "He didn't just happen."

"No, he didn't." Chet watched his son then turned back to Risky. "There were about a dozen of us in the group. Noreen and I hit it off and had a lot of fun that day boating and water-skiing. I saw her on the base a couple of days later. She worked as a teacher in the middle school."

Gratified to see tension ease in Risky's shoulders, he continued. "I found out she'd met my mother and knew the friends we were visiting. I asked her out." He took a breath. "It didn't take long for us to fall in love. Millie warned me against getting in the middle of a married couple, separated or not. It was too late by then because I was head over heels for Noreen. I wanted to marry her."

"Why didn't you?"

Chet went on to tell the story of their affair, Steve's plea to salvage the marriage, and Nori's decision to give it another chance. Broken-hearted, he left Germany. He heard nothing from her until a month ago.

Risky gasped. "You married her, and she died the next day! That's awful." She clasped her hands over her mouth.

Chet's eyes threatened tears, but he blinked them away. "She wanted there to be no question that I would have custody of Christian. Steve's parents told her they intended to take him when she died. They loved Chris and believed Steve was his father in spite of his birth certificate, naming me."

"But her husband must have known."

"He was killed in a traffic accident before Noreen told him she was pregnant." He raised his eyes to the ceiling. "Look, I know I dropped a bomb in your lap with this. I brought him to meet you. I thought if I just told you about him you'd show me the door, and I'd never get a chance to explain." He turned his gaze to the back yard and chuckled sadly when Chris stumbled, and the dogs lost no time jumping all over him.

Risky looked at the boy and shook her head. "He's a beautiful child, Digger. He's going to change your life."

Chet nodded. "He already has. He misses Nori so much, and I'm doing everything I can to fill in for her. That's why I thought if he had a pet, it might take his mind off his constant longing for her. I'm shooting in the dark. Mom is helping when she can, but she has her own life, and doesn't need to be a babysitter for a preschooler." He shrugged and smiled.

His heart squeezed when Mariska put her hand on his arm.

"Daddy!" Chris ran to the screen door. "Daddy, I changed my mind. I like the skinny doggie with no hair the bestest. Can we borrow him, dog lady?"

Risky stood and pushed the door open. "For a few days. Slick likes your daddy a lot, so he'll probably feel right at home in your house. Would you like a Popsicle? I have some in my freezer."

Chris's eyes lit and faced Chet. "Can I, Daddy?"

Chet growled, grabbed Chris and swung him in the air. The boy squealed with excitement. "Daddy, stop!"

"It's almost two, and you haven't had lunch. You need to eat first, and then you can have a Popsicle." He set Chris on his feet.

Risky raised her eyebrows. "So where's the pizza?"

Chet smacked his forehead. "Damn. I knew I forgot something."

Risky touched Chris's cheek. "How about a peanut butter sandwich and a glass of milk?"

Chris sighed, a deep scowl on his face. "Okay." He scuffed his toe on the floor with resignation.

Risky made sandwiches then contemplated Chet and his miniature clone while they sat at her small table eating. Chet often placed his hand on the boy's arm or his head. He seemed in awe of the child, unable to resist touching him. This was the same Chet she often fantasized over, but different. He was a dad. He had a kid and it was clear he was crazy over him.

What an odd turn of events. Still Chester Jensen, the undertaker, but here was a side of him she never suspected. She wondered how he managed with a child tearing through his perfectly clean and orderly apartment. That was something she'd like to see.

They carried their Popsicles out back and sat on the grass under the shade of an ancient eucalyptus. Chris wound down, eyelids drooping heavily over his big blue eyes.

Chet lay on his back, his legs crossed at the ankles, arms under his head. Slick had wasted no time nuzzling into his shoulder and neck, and snored contentedly. "Christian, come here and lie down for a few minutes. You're tired."

"I wanna play with Slick."

"Look, Slick is asleep. You wore him out. Why don't you rest until he wakes up? Then we'll take him home with us."

Sighing with resignation Chris murmured, "Okay." He scooted next to Chet and rested his head on his daddy's other shoulder. Seconds later, he breathed rhythmically and slept. Chet winked at her then closed his own eyes.

There was nothing Risky wanted to do more than crawl right on top of Chet and nestle her nose in his neck. It seemed impossible he could be sexier than ever with the sleeping boy and dog snuggled against him.

Oh, God.

With a sigh, she shook her head at all her sleeping dogs, Chet, and Chris. She lay back and stared at the sky through the leafy canopy of the tree. Her heart sank when the clouds morphed into a semblance of Terry Redmond's handsome, smiling face.

Oh, God.

Chapter Twenty-Three

Risky stood next to the Lincoln and watched Chet buckle Chris in the toddler seat. Slick needed no invitation. As soon as he got past Chet's legs, he bounded into the car and settled in as if it were part of his daily routine.

She pointed her finger at Slick. "You ungrateful little traitor."

Christian stared with wide, worried eyes. "Me?"

She reached in and rubbed his head. "No, not you, honey—Slick. He's way too happy to be leaving me."

Chris looked at the dog then back at her. "He likes me and my daddy." He patted the dog. "Don't worry. We'll take good care of him."

She straightened. "I'm not worried. You have a good time playing with him."

She backed up, right into Chet.

Oh, God.

He put an arm around her waist, leaned over her shoulder and kissed her on the cheek. "Thanks, dog lady. We'll see you next weekend."

A whole week? An eternity. What was she, a pubescent girl with a crush? Lord! Agitated didn't cover it.

The minute Chet drove away she went in the house, leashed her three babies, and headed out for a run. They'd had plenty of exercise with Chris, but she desperately needed to clear her head. Running always helped.

She and Terry were meeting for dinner and a movie later. She wanted to see Terry, wanted to go to dinner with him, wanted to go to the movies with him, wanted him to put his toothbrush in her bathroom cabinet. Really. She did.

She shortened her route, reversing a quarter mile beyond the bend past Oscar's house. He wasn't on his porch glaring at them the first time they passed or when they headed back. Odd. He was always there.

When she got home, she put the small dogs in the back yard and opened the gate for Harley and Shep. "C'mon, kids, let's take a short run and see if we can get old Oscar's nose out of joint." They eagerly followed, not requiring leashes.

She took the same route. Still no Oscar. By the time she doubled back, worry nagged. Where the heck was the old geezer? His truck was parked in the driveway. She passed his house, stopped, turned around, and jogged up his front walk, Harley and Shep at her heels. If he were home, he'd give her hell for letting them follow her inside his yard.

Lights were on, so he must be inside. Uncertain whether or not to knock she stood glued to the ground.

Harley's toenails tapped on the wooden porch, his nose to the ground. He sniffed around the door and whined. The hair on his ruff stood at attention.

"What is it, Harley?" She took a couple of steps forward. Gas! She smelled gas. Bounding up the steps, she banged on the door. "Oscar! Oscar, open up!" No answer. She peered through the front window. Not seeing any sign of him, she left the porch and jogged around to the back.

She pounded on the kitchen door. No answer. On tiptoe, she squinted through the not-too-clean window. "Oh, my God! Oscar, Oscar, open the door!" Risky grabbed the doorknob, jiggled and twisted. The door opened.

The strong stench of gas nearly knocked her over. She gagged and coughed, shooed the dogs back then stepped inside. The oven was on, but she felt no heat. Turning the knob to *off*, she knelt and shook the old man. He didn't respond.

Frantically she looked around for a phone then ran through to the living room and opened the front door hoping for a cross breeze. Back in the kitchen, she shook Oscar again, fearful at the color of his face and lips.

Momentarily unable to decide what to do, she stood with her fingers locked on top her head. She knelt again and checked his neck for a pulse. Whimpering, she dragged him by the arms until his head was hanging part way out the back door. "Come on, please Oscar—breathe dammit!"

Back inside she found a phone in the living room and called 9-1-1. "We need an ambulance on Box Canyon Road. The number? I don't know. Hang on." She ran out the front door and scanned the front of the house. No number. The mailbox! That's where she'd find a number. She located it and hurried back inside. "Two-nine-oh-seven. I don't know his name. A gas leak in his kitchen. Please hurry, he isn't breathing. I'm a neighbor. Mariska Williston."

Shep and Harley paced anxiously around Oscar's still body. Harley pawed at his back, and Shep sniffed his clothes.

Risky rubbed Oscar's cheeks, she didn't know the protocol for gas poisoning. Afraid to make it worse, she moaned with indecision, and kept rubbing and patting.

The dogs howled before she heard the sirens. Risky got to her feet and ran to the front of the house just as the fire captain's car screeched to a halt with the fire truck right behind it. An ambulance warbled in the distance.

Brad Tucker, her old schoolmate and fire captain, saw her and waved. "Risky, what happened?"

"Come through here." She pointed to the front door. "Hurry. I found him unconscious. The house was full of gas. I turned off the stove."

Brad stopped and told one of the firemen to turn off the main gas valve then directed men to follow Risky.

She watched from outside the back door, calming Harley and Shep while the men worked on Oscar. They placed an oxygen mask on his face, monitored his vital signs then lifted him onto the stretcher from the ambulance.

Brad joined her. "Do you want to accompany him to the hospital?"

"I'd like to, but I have the dogs. I need to take them home first."

Brad scratched Shep's head. "I'll take them home and secure them in the dog run. Go ahead and get in the ambulance. I'll meet you at the hospital to take your statement for my report."

Mariska followed the stretcher to the ambulance, and one of the men gave her a hand up. Her breath caught at the sight of Oscar. With the oxygen mask on his face, and a saline drip in a vein, he looked like he was already dead. She touched his arm with her fingertips and clenched her teeth. At the hospital, she followed him inside the E.R.

Terry spotted her and registered surprise. "Mariska, what are you doing here? I called your number and left a message that I'd be delayed."

They followed alongside the gurney. Terry pointed to the exam room he wanted them to use.

"I'm his neighbor. When I didn't see him this afternoon I got worried. I don't even know his name."

Terry asked her to wait outside the room. He'd give her an update once they got the situation under control, so she walked to the small lounge area and took a seat. Acid bubbled in her throat. She stood and paced. Brad Tucker arrived several minutes later. He sat beside her and recorded her statement.

She saw Terry coming toward them and got to her feet. Afraid of his answer, she asked the question anyway. "Is he dead?"

Terry shook his head. "No, thanks to you, he's going to make it. We've got him stabilized, and he'll be moved to the ward in about an hour."

"Oh." She slapped a hand to her chest and blew a pent-up breath. "That's great. Brad and a sheriff's deputy will go to Oscar's house to look for an address book or something to locate a relative."

Terry put his arm around her shoulders and asked, "Do you still want to go to dinner? I'm off shift once I finish his chart and get him moved."

She met his eyes. "I kind of lost my appetite because of this. I hate to leave Oscar to wake up alone. At least until they find a relative or friend. Can we go later?"

He tilted his head. "I thought you didn't know his name?"

She shrugged. "I don't. That's what I call him because he's such a cranky old grouch."

Terry smiled and raised his brows. "So, you're in the business of rescuing people as well as dogs, I see." He turned back toward the trauma room, taking her elbow in his hand. "Come on, you can wait with him until they find a bed."

An hour later Risky flipped through a magazine while sitting in a chair next to Oscar's bed. She jumped when he moved.

"What the hell are you doing here, you goldurned hippie?"

She grinned. "Other than saving your life, you mean?"

"Who asked ya?"

She stood at his bedside. "Actually, it was my dogs. They missed you yelling at them and went to investigate."

"You and them damn dogs. Always giving me fits." His attempt to suppress a smile wasn't lost on her.

"Now, Oscar, what have my dogs ever done to you?"

"The name's Edgar, not Oscar, smart-aleck."

"Edgar, Oscar, what's the difference? You're still a world-class grouch." She patted his arm, prompting him to growl in protest.

He glared through wrinkled brows. "You got one o' them peace signs tattooed on your hinder, hippie girl?"

She smiled and poked his chest. "Why, Oscar, I do believe you're sweet on me."

"I ain't never been sweet on no hippie."

"What's with you and hippies? There haven't been any hippies around since my parents were kids. You're living in the past, old man."

"At least I'm livin'."

"Yes, thanks to Harley, Shep and me."

* * * *

Terry paused in the doorway, and took in the exchange between Mariska and his patient, Edgar Pauley. Mr. Pauley's driver's license had been found by the officers who searched his house. They still hadn't found information leading to next-of-kin.

He strolled to the bed, holding the old man's chart. "I see you're feeling better, Mr. Pauley."

Mariska and Edgar turned their gazes to Terry. Pauley groused, "I'm alive, but I ain't feelin' no better."

Terry tilted his head. "And why is that?"

"Because if this meddlin' hippie had'a been mindin' her own business I'd be resting on a cloud holding hands with my wife instead of this rack you butchers call a bed."

Risky gasped. "Oscar! Did you turn off the pilot light and turn on the gas on purpose?" She flashed Terry a stricken look.

Oscar shifted in the bed. "And if I did, that ain't none of your business."

Terry put his hand on Risky's shoulder. "The sheriff would like to ask Mr. Pauley some questions, Ms. Williston. Would you step outside? After we've moved him to a room, you may visit him there."

Oscar held up his hand. "I don't want her around here. I have a right to my privacy, dammit!" He glared at Risky. "Go on home to your dogs."

Terry saw the hint of hurt on Mariska's face, and stroked her back briefly as he led her from the room.

She gazed at him with sad eyes. "I feel awful, Terry. Did Oscar try to kill himself?"

"It wouldn't appear so from the preliminary investigation of the fire captain and the deputy. They found a pan of unbaked biscuits in his oven. It's speculation until they take his statement." He touched her cheek. "I'm sorry. I can see you're fond of him."

"Yes. No good reason why I should be, but I am."

A tender, compassionate woman, the more Terry came to know Mariska the more he appreciated her. "Shall we pass on dinner tonight?" He hoped she'd say no, but could see how unsettled she was over Pauley.

"I'm sorry. Let's make it later in the week. I need to go home."

He led her to an empty trauma room, embraced her and kissed her tenderly. "Don't apologize. I understand. Your friend Brad is waiting to take you home."

* * * *

She laid her head on his shoulder and sighed. "You're too good to me, Terry. Will you call me later?"

"Yes, soon as I finish up here." He took her hand and they strolled to the waiting room.

Brad Tucker picked up his papers. He glanced at their joined hands and smiled. "Ready to go?"

Risky nodded and led the way out the door.

Brad chuckled. "Nice goin', babe. Good lookin' guy. I never figured you for a doctor though." He slung an arm around her shoulders. "A vet maybe."

She sighed. Better than an undertaker?

Chapter Twenty-Four

Chet's apartment above the funeral home, two nights later.

Chet surveyed the ruins of what used to be his neat, orderly apartment. Chris reluctantly helped pick up some of his toys, but being so distracted by Slick, he'd barely made a dent. He was asleep on the rollaway cot in Chet's bedroom — finally. Slick snored contentedly next to his small form.

Chet stood in the doorway and watched the rise and fall of his son's chest, the flutter of his thick lashes on chubby, pink cheeks. How was it possible he'd had part in creating that small miracle?

He'd known for years that he wanted to have children some day, but hadn't a clue as to the depth of emotion, fear, and responsibility a child wrought. Aware with every breath he drew that he might say or do the wrong thing terrified him.

Something had to give. For one thing, he had to loosen up his compulsion for neatness, or he'd make himself a wreck and an enemy of his little boy. Order was important to Chet, but it was time to reassess his priorities. One thing was certain; he'd have to find a bigger place. A house with a fenced yard for starters, a house big enough for an *off-limits* area. He needed a sanctuary where sanity reigned. He'd find a way to compromise on the rest of it.

First, though, he needed to find a good quality pre-school and get Chris enrolled.

His employees had gone above and beyond, but Chet had to get back to work full-time. He had not only his own future to plan for, but now Chris's as well. He couldn't get distracted, and end up letting his business go down the tubes.

As soon as Bobby and Anita returned from their honeymoon, he'd ask her to put on her real estate broker hat and find them a house.

115

He took another look at the battlefield, formerly known as his living room, shrugged and switched off the light. "To hell with it."

* * * *

Risky's kitchen, next morning.

Risky shifted from foot to foot waiting for Chet to pick up his phone. Her breath caught when a woman answered.

"Hello."

She swallowed and stood dead still. "Um, hello, this is Mariska Williston. I'm calling Chet and Chris to see how my dog is behaving."

"Oh, hello, Mariska, this is Millie. Chester's working this morning. Chris and I are having breakfast. Would you like to come over?"

"No, um, I have to go to work. Do you, uh, have the number for the vet? Where I work? I'll be there until four if something comes up with Slick. If you need me for anything ... if you ..."

Why was she blathering on like a bird-brained ditz? It was Chet's mother, not the queen.

"We're doing fine for now, but do give me the number. From what I've observed so far, you'll have a hard time separating this boy from your dog."

"Oh?"

"Yes, that pup won't let Chris out of his sight. He whined and pawed at the bathroom while Chris bathed this morning." Risky heard Millie's tinkling laugh. "I finally opened the door and let him in."

So much for dog loyalty. Slick always did fight to be the center of attention. From Millie's comment, he wallowed in it now.

She recited the number for the vet clinic. "Maybe Chris will tire of him after a couple of days. He's not four yet, pretty young for the responsibility of a dog."

"Maybe," Millie said. "But so far they're having a lot of fun together. Chester always wanted a dog when he was a boy, but we traveled so much, it was impractical. He was an adult when his father and I gave Beau to him. I think he's enjoying Slick as much as Chris is."

"Chet's so super fussy about everything. I wonder about his small apartment. I can't imagine a lively dog and a little boy there."

Millie's laughter rang through the line. "It's cozy all right. Chris spent several minutes grousing to me, after his daddy left for work, about how Daddy's always telling him to pick up this toy or that book." She giggled. "I confess I'm enjoying Chester's distress more than a loving mother should."

Risky lifted her car keys off the hook by the back door. "Well, I have to get to work. Call me if you need to, our office is very laid-back. They don't make a big deal about personal calls."

"Wait, Mariska. Why don't you come to my house for dinner tonight? Chester and Chris will be there around six. I'd love it if you came."

"I don't think so, Millie, but thanks. I stood Terry up a couple of nights ago. This is his first early day off."

"Ah, that good-looking doctor I danced with at Bob Williston's wedding."

"One and the same."

"Bring him along. The more the merrier. Chester's birthday is next week. I'm baking his favorite cake as a surprise. We'll have a party. What do you say?"

"Gee, I don't know, Millie."

"Please say you'll come. I'd love to see you and that mouthwatering doctor again. I've missed him at the health club the last few times I was there."

Risky couldn't come up with an excuse to refuse.

"Okay, I'll ask Terry and see what he says. How much advance notice do you need?"

"Not much, an hour at most. I'd like to have dinner on the table by seven. After that it's a bit late for Chris."

"Okay, after I talk to Terry I'll call back. If we can make it, I'll get your address."

"Wonderful. I look forward to it, Mariska."

Yeah, well maybe Terry won't be so thrilled with the idea. He probably already had his toothbrush in his pocket.

* * * *

Risky's dad came to the veterinary hospital around noon to see if she could have lunch with him. They hadn't talked since Bobby's wedding.

"Another five minutes and you'd have missed me, Dad. I'm on my way to shop for a token gift for Digger Jensen. I'm clueless what to buy. Any ideas?"

"What's the occasion?"

"His mother's having a small surprise party for his birthday. Terry and I are going to her house for dinner tonight. I hate to go empty-handed."

Dave nodded, his lips in a thoughtful line. "We can talk about it over lunch."

She slung her purse over her shoulder. "Do you want to drive? You came to treat me, right?"

Over lunch, they tossed around some gift ideas. Risky liked her dad's suggestion to buy Chet a box of white handkerchiefs from Men's Wearhouse.

Dave nodded. "I've seen him reach in his jacket and offer one to a mourner at a couple of funeral services." He took a swallow of his heavily sugared coffee. "I doubt he gets many of them back."

Her dad always came up with a solution to any problem she faced. How lucky could a girl be to have such a dad? She tilted her head. "So, what's going on with Anya? She seemed subdued at the wedding."

Dave gazed into her eyes. "That's the real reason I invited you to lunch, to talk about your mother."

Her heart plummeted. Anya had abused her dad's gentle and loyal nature for years. When would it end? No matter how hard Risky tried, she'd never understand their relationship, or the basis for his love and loyalty. He didn't deserve the life he'd chosen, but he *had* chosen it, hadn't he?

"Daddy, you must feel like a frayed old rope after all these years of tugging." She flung out an arm. "Protecting me from Anya," then her other arm, "and caring for her, and loving her no matter what."

Dave's eyes revealed an entrenched sadness. "Honey, I gave up trying to understand it myself a long time ago."

Her hamburger sat like lead in her stomach. "I'm afraid to ask, but what's she done now?"

His smile full of pain, he patted her hand. "She hasn't done anything this time. She's sober and she's trying very hard to pretend she's sane. Her sister, Nadia, has surfaced after all these years." He paused. "She found us and wants Anya to come to Kiev for a visit. She'd come here, but she's afraid to travel so far from home. She doesn't speak English."

Risky sat back. She'd begun to wonder if Nadia was one of Anya's delusions. "Dad, this is amazing. How did she react to this news?"

"Completely stunned when the letter arrived. She called Nadia last night. They talked for over two hours. My Russian is limited, so I had to wait for your mother to translate long after they hung up. Stressed and excited, she couldn't talk about it right away."

"Is she going?" Maybe if her mother went to Kiev she'd stay there. Risky could only hope. That unspoken wish should make her feel guilty, but it didn't.

Dave nodded. "Yes. We decided to go together. Nadia told her that she still resides in the same old apartment building in the Podil district, on the Dnieper River, where they lived as children."

"She's been there all this time?"

"Europeans don't move around as much as American's do."

"I don't know what to say, Dad."

"I'm still coming to grips with it myself." He sat back and put his arms on top the booth's upholstered backrest. "We're leaving next week."

Risky bolted forward and gasped. "Next week! Dad, what's the hurry?

Shouldn't you think about it for a while? Do you have current passports? Who'll run the warehouse? Bobby isn't back from his honeymoon yet."

"Slow down." Dave raised his hands. "She desperately wants to go. The sisters haven't been together in over thirty years. I've never seen such a look of hope in your mother's eyes. I couldn't say no."

"But ..."

"Bobby and Anita return in ten days. The general manager can handle anything that comes up in the interim."

"How long will you be gone?"

"Not sure. I'll play it by ear, but probably at least a couple of weeks."

Risky shook her head, struggled to organize her thoughts. Her dad traveling to the other side of the world unsettled her. Always within easy reach if she ever needed him, they'd lived within a few miles of each other ever since she'd left home eight years ago. Her stomach churned. She lifted her head sharply when Dave chuckled.

"What?"

"Sweetheart, you look like your best friend just died." He shook his head. "You have such a busy life that you'd probably never miss me if I left without telling you. It's just for a few weeks."

She sighed and slumped back. "I know, but it's so far." Ukraine. Holy cow. That was the other side of the world.

Dave slid to the edge of the booth and held out a hand to her. "Come on let's find those handkerchiefs for Digger then I'll drop you off at work. We'll talk about it more when I have our travel plans finalized."

* * * *

Millie's dining room, that evening.

Chet grinned. "Risky, this is a great gift. Thank you."

Chris looked puzzled. "What are they?"

"They're handkerchiefs. Not too many people use them anymore. They're good for tears and runny noses."

"Like Kleenexes?"

He held the box toward the little boy. "Yes, except these can be washed and used again. Feel how soft they are."

Chris stroked with his fingers. "Soft, like Slick."

Quiet as a mouse under the dining table, Slick bounced up the instant Chris said his name. He poked his head between the boy's knees and whined.

Christian giggled with pleasure. "He wants to feel them, too, Daddy."

Risky raised her eyebrows. "It's more likely he wants some of that cake you've been sneaking under the table to him when you thought I wasn't looking. Cake is very bad for dogs. Even if he wants more, don't give him any. Please?"

After a long-suffering sigh, Chris nodded. "Okay. But he really likes it."

Millie tousled his hair. "Remember? I told you not to feed him anything but the food Ms. Williston gave you. If you want pets to live a long, healthy life you can't give them food that's bad for them."

He squinted. "If he gets sick, Dr. Terry can fix him."

Terry laughed. "I'm a people doctor. Dogs have their very own doctors."

Blue eyes huge, Chris stared at Terry. "They do? When I lived with my mama, I went to a kiddy-a-trishun. Is that like a doggy doctor? Because we're not big?"

Chet hauled Chris up and set him on his lap. "You have quite a vocabulary, little man. Terry takes care of people who are sick or in accidents. He works at the hospital."

"I gonna be a doctor when I get big."

"You are? That's great." He hugged the boy and grinned at Millie. "Gramma will like that. Won't you, Gramma?"

Chris struggled and glared at Chet. "You're squeezing me again, Daddy! You'll be sorry if you break me 'cause when I get big I gonna squeeze you 'til you're mashed."

Chet and Terry guffawed. Millie and Risky grinned at each other when Chet growled into Chris's neck and made the boy squeal and kick.

"Daddy, stop or I get hiccapups!"

Millie slapped the table. "Chester! That's improper behavior in the dining room. Move your wrestling match to the den." She stood and picked up the cake dish.

Terry leapt to his feet and gathered some plates. "Let me help, Millie."

She smiled and shook her head as he followed her toward the kitchen. "That's not necessary."

"It's okay. I'd like to help."

Risky sat alone at the table thinking she had the world's worst manners. It hadn't occurred to her to help Millie clear the dishes, but Terry wasted no time demonstrating what a good guest he was. Hmmm. Maybe what he really wanted was to be alone in the kitchen with Millie.

In that case, what was stopping her from joining the wrestling match in the den?

Chet and Chris rolled the ball across the floor, laughed when Slick retrieved it then trotted to Risky instead of them. Each time she'd toss the ball back to Chet, and each time Chris rolled it across the floor, Slick carried the ball to her.

Millie watched from the doorway. "Christian has had enough excitement for one day, Chester. It's time to take him home to bed. You'll be lucky if he's asleep by ten."

Chet rolled his eyes, and Chris pushed out his lower lip.

Risky swallowed. Chet and Chris—mirror images.

Terry tilted his head toward the door, and raised his eyebrows. Risky got the message. "It's time for me to go home, too. Make sure you give Slick a big drink of water before you go to bed, Chris."

Millie stepped aside so Risky could pass. "I'm so glad you two came tonight. I had a good time. I hope you enjoyed yourselves." She gave Risky a light hug and patted Terry's arm.

Terry kissed Millie on the cheek, and shook Chet's hand as he and Chris prepared to leave. "Thanks, Millie. Dinner was delicious. I hope we have the chance to do it again." He patted Chris's head. "I enjoyed meeting you, Chris. You take good care of that dog now."

Chris yawned, already winding down. "I will."

They headed for their cars in Millie's driveway. She stood on the steps and waved as they pulled away.

Risky sighed and dropped her head back as soon as she buckled up. "I'm so stuffed. I ate two pieces of Millie's strawberry cake." She smiled and rubbed her stomach. "How about you?"

Terry backed out to the street, shifted then headed the way they'd come a few hours before. He stared straight ahead, didn't answer her question.

"Terry?"

He whipped his head around as if surprised to see her sitting there next to him. "Sorry. Did you say something?"

Uneasiness crawled through her chest. "Is anything wrong, Terry?" It wasn't like him to be so withdrawn.

He shook his head. "No. Short on sleep. My mind wandered, that's all." He smiled. "What did you say?"

She shifted in the seat and brushed off the knees of her jeans. "It was nothing. I was talking about Millie's cake."

"Great cake, huh? I don't know when I've had better. The woman is beautiful, smart and she can cook."

Risky sniffed. "Sounds like you'd rather be dating her than me."

Terry laughed and squeezed her hand. "Hmm. Is that jealousy talking?"

She brushed away his hand. "No! Don't be silly." To her surprise, she felt the breath of the green-eyed monster, and she gave Terry a sour look.

Terry pulled over and stopped the car.

"What are you doing?"

He flipped the buckle on his seatbelt and shrugged it out of the way. "Unfasten your seat belt."

A little shockwave sizzled through her. "Why?"

"Just do it, please."

Eyes squinted; she unsnapped the belt. "Okay, now what?"

Terry reached for her and dragged her across the seat onto his lap. "Now this." He kissed her with an intensity that caught her unaware. His hand slid down her back and up under her sweater. The heat from his fingers smoldered through her torso.

A spark of passion struggled to flare. Where had it been until now? Suddenly on fire, she returned his kiss with equal ardor. Handfuls of his dark hair in her fists, she pulled him closer, opened when he probed with his tongue.

He groaned when she slid a hand to the neck of his shirt and pushed her fingers beneath the fabric.

His sex-saturated groan rippled through her body. She slid her mouth to his ear. "Terry ..."

A horn startled them. She pushed away from him and stared out the driver's side window. Chet's car idled next to theirs, his window sliding down.

"Anything wrong? You need help?"

Terry rolled down his window. "I don't need your help, Jensen. Get lost."

Chet flashed a two-finger salute, and pulled away.

Mortified, Risky's blush radiated from her heels to the top of her head. She lowered the passenger window and fanned herself.

Terry chuckled. "Jensen has great timing." He refastened his seatbelt and started the powerful engine. "Let's finish this at your place."

Risky sighed with longing. "Yeah." She pressed her palms to her cheeks. "My place."

Chapter Twenty-Five

Risky gasped when Terry parked his Pontiac, jumped out and vaulted across the hood like a movie stuntman. He opened her door and grabbed her hand. Holding her to his chest, he planted a burning hot smooch on her mouth then inched sideways to her front door, holding her close, never letting up on the kiss.

She burned with desire as she pawed the pocket of her jeans for the keys. Her hand trembled when she dragged them free only to drop them on the ground. She pushed back. "Terry, wait, I dr ..."

He tightened his embrace. "I don't want to wait. Do you?"

"No, but I—"

The words died in her mouth when he pressed his erection against her belly and kissed her again. Hands everywhere, his tongue probed deep. He pushed her back against the front door. "Your keys," he groaned. "Give me your keys."

"They're—"

"They're where? I'm dying here, woman. Where are they?"

She put her hands on his chest. "Stop!"

"Stop? What the hell? You've got to be kidding me."

She smacked his shoulder. "I'm trying to tell you. I dropped the keys!"

"Where?"

"Over there." She pointed. "Somewhere." Her stomach fluttered with frustration, her heart raced.

"Show me."

"It's so dark. I can't see them." She dragged him back several feet. "They're around here. Do you have a flashlight?"

He raked his hands through his hair. "That wasn't a flashlight in my pocket, Mariska." He knelt and smoothed his hands over the grass. "I don't believe this."

"You don't have to be a jerk about it," she grumbled. "I didn't drop them on purpose." She crawled around the spot she thought they might be.

Terry sat back on his rump and laughed. Barely audible at first, he gasped then the volume went up. "This is unreal." He reached out and pulled her to his side, fell on his back, and dragged her on top of him. "Ms. Williston, for the record, I've never worked so hard to get laid as I have with you."

She sighed, pressed her head on his shoulder, and couldn't stifle a fit of giggles. She squirmed against him when his hands stroked the length of her back then pressed her hips against his *flashlight*. She reached under his shoulders and rolled him over, putting him on top.

"Youch! Ow!" She wriggled beneath his weight.

"What now?"

"I found the keys, get off me. Ow, ow."

He tumbled off and pulled her up. Patting the ground where she'd lain, he found her keys and jingled them next to her ear. "Bingo!"

He hauled Risky to her feet. "What say we get this show on the road?"

This time she hugged him close and initiated the kiss. Heat and excitement sizzled between her legs. She dug her nails into his back and pressed against him.

Responding explosively, he crushed her, kissed her neck.

Her breath caught. She raced toward her front door. Terry followed her, step for step.

Fumbling and cursing, Terry poked key after key at the deadbolt. Dogs in the house barked. Dogs in the yard howled. Dogs in the neighborhood answered.

Risky made a grab for the keys. "Give them to me, or we'll be out here all night."

She yanked them from his hand, found the right key and opened the lock. "Don't let my dogs out." She bent at the waist to shoo them. "Okay, babies, Mama's home. Back, get back."

Terry grabbed her hips and pressed his pelvis against her bottom. He slid a hand to her abdomen and fumbled for the button on her jeans.

She twisted away, laughing. "Jeez, cowboy, at least wait until we get the door closed." Grinning, she pulled him forward, shut the door, and ran her hands across his chest. "Take a breath, superman, we've got all night."

He yanked her sweater up and over her head. "Where's the bedroom?" Grazing her breasts with his thumbs, he lowered his head and kissed her neck.

"Terry—"

"For the love of—what now?"

"I didn't have time to shower after work. I'm too *doggy*. Do you mind?"

She winced when he closed his eyes and dropped his hands. "It'll only take a minute. I promise."

Her old couch squeaked in protest under his weight when he sat. "It's fine. Whatever. Take your time." He kicked off his shoes, rearranged her pillows and flopped lengthwise, ankles propped on one of the armrests, his head on the other.

She made a grab for the three small dogs. "Oh, no you don't. You're going to sleep in the kitchen. Come on babies, I have a treat for you." She glanced at Terry's sour face. "You too, stud."

He grinned. "Yeah?"

"Yeah. I'll be a nano-second." The dogs scampered after her. She gave each of them a hunk of chicken jerky then opened a drawer, found her corkscrew, and dropped it on the small tray holding a bottle of red wine and two glasses. With her foot, she shoved the kitchen door closed, and returned to the living room.

With a coy smile and a twist of her lips, she set the tray on the coffee table. "Open up this Shiraz and let it breathe for a couple of minutes. I'll be right out, so don't get too far ahead of me, okay."

"You got it." He winked then in perfect imitation of the remark he'd heard Oscar grumble in the ER, he added, "you goldurned hippie."

Risky laughed, grabbed her sweater off the floor and ran to her bedroom.

Five minutes later, every cell in her body vibrating with anticipation, she tiptoed into the living room, dropped the towel, and leaned over the back of the couch.

Dead to the world, Terry breathed with a soft susurration snore. One of his strong, slim-fingered hands rested on the fly of his jeans, the other on his belly. His chest rose and fell in steady rhythm.

Risky blinked, wondering if she was deeply disappointed or a tiny bit relieved. She picked up the towel, wrapped it around her then sat in a chair opposite the couch. After a minute or so, she poured a glass of wine and sipped, watching him sleep.

Such a beautiful man, inside and out, he embodied what every woman wanted. Every woman with a drop of good sense. But as she gazed, a chest-deep sigh escaped her. The burning sexual passion for him faded and died.

In the bedroom, she dragged on a pair of pajamas, jammed her icy feet into fuzzy slippers then carried a blanket to the living room. She placed it over him with care. The hours he worked took a heavy toll. He needed sleep.

* * * *

Jensen Funeral Home

Chet climbed the final steps to his third floor apartment, feet heavy. Slick led, bounding up the top flight with no effort. He danced impatiently for Chet to open the door then gamboled inside, streaked for the bedroom and Chris's bed.

When Chet needed exercise, if he couldn't get on his bike or to a volleyball game, he ran up and down these steps. Chris wasn't heavy, but Chet felt every pound of his small frame when he shifted on his shoulder.

Chet had a heavy heart. It wasn't the weight of his little boy. Mariska Williston was lost to him. Terry Redmond, a formidable rival, had made his move while Chet played sophomoric games, and then got blindsided by the dramatic turn of events in his life.

He held Chris with one arm while he flipped back the bed coverings then laid him on the sheet. The child mumbled and rolled to his side. Chet removed his sneakers, loosened the button on his shorts, and carefully covered him with blankets.

After a quick scratch under Slick's pointy jaw, Chet shuffled to the living room and slumped into his favorite chair. Staring into the dimly lit room, he analyzed what he could have done differently. For one thing, he'd passed up a couple of good opportunities to press forward with Mariska. He blew it.

He knew in his heart that she wasn't a sleep-around woman. So now that she and Terry were intimate, he might as well concede. Move on. Concentrate on his son. Do some long range planning.

Damned if he would!

"Shit!" He tossed a toy walrus. It hit the wall with a thump.

A small cry sounded from the bedroom. "Mama!"

Chet bounded across the room. Gently murmuring reassurances, he lifted Chris, and rocked him in his arms. "It's okay, Christian. Daddy's here. Daddy's got you."

He wailed, "I want my mama!"

Chet sat on the edge of his king-sized bed, the boy in his lap. "I know you do, son. I wish I could bring her back. I wish that more than anything."

"I wanna go home." Chris sobbed. "I wanna see my mama." He struggled against Chet's chest.

Chet's throat clogged, his eyes suddenly filled. Except for an instinct to hold the child, he was at a loss. How would he ever fill the gaping void left by Noreen?

"Shhh, shhh, son, you'll wake Slick."

"I don't like Slick."

"Sure you do."

He flailed his arms. "No. I don't like you either. I wanna go home!"

Chet sighed. Reasoning with a three-year-old was less than useless. "I have an idea, buddy. Why don't we watch Little Bear, or Dora?"

"I'm thirsty."

"Okay, we can fix that." He carried Chris to the kitchen, turned on the faucet and lifted a glass from the cupboard.

Chris struggled. "Let me down. You're too high up." He kicked. "I want down."

"No problem." Chet set him on his feet, filled a glass part way and handed it to the inconsolable child. "Here you go."

Slick's toenails clicked on the tile floor. He stopped and cocked his head as if to ask, what's up?

Chris set his glass on a chair. "Slick's thirsty. The dog lady said give him a drink."

"I'll fill his water bowl." Chet bent to pick it up.

"No!"

"Why not?"

"It's my sponserabel. She said so."

Ready to point out that only a few minutes had passed since Chris said he didn't like Slick, Chet thought better of it, pulled a beer from the refrigerator, and sat at the kitchen table.

Chris padded across the room and poured the contents of his glass into Slick's bowl. From Chet's perspective, half of it went on the floor. About to leap up and grab a paper towel, he caught himself, twisted the cap from the beer and took a long, slow pull.

The spill would still be there after he got his boy back to bed. The puddle would wait. Chet would wait. He'd mop it up later.

He gripped the bottle, hung his head, and sighed.

* * * *

Risky's bedroom

An engine roar woke Risky. Inky darkness surrounded her. She groped for the clock at her bedside, squinting to read the time. Three thirty. Terry's car?

She switched on the lamp and sat up. The sound of tires crunching on gravel, and an accelerating engine brought her to her feet. She stepped into her slippers and crept to the living room.

Her dogs snuffled as she passed the kitchen door so she let them out. Mimicking her confusion, they stood at her feet and stared at the empty couch.

"Looks like Terry left, babies." She spotted a note scrawled on a prescription pad.

> *What a fiasco. Sorry. Early shift. Call you later.*
> *Terry*

His toothbrush and disposable razor sat next to the note.
Oh, God.

Chapter Twenty-Six

Veterinary Clinic, next morning

"You have a phone call, Risky. It's a Dr. Redmond. I hope everything is okay." The receptionist poked his head around the door of the kennel. "Ah, there you are. I thought I was talking to myself."

The black lab was recovering from minor surgery. Risky petted the big dog and monitored his heartbeat. "I'll take the call in the kennel office. Don't worry, it's personal."

She waved as the young man backed out the door. Why would Terry be calling her at work?

She lifted the kennel office phone and pushed the flashing button. "Hello? Terry?" Her throat tightened.

"Glad I caught you, Mariska. I'm on my way to LAX."

That was odd. Why didn't he tell her he was leaving town last night? "Where are you going?"

"A brain trauma symposium at Cleveland Clinic. I was on the wait-list, and a spot just opened up for me. I only got a couple hours notice."

"Oh." That explained it. "Uh, Terry, I ..."

"Great timing, huh? All I can think about is getting my hands on you." A sexy moan then, "I'll be gone two weeks. After the symposium I'm going to visit my parents."

What was she to say? Terry felt the same as last night, but now she had doubts. "Terry, I ..."

"Can't talk now, I barely have time to make it to the airport. I'll call the minute I get back. Keep it warm for me, honey."

He hung up before she formed the words she struggled for.

Warm?

Honey?

Oh, God.

Three hours later, she pulled into her driveway. After Terry's call, the rest of her day was a murky blur. She was in it now. Up to her eyeballs in it. Terry wanted to go full steam ahead on the physical, and she doubted whether or not she wanted to go ahead on any level. How could she explain her sudden cooling off without sounding like a ... a ... Bobby had a crude expression for it—cock teaser.

She shuddered. She wasn't that. She wasn't. She really liked Terry. He was great. He was perfect. He wanted her. She should want him.

Bumping her head on the steering wheel, she gritted her teeth and yowled. Shep and Harley went nuts behind their fence.

Dammit, Digger! Get out of my head! Get out!

Dragging her feet, she walked to the fence to show the two big dogs she was fine. After some serious petting and baby talk, she opened the gate and let them follow her into the house by way of the back door. Mickey, Minnie and Brutus joined the excitement of her safe return home.

One of the best things about dogs was having someone worry and wonder where you were when you weren't home and full of joy at your return. Nothing could beat that.

"Let's all go for a run, babies. Want to go for a run?" Nobody could convince her that her dogs didn't understand every word she said. They made a dash for the front door, looks of happy anticipation on their furry faces. "Okay, I gotta change my shoes, kids."

Brutus did his customary happy dance while she double knotted the laces on her brand new Mizuno Waves.

She did a double take when they ran past Oscar's. A car she didn't recognize sat in the driveway behind his old truck. Lights were on in the house and she saw somebody walking around inside. He was recently home from the hospital, so maybe he had somebody assisting him?

On the way back she stopped outside his fence, tied the three small dogs securely and told Harley and Shep to stay. About to knock she paused. Loud voices from inside sounded like an argument. She hesitated for a couple of seconds then banged on the screen door.

A tall, tanned man, she guessed about fifty, came to the door. "Yes?"

"Is Oscar here?"

"You're looking at him. Do I know you?"

Pulse pounding in her throat, she took a step back.

The grouch's voice called from the living room. "She's asking for me, Oz, not you! Let her in."

The tall man pushed open the screen door. "Okay, Dad. There's no need to yell." He tilted his head. "Dad's over there."

Risky looked past his shoulder. The old man sat in a wheelchair next to the couch. "Git in here, hippie. If you asked for me by my right name—Edgar, you wouldn't of confused my dimwitted son, Oscar, over there.

The tall man rolled his eyes, shook his head and left the room, muttering under his breath.

Risky's eyes popped. "You have a son named Oscar?"

"Didn't I just say that? Or are you just as dimwitted as him?"

Laughing, she shook her head. "I see you're recovered to your fully functioning grouch level. Does it run in the family?"

The real Oscar called from the kitchen, "No. It's just him. The rest of us are nice folks. We take after our mother."

Edgar grinned and winked at Risky. He leaned forward and whispered. "That's what they think."

"I heard you, old man," Oscar yelled from the kitchen.

Edgar shook his head. "Privacy is a thing of the past." He pointed to the wheelchair. "Push me outside. We'll sit on the porch where them big nosy ears can't hear us."

Risky stepped around the wheelchair and grasped the handles. "Why are you in a wheelchair anyway? When Dr. Redmond released you, he said you were fully recovered from the gas."

"Damn doctors don't know anything. Soon as I got home I tripped on the front steps and twisted my bad knee."

"What does that have to do with Dr. Redmond?" She stepped in front of the wheelchair, pushed the door open and held it with her hip as she pulled him out to the porch. "You didn't hurt your knee until you got home from the hospital."

"You always got to argue with me?"

"Only when you're wrong, and you usually are."

She parked the wheelchair next to the wooden rocker and sat.

Edgar pointed to the front gate. "Git them dogs off the road and in here before one o' them gets run over, or next thing I know you'll be suing me for everthing I got."

Laughing, she stood. "What? This shack and all these weeds? No thanks." She went to the gate, opened it and let the dogs in the yard. Harley trotted straight to Edgar and put his big head on the old man's knee.

"Oh, for the love'a God. Git this flea bitten mutt offa me." To belie his words, Edgar smiled, reached out, and ran his hand over Harley's silky noggin. The dog grinned.

"Look at that. Harley loves you, Edgar."

"Shows what poor judgment he has if you ask me." He stroked Harley's head. Shep stood a short distance away, an imploring look in his soft eyes. "Okay, come on, fleabag."

Shep bounded up the step and wiggled with ecstasy under the old man's scratching fingers.

The three small dogs, never having met Edgar, watched warily behind the protection of Risky's legs. She soothed them. "He's not nearly as mean as he sounds, babies."

"Like hell I ain't."

"Give it a rest, Ed. You never had me fooled."

"That's Ed-gar, not Ed, smarty pants."

"Whatever you say, Ed."

The screen door squeaked. Oscar stepped out with two mugs of steaming tea. "Here, Dad, It's getting chilly out here. I don't want you to catch cold." He handed the other mug to Risky. "You too, ma'am."

She rewarded Oz, the real Oscar, with a big smile. "Thank you. I'm Mariska Williston. I live down the road about a half mile." She pointed in the direction of her house then her dogs. "Shep, Harley, Mickey, Minnie and Brutus."

He lowered himself to sit on the top step. "Oh, you're the woman who found Dad." He raised his eyebrows and nodded at the revelation.

"She ain't nothin' but a goldurned, hippie busybody."

She smacked the arm of his wheelchair. "Why, you're welcome, Ed. Always a pleasure to help out a neighbor."

Edgar grumbled in reply then reached up a hand and pulled down on his mouth to disguise his smile.

Oz pursed his lips and cast a he's-not-fooling-anybody look at Risky. "I'm taking Dad up to my ranch in Bishop for a while. My wife loves the old bastard, why I don't know, and wants to look after him until his knee mends."

Ed tugged Risky's arm. "I want it on the record that I'm going against my will. Besides not having no privacy, them damn cow flies drive me nuts up there."

"Dad, I told you we solved the fly problem a long time ago. You haven't been to the ranch in over three years." Oz looked at Risky and shook his head. "I don't know why I bother arguing with him. He never listens to anything I say."

"That's 'cause you never say nothin' worth listening to." Edgar leaned back and took a tentative swallow of the tea. He winked at Risky.

Risky directed her comment to Oz. "So, have you had to put up with this all your life?"

Oz's shoulders shook with a chuckle. "Yeah, the old goat's lucky to be alive. He treats all of us this way."

"All of you?"

Ed cleared his throat. "It was my unlucky lot in life to end up with eight useless kids. All of 'em took after their mother. I loved the woman, but she didn't have a brain in her head."

"Obviously not, Dad. Why would she let you get next to her eight times otherwise?"

Edgar faced Risky. "See what I've got to put up with?"

The love between the two men was warm and heavy. They had a funny way of expressing it though. Risky thought of her own father and the way he'd always protected her from Anya. Her heart warmed. She couldn't imagine a conversation such as this one between them, but she saw the love Oz and Edgar had for each other in spite of it.

"When are you leaving?"

"He's dragging me outta here first thing in the morning. Don't expect to see me alive again. That bunch of circling crows would like nothing better than to get their hands on my property."

"For the love of God, Dad, why do you say such things? I wonder sometimes if you're losing it." Oz rolled his eyes and shook his head at Risky.

She stood and brushed off the seat of her sweats. "I have to get home. My kids are hungry." On an impulse, she kissed Edgar on the cheek. "I'll see you when you get back, you old grouch."

Handing the empty mug to Oz, she thanked him for the tea.

He smiled. "How many kids do you have?"

Ed pointed to the dogs. "Them is her kids, knot head."

Risky started toward the road then turned around. "Do you have a cell phone?" she called.

Oz reached in his pocket and held it up his phone. "I do."

"Why don't you program in my number then? You can let me know when he's coming home. I'll keep an eye on the place while he's gone." She recited her number to Oz, and he punched it in.

She picked up the leashes for the three small dogs and let her 'kids' out of the yard. "Bye, sweetie pie." She waved at Edgar.

Instead of returning her wave, he flapped his hand as if to say beat-it.

She laughed and led her dogs down Box Canyon road toward home.

Chet ran down this road with her that day so long ago. Every time she turned the bend past Oscar's house, she remembered how fluttery her chest felt with Digger pounding along beside her and the dogs. His blond hair flopped with every long stride. His muscular arms gleamed with sweat, and the damp shirt stuck to his flat belly.

Oh, God.

Her phone rang as soon as she put her key in the door. Breathless, she answered. "Hello?"

"Dog Breath?"

"Chet?"

"What's up? You sound out of breath?"

She shooed all the dogs out the kitchen door into the yard. "Yeah, I just got back from a run with the dogs." Her heart thumped through her chest like an invading army, and not just from the run. "Everything okay? Chris? Slick?"

"We're great. I called to ask you if you'd like to meet me and my little guy for pizza tomorrow after work. He's been wheedling for pizza, and I promised him we'd go if he picked up all his toys and books for a solid week. He did." Chet chuckled. "Now I have to pay up."

"A week? Wow, that's a long time for a four-year-old to remember." She pictured the little boy's blond, blue-eyed face, so like his dad's.

"Speaking of four years, Millie and I are taking him to Disneyland for his birthday next Saturday. Want to go?"

She paced, a wide grin cracking her cheeks. "Chet, you're not going to believe this. I've never been to Disneyland."

"What? You're right, I don't believe you. You were born here, weren't you? Are you telling me that you've lived two hours from Disneyland your whole life and you've never been there?"

"I almost went once with Bobby, when his high school class went for senior ditch day. But my dad had this strange hang-up about truancy. I figured it would still be there when I got around to it."

"Well, hey, here's the perfect excuse, Christian's fourth birthday."

"What day?"

"Thursday the fourteenth, but we're going on Saturday."

The fourteenth? What a weird coincidence. "Uh, Chet?"

"Yeah, doll, what?"

"Thursday is my birthday."

"No."

"Yes. It is. I'll be twenty-seven. A spinster already." Especially since there was no chance she'd marry Terry, or an undertaker for that matter.

"That settles it then. You have to go with us."

"I don't want to horn in on the little guy's celebration." It would be nice to see Chris's eyes light up at Tinkerbell's flight, the glittering lights, and the parade. If it were half as spectacular as they showed on TV, it would be worth the lousy traffic to get there.

"You have to say yes, or I'll sic my mother on you. She will insist when she finds out it's your birthday too. And I will tell her, doll."

Every time Chet called her doll, she got all warm in her girly plumbing. The guy was dangerous, but she could think of nothing she'd rather do more than go.

"Okay. I'll think about it. I'll let you know over pizza tomorrow. Where should we meet?"

"Chi Chi's of course. Best pizza in Simi Valley. How's six?"

Last time she went there was with Terry. That's when she fell in love with his car. Maybe she would give it another try with him. She hated to give up that great old Pontiac.

Chapter Twenty-Seven

Chi Chi's Restaurant, next evening

Chris insisted on sitting on the same side of the booth as the *dog lady.* Risky scooted over to make room for him. "I gonna eat a whole pizza!"

Risky smiled and ruffled his golden curls. "Well, you can try, but guess what? You can take home what you can't, and eat it tomorrow."

Chet tapped Chris on the head with his menu. "I love cold pizza and beer for breakfast. Want to try it?"

Risky and Chris pulled identical faces of disgust. "Eeew."

Chet's expression was feigned shock. "What's so bad about beer and pizza?"

"I don't like beer," Chris declared. "It's yucky."

Risky bumped Chris with her shoulder. "When did you taste beer?"

Puffing his chest with pride, he declared, "My daddy let me taste it, but I like milk better."

She wrinkled her nose. "And you should. It's good for you, and it also tastes good with pizza. I'll ask the server to bring you a nice big glass." She looked at the menu. "What kind of pizza do you like?"

"The round kind."

"Me too. Anything on it?"

"Cheese on top."

Chet handed Chris the kid's place mat and a small box of crayons. "Draw a picture of Slick for Risky. Like the one I put on the refrigerator."

"Okay." He slowly unpacked the crayons, studied the blank square reserved for original art, and then drew.

Risky watched Chet's face. The pride and love in his eyes melted her heart. As she stared at him, he raised his eyes, and his expression changed.

136

Those sexy blue eyes took on a glint of hunger. She was pretty sure it wasn't for pizza. He smiled. She blushed. Message received loud and clear. He tapped her foot ever so softly.

Oh, God.

* * * *

Totally turned on when she told him Redmond would be out of town, Chet vowed to take full advantage of the coming week, starting tonight. He wanted the willowy, unconventional Mariska Williston, and he would make it happen.

Those dark chocolate eyes of hers betrayed her air of cool friendliness. Her blush and the way she'd placed her hand on her cheek at the slight tap of his toe gave her away. He remembered that sizzling encounter the day he fixed her sink. Hell, he remembered it every day since then, and reacted physically every time.

No other woman lit his fire like Mariska. Sure, he'd been in love with Noreen, but he was a lot younger then. Many women had come and gone in the past years. But Mariska Williston—damned if he'd sit on the sideline and let another man take what was his.

She took a sip of beer and cleared her throat. "Did I tell you my parents left for Kiev?"

"Wow, the Ukraine? No."

"They went to visit my mother's sister. The two girls lost track of each other when they were teenagers."

Chris held his drawing. "Here's Slick." A big smile stretched across his innocent face.

Risky's eyes went wide. "That's really good, Chris." She nodded at Chet to show that she really meant it. "It looks just like him."

He handed it to her. "You can have it for your 'frigerator. Your other dogs can 'member him when they see it."

"What a good idea. I'll do that." She carefully folded the place mat so as not to crease the picture and tucked it into her bag. "They'll be so happy to see him again. Thank you."

"Welcome."

Chet beamed with pride. "I think this young man is a budding artist. What do you think?" He touched her toe again.

Her blush brightened. "I agree, absolutely."

He reached across the table and picked up the crayons and empty box. "What say I take these home for you, son? Our pizza should be here soon."

Risky's discomfort encouraged him. Attraction was there, no matter how she tried to hide it. He'd change the subject and let her off the hook for a while.

"So, how did your mother and her sister become separated?"

She took a breath. "I'm not really sure. I don't think even Dad knows the true story. She told so many lies about her life that she's tripped herself up a couple of times." She shook her head, raised her eyes to Chet. "I wish she'd stay there. Does that sound awful?"

He reached for her hand. "No, Mariska, because I'm sure there's a very good reason for you to feel that way."

Chris wrinkled his brow. "Lying is bad. My mama said never ever to tell a lie."

Risky hugged him to her side. "That's very good advice your mother gave you. Oh, look, here's our pizza. Round and covered with cheese, just the way you like it."

Chet intercepted the little boy's hand. "No! It's hot. I'll put a piece on a plate for you. Be sure you test it with your finger before you put it in your mouth. Okay?"

Chris rolled his eyes and sighed. "Okay, but I'm hungry."

Risky pointed to his glass. "Have some milk while you wait for it to cool. Or would you rather have a sip of my beer?"

"Daddy, the dog lady is funny, huh?"

Chet tapped the neck of his beer bottle against Risky's. "Yes, she is."

Risky grinned at Chris. "Tell me what you want to see at Disneyland."

The child chattered away about all the things he wanted to see and do while Chet placed a slice of pizza on a plate and set it in front of him. By the time he stopped talking it would be cool enough to eat.

"And I want some mouse ears, and a baseball hat, and a hot dog, and a ride on the Magic Teacups."

"That sounds like so much fun. But let's take the Teacup ride before we have a hotdog, okay."

His eyes lit up. "Are you going with us?"

Chet's chest warmed. She hadn't told him whether or not she'd decided to go. "Yes, and guess what, Christian?"

"What?"

"Miss Williston has her birthday on the same day as yours."

His little brow wrinkled. "Can two peoples have their birthday on the same day?"

Risky patted his head. "Oh, yes they can, but we're going to celebrate *your* birthday. I'll have my birthday when my daddy gets back from his trip."

"Can Slick go?"

She pressed her lips together and shook her head. "No."

"Why?"

"They don't allow dogs there."

"But they allow mouses."

Chet and Risky laughed at the boy's innocence. He hailed the waiter and ordered two more beers then tapped his finger on Chris's plate. "I think it's cool enough to eat now."

He gazed at Mariska, and enjoyed her slow blush when he widened his grin. "Dog lady and I'll think of a way to celebrate her birthday."

Chris paid no attention to his comment. Pizza was first and foremost in his mind.

Risky gave Chet a warning frown. "Stop it, Digger."

He waggled his eyebrows. "Stop what?"

"You know what."

"Can't a man have any fun?"

"Not if I can help it."

He nodded slowly, quirked his lips at her flaming cheeks. "You can't."

* * * *

Risky choked on her beer.

Oh, God.

Why had she agreed to leave her car at the funeral home and ride to the restaurant with them? If she had her own car she could make a quick getaway as soon as dinner was over then she wouldn't be alone in Chet's company. She wasn't alone with him exactly, and he'd never try any funny stuff with Chris around, would he? No. If he even put one hand on her, she'd probably fall on her back like Brutus begging for a belly rub!

By Saturday, she'll have had plenty of time to calm down. It was dangerous to be in the same room with him. At least on Saturday Millie would be there as another buffer between her and Chet. Yes, okay, by Saturday she'd be past this fluttery, dizzy *thing* she had for him. Whatever it was, it made no sense.

Terry, she had a budding relationship with Terry. She wanted to give that a chance. Terry had it all. Yes, he did. He was everything she'd ever wanted in a man. Handsome, intelligent, kind, and classy. Good kisser. Great job, great car, good dancer, masculine, funny, sweet, sexy.

Chet was a real good kisser, and he had those other things, except for his car, and his job.

Dammit! What was wrong with her? Okay, maybe she should just give up. Quit resisting her attraction to Digger. Hop in the sack with him and get it out of her system. Her heart pumped, and warm weakness oozed through every muscle in her body.

No! That's craziness. Stop it. How could she ever face Terry again if she did that? Eat your pizza, Mariska. Concentrate on the little angel sitting next to you, not the sex oozing devil facing you.

He rubbed the toe of his shoe up her leg.

She gave him a sharp kick.

* * * *

Chet coughed out a bite of pizza. "Ow!"

"What's wrong, Daddy? Is it too hot?"

He nodded. "Yes. I think I better slow down."

He enjoyed her discomfort. She wanted him. No matter how much she resisted, she wasn't fooling him, herself maybe, not him. Planning the next move sent a hot buzz through his legs. He'd hold that feeling, it was too good to let go.

"Mariska, we were talking about your mother."

Her gaze flew to his. She swallowed her food. "Um, yeah, my mother."

He sincerely wanted to know more. "Why did you say that you wish she'd stay?"

A look of mild panic filled her eyes. "Um ... she ..."

"I only met her that one time. At Bob's wedding. She's very exotic, beautiful really."

"Yeah, well." Her throat sounded clogged.

"Dave has never said anything about your relationship with her."

"Dad doesn't talk about our family." No, he never spoke to others about the three of them, and except for his unmistakable, and often expressed, love for Risky, he didn't talk in depth about Anya to her either. Dad lived in a morass of denial, devotion and love for her mother. He nurtured undying hope that Anya would someday be sane and well. He lived to see her sane and well. Risky had finally accepted that fact. She'd never fully understood it, but there it was. Her father loved her. He'd done his best to protect her. When Anya was in *the place,* Daddy was relaxed, loving, humorous and able to work successfully with his difficult brother in the family business. But when her mother was home, they existed on a precipice of fear, anticipating her next monstrous episode of insanity.

* * * *

"I can see you don't really want to discuss her."

"No." She tilted her head and glanced at Chris.

"Oh. Okay." He touched Chris's hand. "Did you tell Dog Lady about your new school, son?"

Risky brightened. "You're going to school? That's great."

He scowled. "I gonna start after my birthday, but Slick not gonna like it. He'll be lonesome."

She ruffled his hair. "Don't worry about Slick. Dogs have a secret. When you're not there they sleep all the time. They love to sleep all day long."

"They do?"

"Yes they do." She wiped a thread of cheese from the corner of his mouth with her napkin. "Now tell me about the school? Have you visited?" Her motherly gesture made Chet smile.

Chris nodded his eyes big and serious. "It's a baby school. I not going to real school yet, but I can read. My mama taught me."

Chet got a hitch in his chest. "Remember the teacher said you could help her teach the other boys and girls to read." His love for this child, a son he didn't know about such a short time ago, grew bigger every day.

He and Millie commiserated about how much they'd missed, but he wouldn't fault Nori. She did what she thought best for all of them.

They talked and laughed while finishing their pizza and drinks. Chris soaked up Risky's serious responses to his conversation. He obviously missed daily contact with women. The teachers at the pre-school were all women. Chet hoped they would help fill the huge gaping hole left by Noreen. They knew his story and looked forward to nurturing him.

"It's almost your bedtime, my man. What say we head home, take Slick for a walk in the garden then get you in bed?"

His small shoulders hunched with reluctance, the little guy nodded. "Okay. I can't eat any more. I'm full."

Risky laughed and poked her finger against his tummy. "See, you did eat it all. We don't have any left to take home. I guess your daddy will have to have something else besides pizza and beer for breakfast tomorrow."

Chris took Chet's proffered hand and giggled. "Yeah, Daddy. You gotta cook oatmeal again."

Risky took the passenger seat in Chet's car while he buckled Chris in the back. He patted his son's head, and for good measure, gave Risky a pat. She jerked with surprise. He chuckled at her reaction to his touch.

Chris babbled all the way back to their apartment. He told Risky a long dramatic story of heroic Slick chasing away the boogey man while he slept.

Chet glanced at Risky and grinned.

She smiled back with a look of resignation. "I think I've lost one of my babies."

"Looks like. I don't know how I could separate them at this point."

She shrugged. "Slick came to me by way of a family with three kids. They relocated outside the U.S. and couldn't take him. I think he's happy with you two. He probably missed all the squeals of excitement and commotion of children. I'm okay with it."

He squeezed her wrist. "I really thank you for that, Mariska."

Her answer was a sigh. He caught her glance at his hand on hers. She didn't pull away.

When he glided into his parking space at the back of Jensen and Jensen, he tilted his head to the back seat.

She turned and grinned at the sleeping angel. "He went out fast. It's only been fifteen minutes since we left Chi Chi's."

"I'll carry him upstairs. Would you bring his car seat up? Millie's taking him in the morning. She'll need it."

Risky slid from the car. "Sure." She waited while he lifted Chris then unbuckled the seat and pulled it free.

Chet heard her quiet footsteps following him up the stairs. The boy was light as a feather, asleep, head lolling on his shoulder. He quietly unlocked the door and shushed Slick before he barked.

"Digger, go ahead and put him to bed. I'll take Slick down to do his business."

"You got it, Dog Breath. I owe you one."

"No, this one's on the house. Come on, baby, your former mama's going to take you for a walk in the flowers." Her smile got Chet's heart rate jumping.

By the time she and the dog got back upstairs to the apartment, Chris was tucked in bed, the teakettle hissed on his stove, and a bluesy, sexy, CD played on his stereo. The song — *Do It Again*. Nice. The mood he wanted.

Breathless, she led Slick inside and unhitched his collar. "Okay, thanks for dinner. I'll see you on Saturday morning at eight."

"Not so fast. Sit down and relax. I'd like you to try this great spiced tea I order from Hong Kong. It'll help you sleep like a baby."

"No, I—it's late. I should go." But she didn't go. She hesitated then closed the door. "Oh, well, I'm a big girl. Nobody's got a stop watch on me."

She was a big girl all right. A big girl he had plans for. "Okay, good. Relax, kick off your shoes. I'll be right back." A hum of anticipation heated his gut.

Chapter Twenty-Eight

Why was she still here? Nuts, she was nuts. That's all there was to it. Hopelessly nuts. Only one thing took the edge off. Chris asleep in the next room. Chet left the bedroom door open. So he wouldn't try anything, right?

She'd drink the cup of tea, thank him for a fun evening, and be on her way.

She watched his back as he left the room. He wore a form-hugging tee shirt, khaki pants, and no shoes. A swirl of dizzying warmth wound its way around every limb then up her torso and settled in her chest and neck. What was that music? What did the singer just croon so breathlessly? *Do it again?*

Oh, God.

He padded back into the living room and set the steaming mugs on the coffee table. "Here we go. Said I'd only be a minute."

"What's that?"

"The tea from Hong Kong."

"No, that." She pointed to the stereo. "Who's that on the CD? What's that song?"

He sat next to her and grinned. "Do you like it? Classic Diana Krall. I get turned on every time she sings that one." He picked up the CD case from the side table and handed it to her. "I have all her CD's. I've almost worn this one out."

She snatched it from him with trembling fingers, careful not to touch him. No, she couldn't touch him. Not now. Too dangerous. He was turned on. He just said so. Drink the tea and skedaddle. Get the heck out of Dodge. Leave before any fireworks start.

Chet's shoulder was warm against hers. "Try the tea. It's a special blend." He grinned when she cast him a suspicions look. "What?"

"What's in it?"

"You think I'd drug you? Come on, Risky."

She stared at him with raised eyebrows, her lips pressed together.

He leaned forward and switched the mugs. "Okay? The base is white tea. The old lady adds chamomile, a touch of ginger, some mysterious oriental herbs, and cinnamon. I love cinnamon, always have."

That's why he was always sniffing her hair. Great. She practically drowned herself in the stuff when she washed her hair this afternoon. He leaned in. She jerked with surprise and bumped his chin with her head. "What are you doing?"

He rubbed his jaw and smiled. "Smelling delicious you."

"Look, Chet, Terry and I—Terry's out of town and I probably shouldn't ..." Her breath caught in her throat. Chet buried his nose in her hair then kissed her head. His hand caressed her cheek as his lips moved to her forehead then her eyes, so slow, so ...

Oh, God.

"Mariska, I want a chance with you. I know you and Redmond are sleeping together, but ..."

She pulled back, but didn't take her hands from his chest. How did they get there? Like a magnet for her hands, she didn't realize they were on him until this moment. "No, Chet, we're not, we ..."

He held her face in his palms, stared into her eyes. "You're not what?"

Risky's lips burned, puffy and dry. Without thinking, she extended her tongue to dampen the bottom one. She found it difficult to inhale or exhale. Would she die of asphyxiation staring into Chet's beautiful eyes, his Nordic cheekbones, wonderful mouth? "We ... uh ... haven't ..."

His hungry kiss stopped her heart and her words. He dragged her onto his lap and pushed her back against the pillow, grumbling. She couldn't understand his words, but they set her on fire. His meaning sharp and clear. She should struggle, she should leave, and she should stop him right now. She should—

She struggled all right, but to position her body so she could get both her arms around him. One hand gripping his shoulder and the other running through his thick blond hair, she whimpered with desire.

Chet lifted his head and gazed into her eyes so deep she thought she'd drown in the bottomless blue then he smiled and ran his tongue over her mouth. "I want you, doll. You know I do."

She whimpered. "Don't call me that, please."

"Why?"

"What did you put in the tea?"

"Nothing, but you didn't drink any. Remember, doll?"

She groaned and threw her leg over him. "Chet, when you call me that all I want to do is tear your clothes off and climb all over you." She gripped his hair until he winced.

He chuckled. "Feel free." His hand glided over her hip and bottom. "You have the sweetest ass I've ever held in my hands."

She stroked his face and neck. "We shouldn't."

"Why not? We both want to."

"Chris is a few feet away."

"He's asleep."

"But ..." Again his kiss stopped her words. By primal instinct, she tugged his tee shirt up and ran her fingers over his back. Oh, his back. She clamped her lips to his chest. Doomed, she was doomed.

* * * *

Chet sat up and lifted her with him. Slim as a reed, she had more sexuality in her light-as-a-feather body than any other two women he'd ever known. This was meant to be. He stood and set her on her feet. She offered no resistance when he removed her blouse and her bra. Her fingers gripped his biceps when his lips trailed from her neck to her breasts. Perfect, small breasts beckoned his tongue and his hands.

Fearing spontaneous combustion if he didn't get inside her soon, he lifted her and walked toward his bedroom.

She stiffened. "Chet we ..."

He brushed her lips with his. "Shhh, it'll be okay. We have to do this. It's the right time, doll." His pulse thundered in his groin. "I have to do this."

On a resigned sigh she dropped her head on his shoulder. "I know. Me too."

At the side of his bed, he lowered her to her feet. His head dropped forward when she lifted his shirt and tugged it off. Her slender hands explored, barely touching him, driving him mad when she pressed her bare breasts to his chest. He groaned. "Thank you, God."

She raised her head, smiled into his eyes, and whispered, "Shall we get naked?" Her remark, emphasized by her hands tugging at his waistband, sent a shockwave through him.

He pushed downward on her shoulders until she sat on the edge of the bed. With trembling fingers, he pulled off her shoes and socks then stood and stepped out of his pants.

Risky stared then raised her eyes and grinned. If he had to take an oath later, he'd swear fire sparked from those gypsy dark eyes as she touched him, drove him close to the edge.

He backed out of her reach. "Get your jeans off, doll." He pushed her hands away as she fumbled with the zipper then slid her pants down her hips.

She chortled with surprise when he flipped her back by whipping them off by the bottom hem. He reached to put his hand over her mouth, but she already had her fingers pressed to her lips and head tipped to peek at the sleeping Chris.

Chet grinned at her white cotton boy-leg panties, the sexiest turn-on he could imagine. He straddled her, prepared to remove the last stitch of her clothing.

Risky shrieked and bolted upright, her arm extended straight to the end of the bed, dark eyes huge in her pale face.

"Daddy?"

Chet's heart thundered. "Chris?" He dropped his head and watched his erection die an ignoble death.

"Daddy, I'm cold. Can I sleep with you and Whisky?"

Risky tugged on the sheet to cover her breasts. "Sure, honey." Chet shifted off her. "You can sleep with me and your daddy."

Chet turned, slid under the sheet then extended his hand and beckoned the boy forward. "Come on, son. Right up here."

Chris scrambled on the bed and crawled between them, lifted the sheet and slid under.

Chet rolled his eyes when Risky twisted her lips at him. She suppressed a giggle and slid down next to Chris. "Warm now?"

"Uh huh." He rolled his head on Chet's shoulder. "Night, Daddy. Night, Whisky."

He slapped his forehead when Slick joined them and hunkered down into the miniscule valley of space between him and Chris. He rolled his eyes once more when she entwined her foot with his.

She grinned wickedly. "Isn't this nice?"

"Perfect, just perfect."

* * * *

Hours later Risky tapped his foot, waking him instantly. He startled. "What?"

"Shhh. I have to go home, Digger."

"What time is it?"

"Almost five I think." She slipped from the bed and tiptoed to the bathroom.

After a couple of minutes, he followed her. She stood in the gray light, brushing her teeth with her index finger. When she bent over the sink to spit, he stepped forward, grasped her hips and pressed against her.

She raised her head and gazed at their reflection in the mirror, watched his wonderful hands slide up her sides then to her breasts. Sighing, she relaxed against him, head rolling on his shoulder.

"I don't want you to go, doll."

"I have to, Digger. I never got home to take care of my dogs. I don't like to leave them out all night. There're so many coyotes in the hills. I need to shower and get ready for work."

His lips trailed her shoulders and neck. "I know." He shoved the bathroom door shut with his foot.

The latch click thundered in her ears. He knelt and slid her panties past her jittering knees, to the floor. His lips trailed back and forth across her bottom. "Chet, please."

"A minute." He stood, lowered the lid on the toilet then sat. "Give me a minute." Tugging her hands, he pulled her forward. Hands behind her knees he urged her to straddle his lap then crushed her against his chest.

Gasping as a stab of desire streaked right to the place he explored with his fingers, she dug her nails into his shoulders. "Chet, you're killing me. We can't do this right now."

He grazed her collarbone with his teeth. "I know, dammit. I know, but I had to touch you."

His wristwatch alarm went off startling both of them. He nearly dumped her on the floor, but grabbed her in the nick of time.

She clutched his neck, caught her breath then giggled.

Chet snapped off the annoying tone and raked his fingers through his hair. She stepped back, reached for his hands and tugged until he stood. "Do you usually get up this early?"

He blew out a breath and shook his head. "Nah, busy work day ahead."

"Oh." She didn't want any details. "Okay then, I'll just grab my clothes and get out of here."

He grasped her hand. "Come back here this evening. I'll get Mil to keep Chris overnight. This isn't finished."

She bit her bottom lip. "It hasn't even started, more like it."

Chet pulled her against him, insistent hands caressing her bottom, lifting her until their eyes were even. "So? You coming?"

She nipped his bottom lip. "Not at the moment, but I expect to later."

Chapter Twenty-Nine

Chet's Apartment, 8:00 a.m.

Chet let Chris answer the door. He left his bedroom, and checked the shine on his shoes then stuffed a handkerchief in his breast pocket.

Chris greeted Millie. "Guess what, Gramma?"

"What, sugar?"

"Me and Whisky and Daddy and Slick all slept in Daddy's big bed last night." He raised his arms in anticipation of Millie's hug.

Millie cast a sideways glance at Chet when he entered the living room. "Is that so?"

"Yes, 'cause I got cold, but they didn't have any jammas on. They were all hot."

"Why don't you go in the kitchen and finish your breakfast, sweetheart? Gramma wants to talk to Daddy."

Chet preempted her inquiry when he strode across the room. He raised his hands palms out. "Nothing happened, Mil. Nothing."

She cocked her head, a look of disapproval on her lovely face. "I didn't know that's what you had in mind when you said you wanted to get her in your bed, Chester."

"Gimme a break, Mom. It's a long frustrating story."

"I can't wait to hear it."

"You'll have to wait until later. I have to get downstairs. We have three funerals today." He leaned in and gave her a hug and a kiss on the cheek. "I need a big, really big favor."

She brushed her hands down his lapels and straightened his tie. "What's the favor?"

"Could you keep Chris overnight?" He flashed his most pleading please-

148

mommy expression. "I'll be in your debt forever."

"Stop it." She slapped his shoulder. "You're already in my debt forever. I won't ask why, but if I do take Christian, you'll have to come get him no later than nine tomorrow. I have a tennis date with a very handsome, eligible gentleman."

He picked her up and swung her around in a circle. "You're the world's best mom." After setting her on her feet, he reached behind the sofa and handed her a small gym bag. "His things."

"Chester, you knew I'd say yes. I'm such a pushover where you're concerned." She set the bag on the car seat and went to join Chris at the kitchen table.

Chet was almost out the door when he turned. "Oh, one more thing." He took Anita Williston's business card from his pocket. "If you find the time, please call Bob's wife and ask her to find me a house. Like yesterday."

"You're buying a house?"

He swept his hand around the small apartment. "This isn't working anymore. I need a place with a big yard and at least three bedrooms. Oh, and a dog-friendly neighborhood."

She hugged him. "Chester this is wonderful! Do you remember Ed and Molly Jenkins, my neighbors three doors down? You've met them a few times at our annual Fourth of July street party."

"Yeah." He wrinkled his brow and nodded. "Ed recently retired didn't he?"

"Yes, they're putting their house on the market. They plan to move to Crescent City to be close to their grandchildren. Our tract is zoned for horses and small animals. It would be perfect for you and Chris and ..." She tilted her head and raised an eyebrow in silent question.

"Me and Chris. Sounds great, Mil. Maybe I can drop by and talk to them when I pick up the little guy tomorrow."

"I'll call Molly." She walked over to him and kissed him on the cheek. "I'll see you in the morning. Better luck tonight, sweetheart." Her broad stage wink made him laugh.

"I gotta go. I'm running late." He waved to Chris. "Bye, son. See you later. Be good for Gramma, okay?"

"Bye, Daddy. Don't forget to kiss Slick."

Chet laughed, scooped up the little dog, and kissed his head. Things were looking up. He had a nice bounce in his step as he jogged down the stairs.

* * * *

Risky's house, 6:30 p.m.

How many things would she take from the closet then put back? It probably didn't matter what she wore. Chances were whatever she decided on would be on Chet's apartment floor within minutes after he closed his door.

In that case, why not have some fun with it? She picked up her unscented skin cream and carried it to the kitchen. Her big Costco jar of cinnamon was getting low, so she quickly jotted it on her shopping list. A little cream, a little cinnamon. Give it a whip with a fork and voila! She carried the concoction back to her bedroom.

She fluffed her hair, added a little spiking paste and played with it until she had the look she wanted. Next, she slathered the cinnamon cream all over her body. Chet would drool like a bloodhound. She imagined his reaction, and her middle warmed and buzzed. Now for dark eye makeup and deep purple lipstick, like the way she dressed for Jack's funeral. The first time Chet saw her.

After pulling on her black lace thong, she donned thigh-high black stockings and her dangerous looking ankle strap shoes. No bra. She slipped on a silky black tank top and her short, tight, black leather skirt.

A slow turn in front of the full-length mirror on the closet door brought a tickled smile to her lips. "Chester Jensen, you'll never be the same after tonight. I promise."

* * * *

A little past seven, she parked next to Chet's Lincoln at the back of Jensen and Jensen. She grabbed the bottle of merlot off the passenger seat, straightened her shirt and climbed the two flights of stairs to his apartment.

The door was slightly ajar. Bluesy music played on the stereo. A different singer this time. Risky pushed with her fingertip and peeked inside. "Digger?" She heard the shower turn off. "Digger?"

"That you, doll? I'll be out in a flash."

Risky set the wine bottle on the coffee table and strolled to the bathroom door. Stealthily she pushed it open. Chet stood behind the foggy glass shower doors slicking water off his body. A floating feeling invaded her chest. She covered her heart.

Oh, God.

He pulled a towel over the top and started drying off. She pushed the door all the way open, propped her shoulder on the frame, crossed her arms, and crossed her feet at the ankles. All vamp. All for you, Digger.

Chet slid open the glass door, and stepped out before he spotted her. He went stock-still. His eyes swept her. "Jesus God in heaven! Kill me now."

He put his hands on his hips and took his time with a slow, appraising, once over. He sniffed the air. "I can smell you, witch. You're taking your life in your hands showing up here looking like that, and smelling like that."

She grinned and backed up. "Ooh, you're scaring me."

Returning her grin, He took a step forward. "Where's your whip?"

She raised her hand in the shape of a claw, and took a coy step back. "Don't need one."

"You sure? Because I'm thinking I'll take you apart piece by piece. Slow, steady torture, 'til you beg me to get to what we both want." He took another step forward.

Risky's heart pounded. Heat built and melted her insides, turned her knees to pudding. She bumped against his dresser and stopped. "Come and get it if you think you're man enough, blondie."

He was on her in an instant. His hands gripped the sides of her head. His intense blue stare took her breath away. "Don't move. Don't make a sound. You're mine, you understand?"

She nodded mutely, a sob of passion caught in her throat. His kiss almost brutal, he pressed her back against the dresser, put an arm around her waist and pulled her against his chest. She loved the damp, clean scent of his skin, and wanted her mouth all over him.

Hands on her shoulders he stepped back and went to his knees. She gasped when his hands slid up her legs and under her skirt then caressed her bottom. His touch burning, but gentle. He fingered the stretch lace tops of her stockings, her microscopic underwear, and her inner thighs. She grabbed a handful of his hair. "Chet."

The zipper on her skirt slid down, slipped slowly past her black stocking clad legs and dropped it to the floor. He ran his hands over her feet and left her shoes on. Stopping for a breath he gazed into her eyes then brushed his lips on the tender skin of her abdomen, and nipped and pulled the top of her thong with his teeth.

Her trembling hands skittered over his shoulders then his sides and chest as he stood and smoothed his palms across the outside of her tank top, caressing her back then her breasts. She gasped when he moaned and carefully grazed his teeth over her nipples.

Lowering her arms after he pulled off her top, she grasped his butt and pulled him against her.

He chuckled. "You want something, doll?"

She sighed. "You know I do."

He cupped her face and tilted it so he could gaze into her eyes. "Say please."

"Please, Chet." She bit his chin. "Pretty please."

"Sure you don't want to stop and have some supper first?" He jumped when she bared her teeth and dug her nails into his butt. "I guess not."

His hands on her shoulders he turned her, pointed her to the bed. "I want to watch your ass when you walk to my bed, doll. I want to watch and remember." He gently snapped her thong. "Don't take this off."

She hoped she could make it. Barely able to breathe, legs unsteady, she stepped forward ever so slowly. Digger drew a sharp breath, igniting a fire between her legs. At the edge of the bed, she stopped, flaunted a sultry look over her shoulder then deliberately crawled on top the sheets. It wasn't like she did the nasty sex kitten routine on a regular basis. This was an exciting first, and she wanted to do it for Chet. Her elbows and knees threatened to give out at his deep feral growl.

* * * *

Faint purple dawn light streamed through the small window above Chet's steaming shower. Hot water sluiced over their heads and shoulders. He held her tight against his chest; sure, she could feel his heartbeat pounding against her back. He nuzzled her neck and jaw, slid his hands down her belly and stopped at the mound between her legs. He pressed her tighter against his pelvis.

"Please, Digger." Risky moaned the words. "No more."

He didn't let up on his embrace. "First you beg me to start then you beg me to stop. There's no pleasing you, is there?"

Slipping around in the slippery circle of his arms, she gripped his butt and kissed his shoulder. "Oh, I'm pleased, more than pleased." She tilted her head back. "But I'm also starving and exhausted." Her forehead dropped on his chest.

He smoothed her back and shoulders. Turned off the water and handed her a towel. "I'll save some for your birthday party tonight then."

She startled. "My birthday party? When was this planned?"

He grinned at black mascara smudges beneath her eyes. "Just now." He took her towel away and turned the water on again.

"What are you doing?"

Chet put a drop of shower gel on the tip of his finger and very carefully smoothed it over the soft skin under her eyes. "Making you presentable, doll. We can't walk into Denny's for breakfast with you looking like you've been shagging me all night."

Risky ran her hand down his belly, caressed him and grinned. "I have been shagging you all night. I'm surprised this thing still works."

He turned off the water. "Careful or you'll find out." He handed her a towel then turned to dry his head and shoulders. "Watch it!" He jerked when she bit his bottom.

Risky stepped out of the shower before he could grab her, and ran to the bedroom. "Digger, do you have a shirt I can borrow? I don't want to get picked up for solicitation by wearing my dominatrix getup so early in the morning. All the SVPD guys show up for coffee at Denny's." She stepped into her thong, but passed on the black stockings and spike heels.

Naked, he entered the bedroom. "I've always wondered. Why did you dress like that for Jack's funeral?"

"Oh, I don't know. Just a poke in the lecherous old bastard's eye, I guess. Bobby didn't care. He knows me."

Chet opened a drawer and took out shorts and a pair of gym socks. Everything in the drawer was as precisely arranged as a display counter at Macy's.

From the corner of his eye, he caught Risky's smirk. He shrugged. "Hey, look at it this way. I'm somebody who never has to be picked up after."

He enjoyed the view of her ass as she wiggled into her skirt then pulled the tank top over her head. Bending in front of the dresser mirror she rubbed and fluffed her curly hair then smoothed a finger over her eyebrows.

Chet tossed her a white dress shirt. "Jesus, woman, you're even sexier without the gunk on your face and in your hair." He winked. "Wanna go back to bed? Some more action spiced with your dirty talk would get my day off to a great start."

She pressed her lips into a tight circle, rolled up the sleeves of his shirt and knotted it at her waist. "I don't indulge in dirty talk."

He chuckled. "Like hell, but I'm into it."

She jabbed a finger in his chest. "Feed me before I'm forced to hurt you."

"Hurt me, please."

"Later. I'm going down to my car to put my Mizunos on." She picked up her discarded clothes and headed for the door. "I'll meet you at Denny's. Hurry up. I have to take care of my babies before I go to work."

Chet dragged on his gym socks and jammed his big feet into a pair of loafers. He grabbed his keys and followed her out the door wishing she'd turn around, climb back up those stairs and hurt him.

Chapter Thirty

Veterinary Clinic

Risky leaned against the doorframe. "That's the last one for today, Larry. I'll take the two orphans home with me. You took their pictures and posted them on the bulletin board, right?"

"Done and done." Dr. Larry removed his animal print lab coat and hung it on a peg. "I'll ask our webmaster to add a lost dog and pet adoption page to the site. That might help move them through here faster."

She nodded. "Good idea. We get a lot of people in here looking at the board, especially if they've lost a pet. Once the new page is up we can link it to the Humane Society."

"Hey, didn't I see you having breakfast early this morning at Denny's? With Chet Jensen?"

Oh, God. "You friends with Chet?"

"Yeah, we're both in Rotary. He took care of my mother's funeral last year. Good man." His speculative look unnerved her. "Are you two ...?"

"Are we what?" What did she expect? Anyone who knew either of them, and saw them having breakfast in the wee hours would naturally think there might be something going on between them. As in — yeah, baby.

Larry had the decency to blush. "Forget it, Mariska. It's none of my business."

"Right."

He jammed his hands in his pockets. "Could you come in early tomorrow? I have two surgeries scheduled, and Marnie just went home sick. I'd just as soon call her and tell her to take the day off, and not, you know, spread anything around the clinic."

"Sure. What time?"

"Seven?"

She grimaced. "Yikes, that means getting up at five again." She noticed the brief jerk of his eyebrows. *Why not just give him a blow-by-blow of your wild night with Digger, Mariska?* As usual, she had her mouth in motion before her brain was in gear. Her face got hot. "No problem. I'll be here."

"Thanks." He placed a hand on her shoulder. "That's a great help." He jingled his keys. "I'll help you leash those dogs and get them in your car."

Her cell phone vibrated in her back pocket. Bobby. She'd let it go to voicemail for now and answer once she got the strays settled in the back of her beat-up SUV.

Larry helped her wrangle the nervous dogs then waved goodbye as he pulled out of the parking lot. The sun was low, so she had to get home, take the dogs for a run then touch base with Chet. She punched the message button on her cell.

"Happy birthday, Dog Breath. It's Bob, the man who loves you, baby. Call me back as soon as you can. Anita and I want you here for dinner tonight."

That put a kink in her plans to celebrate with Chet. She punched in Bobby's number.

"Hey, gorgeous, that was quick."

"Hi Bobby. Jeez, I haven't seen you and Anita since the wedding. How's married life?"

"I highly recommend it, cuz. Can you come over for dinner later? I already called Digger. He and the boy are coming. Since it's your birthday it would be nice if you could join us."

Now why in the world would Bobby presume to invite Chet and Chris? Her face burned at the thought of Chet and Bobby having a conversation about her. First, her boss had suspicions, now Bobby? Maybe the SVPD put out a BOLO following their zero-dark-thirty foray into Denny's. Things were happening too fast. Terry would be back in a few days. What had she started?

"Uh, okay, but I can't make it before seven. I've got two nervous strays to introduce to my other dogs, take my kids for a run, feed them, shower ..."

"Okay, I get it. Seven is fine. See you then."

"Uh, Bobby?" But he'd already disconnected. She sighed, dropped the phone in her bag, and backed out of the clinic parking lot.

* * * *

Bobby's condo, 7:00 p.m.

"I'll get it," Chet shouted. "It's gotta be Mariska." He pulled the door open, and his smile quickly faded. It was Risky all right, and the glare on her face would stop a charging moose. "What's the matter?" She ignored his hand.

Hissing like a snake, she spat, "What did you tell Bobby?"

He scratched his head. "What did I tell Bobby?"

"That's what I asked."

"What did I tell him about what?" He backed up at her thunderous look.

She grabbed the front of his shirt and pulled him forward until they were standing on the front step. "Close the door, Digger."

Absolutely in the dark about what had morphed her into a shrew, Chet closed the door and faced her. "Risky, what's going on? Are you mad at me about something?"

"Should I be?"

Whoa, this was a side of her he'd have to give a lot of thought to. He threw up his arms and shoved his face close to hers. "Cut the bullshit, and tell me why you're acting like an avenging angel."

Through gritted teeth she said, "What exactly did you tell Bobby about us?" She jabbed a finger in his chest.

"About us?" Chet put his hands on his head and rolled his eyes. "Nothing. I don't kiss and tell, doll, if that's what you think."

"Why did they invite you to dinner tonight—on my birthday?"

"Oh, for chrissakes! Bob's my best friend. I was his best man, remember? They just got back from their honeymoon. Anita wanted to show off her new cooking skills. They'd like to get acquainted with Chris. It just happens to be your birthday. Anything else?"

The starch went out of her back, and she exhaled. Her lips trembled, and he touched her crumpling face.

"Oh, Chet, you don't know—I can be a real bitch sometimes."

"So I see." He smiled. She stepped into his arms.

The door flew open and Bob looked out. "Hey, what's ... Oops, sorry." The door clicked shut.

Chet chuckled and rubbed her back and bottom. "Now you've done it, Dog Breath."

She sighed against his neck. "Kiss me, Digger. I need a kiss." She didn't have to ask twice.

"Why were you so upset, doll? All Bobby ever knew, until this minute, is that I was attracted to you. I told him months ago."

"I don't know." She sighed with surrender. "I love Bobby, you love Bobby, and he loves both of us back. Why should I care if he knows I'm crazy for your body, for you?"

His heart tripped and stumbled in his chest. "You are?"

"You have to ask me that after last night? Come on, you're no dim bulb, *Jensen the undertaker*. Tell me you don't feel the same, and I'll get back in my car and go ho—"

The kiss had all Chet's feelings packaged in it, and it was a doozie. If steam wasn't shooting out of his ears, he was left to wonder why. His libido soared and his heart threatened to explode.

"Daddy? Are you and Whisky gonna eat dinner?"

* * * *

Risky sighed with contentment. "Anita, that was so good." She squeezed Anita's hand. "You should forget about real estate and go in the catering business."

Bobby beamed at his new wife. "That's what I said." He told them she'd taken a French cooking class while he went fishing almost every day during their honeymoon on Bora Bora.

Anita patted Bobby's cheek. "I hate fishing. Good thing the hotel offered the class. That's what saved the marriage from going in the tank before the honeymoon was over." She grinned at Mariska. "The French Chef was pretty hot stuff. Think Nicolas Duvauchelle."

Risky swooned. "Oh, my God. I would have been so busy wiping the drool off my chin that I'd never have learned to so much as poach an egg."

Chet and Bobby exchanged clueless-male glances and shrugged.

Chet turned to Christian. "Did you like Anita's dinner, son?"

"It was okay, but I like pizza better."

Bobby laughed. "Nothing like the honesty of a kid, is there? Tell me, Chris, what have you and your dog been up to lately?"

"Me and Slick got to sleep in Daddy's big bed with him and Whisky."

Risky dropped her head in her hands. "Oh, God." Where in heck was that sinkhole when you needed to be swallowed up?

A moment of silence was broken by an outburst of laughter from Bobby and Anita. Bob stretched across the table and punched Chet in the shoulder.

"Okie dokie." Anita stood. "Time for birthday cake. Who wants to help me in the kitchen?"

Chris hopped off the big phone book on his chair. "I do, but don't give cake to Slick. It's bad for dogs."

Bobby shook his head, gave Risky a lascivious wink then said, "I think I better go help the wife. Is it safe to leave you two alone?"

Risky glared and raised a fist. "Stuff it, Bobby."

He raised his hands and backed out of the dining room.

Chet trailed his finger down her cheek. It sent a streak of heat that made a direct hit on her bottomless lust for him. When did she turn into the Queen of Horny? She gave him a smoldering look and pushed his finger into her mouth.

Chet gasped. "Jesus, doll. I gotta get you back in my bed."

She grinned. "We have a little two-legged impediment, wouldn't you say?"

"I'm working on that."

She pushed his hand away when the sounds of *Happy Birthday* were heard, and the swinging door to the kitchen opened. Bobby carried a beautiful cake, blazing with candles. Christian grinned at her, a telltale smear of blue frosting on his cheek. She sat back and smiled as a chorus of off key singing and birthday wishes filled the room.

"Just take a small piece," Chet admonished Chris. "We'll take the rest home, and you can have more tomorrow."

Through a mouthful of cake and lips covered with icing, Chris mumbled. Risky saw his eyelids beginning to droop. She smiled when he refused all Slick's whining begs from under his chair.

Chet rose to help Anita clear the dishes. Bob put his hand on Risky's shoulder. "Sit still, birthday girl. We'll get it."

She beckoned Chris. "Come and sit on my lap, honey. Tell me about your sleepover with Gramma." He climbed up, and she wiped his face and hands with her napkin. "Wasn't that good cake?"

"Um hum. I didn't give Slick any."

"I noticed. That was very good. Now he won't get a tummy ache."

"Gramma and me went to the petting zoo. I got to ride a pony and eat a taco." He picked up the napkin and rubbed her lips. "You got frosting on you. I fixed it."

"Thank you."

"Nita told me a secret."

"She did? If it's a secret, you're not supposed to tell me." She kissed the top of his head. A wave of affection engulfed her. She whispered, "I love you, Chester Christian Jensen."

He put his small hands on her cheeks and kissed her lips. "Love you too, Whisky."

Tears sprang to her eyes. She looked up with trembling lips as Chet came back in the dining room.

A look of concern on his face, he asked, "Something wrong?"

She shook her head. "No. Something good. Chris loves me."

Chet's blue gaze stole her breath. "Like father, like son."

A clog in her throat threatened to choke her. Happiness and fear warred inside. He didn't really mean that. He couldn't love her. Yet. They hadn't spent enough time together, time to know each other.

Bobby and Anita joined them. Bob patted Chris on the head. "Anita told me you had something to tell me, Chris. What is it?"

Chris slid from Risky's lap and moved to Anita's side. He tilted his chin up and looked at her, his eyes solemn and serious. "Is it okay to tell the secret now?"

She put her hand on his head. "Yes, you can tell the secret now." She turned a loving gaze to her new husband.

Chris puffed out his chest, full of importance. "Okay." He put his finger on Anita's stomach. "There's a baby in here."

Risky gawked at her cousin. Poor Bobby looked like he would faint. She was afraid he was having a heart attack when he gripped his chest. New tears burned Risky's eyes as Bobby embraced his bride and rested his cheek on her head. She didn't realize until that moment that Chet was gripping her hand.

"Congratulations. That's absolutely great news." He smiled at Risky. "Isn't it, doll?"

She squeezed back. "The best ever," and rose from the table to embrace Bobby and Anita from behind, her cheek on Bobby's back. "Nice going, cuz. Wait 'til Dad finds out, he'll be so happy for you."

Anita pulled away from her husband and put her arms around Risky. The girlfriends sobbed. Chet and Bobby indulged in a strong handshake and a flurry of back pounding, followed by an exchange of playful punches.

A small voice piped up. "This was the bestest birthday party. Huh, Daddy?"

Chet swooped Chris up and twirled him overhead, careful to miss the chandelier. "Yes, a great party. Now it's time to get you home to bed, little man. Tell Anita thank you for the great dinner and cake."

"Thank you, Nita."

"You're welcome, sweetie. You're a very good secret keeper. Have a fun time on your birthday at Disneyland."

"Yes." He clapped his chubby hands. "Whisky's going with us, and Gramma too, but Slick can't go. They only allow mouses."

Risky helped Chet gather up Chris's things and snapped the hook on Slick's leash. At Chet's car she waited while he buckled Chris's seat belt then she let Slick jump in.

"I'm not coming over tonight, Digger. I have a real early morning at the clinic tomorrow. I need to sleep, or I might accidentally kill a patient while I'm assisting Dr. Larry in the surgery."

His wonderful arms around her, she melted against him. "I'm working on a plan, doll." He kissed her. "I'll know more by Saturday. We'll swing by and pick you up at eight, okay?"

Brushing her lips against his, she smiled. Digger had a plan.

Chapter Thirty-One

Disneyland

Millie and Risky smiled and waved at Chet and Chris when their little car bumped and chugged off on the Seven Dwarf's Mine Train Ride.

Risky touched Millie's arm. "Let's grab that seat over there in the shade before somebody else gets it."

"What a good idea. This place is great for kids but hard on grandmas." She held her hat against a puff of wind and led the way.

"Please, you're in the best shape of any grandma I've ever known. Were you a child bride?"

Millie sat, sighed and patted the spot on the bench next to her. "I was eighteen when I met Chester's father. He was a thirty-year-old captain, and so handsome in full military dress that he took my breath away. Chester is the spitting image of him."

"And Chris is the spitting image of Chet."

Millie smiled and nodded. "The second I saw that child in Germany, I knew he was my grandson."

"That must have been some shock." Risky tried to picture Millie's face when she met Chris for the first time.

"I'll say. I was furious with Chester for keeping him a secret from me. I didn't know he'd had no knowledge of the boy's existence for more than a few hours. I still have some resentment toward poor, tragic Noreen. Because of her, we missed more than three years of that precious child's life."

"I can't imagine what she went through all that time."

"Chester was so in love with her. I warned him against involving himself with a married woman – told him it would end badly. He was devastated when she went back to her airman husband. It took him more than a year to get over her. So sad."

"Yes, but now you have Christian. He's special."

"He is. He had me wrapped around his little pinky within minutes of our first meeting." Millie chuckled. "Ironic isn't it? I insisted Chester call me by my first name instead of Mom, and now I'm thrilled to be a grandmother."

Risky shifted. "Millie, may I ask you something? You don't have to tell me if you don't want to."

"Of course, Mariska. What's your question?"

"What did you think when Chet told you he wanted to be an undertaker?" Risky couldn't help grimacing when she said the word.

"At first I thought he was teasing me. He'd been working with his uncle at the funeral home all summer, but it never occurred to me that he'd want to pursue it as a profession. I'm ashamed to say that I was horrified."

"What did you do?"

"When I started in on him, his father took me aside and set me straight. The Colonel rarely ever laid down the law to me. I wasn't one of his Marines, after all."

"What did he say?"

"He told me he was proud the man Chester had become. As a fully functioning, intelligent adult, he was at liberty to make his own choices in life without the aid of his mama. His son's decision to pursue a noble and necessary vocation was his choice and no one else's. I've accepted it, but I still don't particularly like it."

"Wow."

Millie sighed and patted Risky's arm. "I know you have a problem with it."

"I don't want to. I shouldn't really." No, she shouldn't. She thought she'd got past that long ago, but apparently not.

"You're allowed your feelings, Mariska, but it helped me to look at it this way; Chester is there to help people through the most tragic and sorrowful periods of their lives. Even though we all know death is inevitable, we're never really prepared for the reality when we lose someone we love. He's strong, respectful and dignified when they're in desperate need, when they're numbed with grief and confusion. I'm very proud of him. The Colonel would feel the same."

Risky pressed her lips together and considered Millie's wisdom. She so wanted to come to terms with it. Her hang-up made a prisoner of her. She didn't want it to spoil her budding relationship with the most exciting and wonderful man she'd ever known.

"Here they come." Millie waved.

Risky smiled at Digger and Chris, their identical grins and matching tee shirts.

* * * *

Chris cried with protest when Chet told him it was time to go home. He lifted the boy in his arms and patted him on the bottom. "We'll come back again. Lots of times."

"Promise?"

"On my honor as the proud son of a proud Marine." He snapped a salute. "Can you do that?"

Chris mimicked his father, his salute pretty sharp, even though he did it left-handed.

Chet hugged him. "That's my man."

"Don't squeeze me, Daddy."

"Oops, sorry. I forgot."

Millie and Mariska, close behind, laughed at the exchange. "Chester, I'm particularly fond of those shirts you and Chris wore today. Where did you get them?"

"Don't blame me, Mom. Mariska gave them to us."

Risky took exception to his remark. "What's wrong with 'I'm with my son, and I'm with my Daddy'?"

"Nothing, doll. We love these shirts don't we, Chris?"

"Yes, now Daddy won't get losted."

They hopped a parking lot shuttle and soon arrived at Chet's car. It took several minutes to unload all their purchases into the trunk before they could get on their way. Chet sighed and stretched his neck before starting the car. "Long day. More exhausting than a volleyball game with college kids in overtime."

He reached across the front seat, lifted Risky's hand and kissed her knuckles. "You okay, doll?"

"I'm great. When can we go again, Daddy?"

Millie, sitting next to Chris's car seat in the back, added her own comment. "I'm really enjoying the name Daddy as applied to you, Chester. It suits you."

Yes, it suited him fine. He loved being a daddy. Surprised at how his feelings were different on the subject of fatherhood, from the old days when he thought about it in the abstract, some-day context. Having spent his entire life until age thirty-two as a son, he was suddenly thrust into fulltime fatherhood.

He glanced in the rearview mirror. "He asleep yet?"

"Yes," Millie answered. "The little angel."

"You're a lucky guy, Digger."

"Oh, I know it. First Christian and now you." Her deep blush and furtive glance in Millie's direction warmed his heart. He squeezed her hand and winked. He loved it when she couldn't come back with a sassy comment.

* * * *

They pulled into the parking lot behind Jensen and Jensen. Risky was shocked to see Bobby and Anita. Chet parked in the space next to them, and Bobby and Anita got out of their car and waited. The look on Bobby's face sent a stab of fear through her heart.

When she stepped out of Chet's car, Bobby reached out and embraced her without saying a word.

"Bobby? What's happened? You're scaring me." She pushed back so she could see his face. "What?"

Anita put her arm on Risky's shoulder. "It's your father." Terror struck Risky like lightning. "He's been hurt, but he's alive."

Risky's body seemed to deflate. Her vision fogged from a light mist to black. Gasping to breathe, she gripped Bobby's arms fiercely. "Bobby, please, what happened? Is it serious? Is he going to be okay? Where is he?"

Bobby rested his forehead against hers. "He's still in Kiev. We have a lot to talk about, and a lot to do. Let's go upstairs." He turned her in the direction of the stairs.

Anguish filled her. "Bobby, what am I going to do?"

Chet stepped between them. "Bob, please bring Chris upstairs. Anita, will you help Millie with the bags?"

Bobby and Anita stepped away leaving a cold chasm in Risky's chest. "Chet, I ... I ..."

"Can you make it up the stairs, doll?"

She stumbled on the first step. Chet lifted her in his arms and carried her up the two flights to his apartment. She clung to him while he took the keys from his pocket and unlocked his front door.

Inside he set her on the couch and went to the kitchen to get a glass of water. "Drink this. Take a few calming breaths. Hear Bobby out before you panic. All right?"

She nodded mutely.

"I'm here for you, sweetheart. We'll figure out what to do."

His hand on her cheeks, as he knelt before her, gave her some strength. The others came through the door, and Bobby took Chris to the bedroom. Millie followed him.

Anita sat next to Risky and took her hand. "Bobby'll tell you everything, honey. He's been working on a plan for the last three hours. Relax, if you can."

Bobby returned to the living room, and Anita got up to give him her seat. Chet remained kneeling before Risky, holding her hands.

"Okay. Here's the situation, Uncle Dave was stabbed and ..."

Risky shrieked, "Stabbed! Oh, my God, oh, my ..."

Bobby shook her. "Be quiet and listen to me! We don't have a lot of time. Keep it together. I'll tell you all I know, and what we've done so far." He gazed into her eyes. "Okay?"

She raised her hands to cover her face and nodded. If anything happened to her father, she didn't know what she'd do. He had to be okay, he had to be.

"The American Embassy called me. The details are sketchy and unconfirmed." He stroked her hair. "An altercation occurred between Anya and her sister. Anya attacked Nadia with a knife. Uncle Dave intervened."

Risky gasped and clutched her throat.

Chet mumbled, "God Almighty."

"Dave was severely injured. They took him to the American Medical Center where he underwent emergency surgery. So far he seems to be responding."

Risky gripped handfuls of her hair. "I have to go. I have to go to Daddy."

Bobby patted her leg. "Yes. The American Ambassador has arranged an emergency visa and a temporary passport for you. I've booked flights leaving tomorrow afternoon. Anita will go with you."

Alarm rang through her. "But, Anita, you're ..."

"I'm going with you. I'll be fine. My passport is up to date, and they'll have a visa for me. American consular officers will meet us, and be available to us while we're there."

"What happened to Anya?" Her hatred for her mother couldn't have been stronger. The woman was a monster.

Bobby took her hand. "She was arrested and taken to Lukyanivska detention center. She's a citizen of Ukraine. It's out of the hands of the American authorities."

She wrung her hands. "I don't know what to do. What should I do?" Anguish, so strong it was physically painful, consumed her mind and body.

Bobby pulled her to her feet. "I'll take you home so you can pack and get some sleep."

Risky glanced around the room unable to focus her thoughts. A curl of nausea swelled in her throat.

Millie caught her eye from the bedroom doorway, shock and sympathy on her beautiful face. "Chester, you go with Mariska. I'll stay here tonight." A wave of relief and gratitude engulfed Risky. Tears stung her eyes as the gravity of the moment began to sink in. "Thank you, Millie."

Chet stood. "Right. Come, I'll take you home. Bobby and Anita can follow us, and we'll all sit down and figure out the next few hours." He embraced her briefly then led her toward the front door.

* * * *

They walked into Risky's house, and she burst into a new wave of tears when the dogs greeted her. Chet left the door ajar so Bob and Anita wouldn't have to knock. He led her to the couch, sat next to her and beckoned the dogs to join them.

"Chet, what am I going to do with my babies? I can't leave them alone. I don't know what ..."

"You don't need to worry about them. Chris and I'll move in here and take care of them while you're gone."

"You'd do that?"

"I'd do anything for you, sweetheart. You know that, don't you?" He kissed her cheek. "I love you."

Her chest bounced with a sob. "You scare me when you say that." A tear leaked from one of her big brown eyes.

"Why? This isn't the first time I've said it." He loved her. Yes. He wanted to marry her and keep her and all her quirks and insecurities, and her pack of mismatched dogs within arm's reach, for the rest of his life.

"Chet." She put a hand over her mouth.

"You don't have to say anything. All you need to do right now is listen to Bob's plan and get yourself overseas to be with Dave and take care of him until you can bring him home. All right?"

* * * *

Hours later, limp with exhaustion, she showered and went to bed. He took care of feeding the dogs and getting them settled for the night. After his shower, he crawled into her bed and cuddled her in his arms. He remembered the agony he and Millie had gone through when those Marines, in full dress uniform, arrived at their door to inform them that Sir had been killed in Afghanistan.

The woman he loved was in pain and terrified at the thought of losing her father. He'd have a long talk with Bobby after she and Anita left in the morning. He wanted to know so much more about Mariska's childhood, and especially about her mother, Anya. What events had shaped her?

* * * *

Early the next morning Risky and Chet went for an abbreviated run on Box Canyon Road. Shortly after they finished breakfast, she heard tires on gravel. Bobby and Anita had arrived.

She opened the front door and watched Bobby unload Anita's luggage and set it on the ground at the back of Chet's car.

Chet grabbed his keychain, and from inside the house, he popped open the trunk. Bobby placed his wife's luggage inside next to Risky's. He and Anita entered the house.

Anita embraced her. "How are you doing this morning?"

"I'm much calmer, thanks to Digger. He's been wonderful. I'm so grateful to him for taking over, for helping me get ready to go."

Anita beamed into her eyes. "He's a rock. I've been half in love with him for years. Don't tell Bobby." She smiled and glanced at her husband.

Chet embraced her. "Bobby already knows, beautiful. The feeling is mutual." He picked up Risky's flight bag. "Ready?"

"I need to kiss my babies goodbye. It won't take a minute." She hurried to the back yard.

They had an early flight to London then a lengthy layover before continuing on to Kiev. It would take a very long day to eat up those six thousand plus miles. She rubbed the heads of Harley and Shep, and put the three small dogs in the outside dog run with them.

"You big boys keep the coyotes away from my babies, you hear? I hope I'll be back soon, but Chet and Chris will take good care of you, okay?" The dogs stood quietly. They sensed her unease, and by doing so, warmed her heart. "Bye, kids."

* * * *

Next in line at the ticket counter, Chet waited with his arm around Risky's shoulders. "Don't worry about anything here, doll. Private First Class Jensen, and buck Private Jensen are on the job."

"Chet, you have a business to run. I'm taking advantage of you."

"Like the rest of my life, until you, and then Chris came on the scene— my business runs like clockwork. I have a loyal staff. The world won't stop if I step off for a while."

Her brown eyes focused on his. "It would stop for me."

Those few words made his heart soar, and gave him hope. He squeezed her slender hand in his.

The passenger in front of them stepped away. Chet moved aside so Anita could join Risky at the counter. They handed over their identification. Risky's passport would be waiting for her at immigration in London Heathrow. Bobby had arranged for an English friend to pick it up at the American Embassy and meet their flight. In the meantime, she had an affidavit from Homeland Security to get her that far.

Risky looked at her boarding pass. "Business class?"

"Yes ma'am. That's how the reservation was confirmed."

She and Anita picked up their baggage claim checks and stepped away from the counter. "Bobby? You paid for business class? That costs a fortune."

He grinned at her. "Hey, my wife is in delicate condition. I didn't do it for you. You I'd put in the last row, by the toilet."

"I ever tell you what a jerk you are?"

"Many times, cuz."

Chet picked up the women's hand luggage and chuckled at the byplay between Mariska and Bob. As an only child, he'd always longed for a sibling, or at least a few cousins. "Shake a leg, world travelers. You still have to navigate security. We don't even have time to get a cup of coffee."

* * * *

After a grueling fifteen hours of travel, Risky and Anita stepped off the plane at Boryspil International Airport, Kyiv. They proceeded to immigration and waded through a confusion of activity and officials before they exited to baggage claim.

A western looking man held a sign with *Williston* in bold black letters. She and Anita approached him. Slightly behind the man a middle-aged blond woman hovered. A shockwave went through Risky. She had the eerie sensation of looking in the mirror. Except for the hair and the age difference, she was looking at *herself* in the mirror.

The man stepped forward. "Ms. and Mrs. Williston? I'm Stevens, an officer in the U.S. Embassy." They nodded. He stepped aside and said something in Russian to the woman.

Tears sprang to the woman's eyes, and she shyly approached. Through trembling lips, she asked, "Mariska?"

Risky swallowed. The only other word she understood was Nadia. This was her mother's younger sister. Not sure what to do, she extended a hand and nodded. "Nadia?"

They rode in an official consulate car. Stevens sat next to the driver and tried to keep up with the translation of Nadia's words. "She wants you to stay at her apartment, but I advised her that it would be better, under the circumstances, if you stayed at a hotel. At least until more of the investigation is completed."

Nadia gripped Risky's hand and continued her excited chatter. Nadia had a large bandage on her arm.

Risky's heart pounded with fear for her father. "Tell her I said thank you, and that I hope to spend some time with her once I've checked in on Daddy."

Nadia understood her priority and bobbed her head in agreement when Stevens translated. He instructed the driver to drop Nadia at her apartment building, and told Risky and Anita they would go on to the embassy and from there to the hospital. The hotel had been arranged, and an employee of the Radisson Blu staff would convey them back to the hotel when they were ready to leave the hospital.

He handed Risky a card from the hotel manager. "Any member of the staff at the hospital will place the call for you. I've written instructions on the back of the card. Your luggage went directly to the Radisson, and will be in your room."

Chapter Thirty-Two

Risky's House, four days later.

Chet's bare back gleamed with sweat as he pushed, shoved, and wrestled with Risky's old-style hand mower. Her large back yard needed a haircut, and it looked like he was the man to do it. Chris played with his soldiers on a patch of dirt in a far corner near the dog run. Harley and Shep had two new temporary companions, the orphans Risky brought from the vet.

"First you were the plumber and now the gardener. Is the funeral business that bad, Jensen?" Terry stood inside the back gate, hands on hips and surveyed the scene.

"Hey, Redmond. Yeah, you guys at the hospital must have had some continuing education on how not to kill as many people as usual." Chet pulled his wadded tee shirt out of his back pocket and mopped his face and neck.

"Where's Mariska? She's not returning my messages."

"She's in Kiev, Ukraine. Her father was gravely injured in an attack. She and her cousin's wife, Anita, went over there to be with him. They're hoping to get clearance to have him released from the American clinic. You'll probably be seeing him in your hospital in the next several days."

At that moment, the back screen door opened and Millie stepped outside. "Terry! How nice to see you. I just finished making lunch. Will you join us?"

Chet noticed that Terry's smile reflected his appreciation of Millie's many fine qualities. Redmond hesitated a moment. "If you have enough, that would be great. I don't want to horn in on such short notice."

"Nonsense. We have plenty. Christian! Come and get washed up, sweetheart. Lunch is ready." She waved. "Your soldiers will wait for you."

She pointed to Chet. "Chester, you put on a shirt before you come to the table."

170

He saluted. "Yes, ma'am, Sergeant, Jensen." He laughed and pulled his shirt over his head, went to the hose and washed his hands and face.

Millie held her hand toward Terry. "Come in, you handsome thing. We have a lot of catching up to do." She grabbed Chris as he tried to get around her. "No you don't, young man. Have your daddy wash those filthy hands before you come in here. And brush the dirt off his pants and shoes, Chester."

"Toss me a towel, Mil." Chet laughed to himself as he cleaned up his little boy. He remembered what a stickler she was when he came home dirty. Shoes outside, all dirt brushed off, hands clean. "Gramma won't let either of us have lunch if we don't get washed up."

Chris wrinkled his nose. "She's always washing me."

Laughing, Chet rubbed Chris's little hands and face with the towel. "I know what you mean, buddy. She never let me get away with anything."

Crowded around Risky's small kitchen table they brought Terry up to speed. For several minutes, Chet related what happened as far as they knew. "Dave suffered critical blood loss and multiple stab wounds. As of yesterday he regained consciousness, and seems to be improving." He held up a hand with fingers crossed.

"Her mother did that?" Terry's astonishment was painted all over his face and demeanor. "Do you know why?"

Chet raised a hand. "Are you finished with your sandwich, son?"

"Yes." Chris sat quietly, a glass of milk in his hands. He'd been listening to the adult conversation with great interest.

"You may be excused. Remember how I showed you to fill the dog dishes for Harley and Shep?" The boy nodded. "Okay then. You can feed them all by yourself this time."

Filled with wide-eyed excitement, Chris jumped up and headed for the back door. As an afterthought he tossed a hurried "Ascuse me," over his shoulder.

Chet turned back to Terry. "I don't like to go into too much detail around my kid."

"Of course, I understand." Terry leaned forward on his elbows. He nodded his thanks when Millie refilled his glass.

Millie shook her head. "Such a tragic thing. Poor Mariska was devastated when she left. We know so little about her mother, her childhood."

Terry nodded. "I first met her mother in the ER then again at Bob Williston's wedding. A stunning woman. She barely said two words all evening. Mariska resembles her. I sensed tension between them."

A sharp stab of jealousy pierced Chet's chest. Here was his competition in the flesh. Despite their intimacy, Risky had made no commitment to him. He'd fight for her. Redmond would not walk in and take her away.

"Here's what we do know, Terry. Anya and her sister couldn't get along when they reunited, after so many years apart. Nadia asked Anya and Dave to leave after a few days. Dave moved them into a hotel. Somehow Anya got her hands on alcohol and went on a real bender."

"Is she an alcoholic?"

"Yes. She's also been in and out of mental and rehab facilities all of Risky's life. Mariska told us that her father had nearly bankrupted them over the years with her expensive care. Anya would often disappear from their home or walk away from a rehab facility and be gone for days, weeks or months, with no clue as to where she'd been when she finally showed up back on their doorstep."

"I had no idea." Terry shook his head and glanced first at Chet, and then Millie. His gaze swept the room. "Are you living here ... together ... with Mariska?"

Chet didn't miss the combative glint in Terry's eyes, and he was so tempted to say yes he and Risky were together. *So, Redmond you can just butt out now.* "No. Chris and I are house and dog sitting while she's gone."

Millie tapped Terry's arm. "I'm having the best time in this old fashioned kitchen." She pointed across the room. "Have you ever seen a stove like that? This place is a treasure trove. I come over every now and then to fix lunch or dinner, or to take Chris while Chester's at work."

Chet and Millie both caught the blatant look of relief on Terry's face. Chet locked gazes with her briefly then continued his story.

"When Dave first met Anya she was barely twenty. He was thirty-five. She enchanted him with her beauty and her Russian accent. She told him that when she and her sister were in their teens they'd been kidnapped by sex traffickers.

"She managed to escape after several months, but was sure Nadia had been murdered. Somehow, she made her way to the U.S., and worked as a waitress in a Russian Tea Room in West Los Angeles. She longed to be a ballerina and was enrolled in a dance academy at the time.

"She told Dave a tragic sob story about how she would have to drop out of class because she couldn't afford to pay rent on her apartment, and tuition. Her green card would soon expire, and she was in danger of being deported.

"By this time he was in love with her, and offered to pay for her dance classes. She asked if she could move in with him. A few months later, they were married. She was pregnant with Mariska, and gave birth to her six months later."

Terry shook his head and sighed. "Sounds like a movie plot, doesn't it?"

"Sadly, that sort of thing probably happens more than we know. In any case, after a time Dave began to doubt her story, but he loved her and told himself her past didn't matter."

Millie moved to the refrigerator for more iced tea. "Mariska told Chet a few days ago that when she got a break from Dave's bedside, she visited Nadia. Nadia told her they were never kidnapped. Anya ran away from home after an altercation with their father.

"It's still a mystery how she made her way to California. Nadia said Anya was erratic and troubled all her life. The reason she ran away that last time was that her parents planned to have her committed to a mental hospital. They couldn't handle her any longer."

Chet took up the story. "I guess it took Dave a while to admit she was an alcoholic. He watched her very carefully when she was pregnant, didn't allow her to drink or take any drugs until Mariska was born. They fought constantly. She physically attacked him many times, but he never stopped loving her, and never gave up hope he could help her."

Terry sighed and leaned against the back of his chair. "I see why Mariska is so alienated from her. She would never talk about it, and I never pressed her." He clamped his lips together and shook his head. "I admire her ability to put it behind her, and get on with her life."

Chet nodded his agreement. "Here's the topper. Anya swore to Nadia that Dave was her kidnapper. That he'd forced her into marriage after raping her repeatedly. The reason the sisters fought is because Nadia didn't buy that any more than the other lies she'd told all her life."

Millie began to clear the table. "Can you imagine?"

Chet stood. "I've got to finish mowing out back. Also Chris has been quiet for too long." He paused at the back door. "I expect Risky to call late tonight. I'll tell her you're back in Simi, and asking for her." He be damned if he'd do any more than the minimum required by common courtesy. Risky was his, and he intended it to stay that way.

He was nearly finished with the mowing when Millie and Redmond finally came through the back door. They talked for a few minutes then Terry kissed Millie on the cheek and waved goodbye to him and Chris. Chet nodded and continued pushing the rusty old mower across the last few strips of un-mowed lawn.

Later that evening Chet sat on the toilet seat lid, laughing while Millie bathed Chris in Risky's old claw-foot bathtub.

She screamed when Chris splashed water on her. "You little devil!" Chet came to her rescue and took over the last of the bath.

Once Chris was in his pajamas, the three of them sat on the couch with Mickey, Minnie, Brutus and Slick, and watched a basketball game. Chris was new to basketball and chirped a constant stream of questions while Chet tried to concentrate on the game.

Finally he switched it off and bundled Chris into Risky's bedroom. He'd brought the rollaway cot from his apartment and squeezed it in between the dresser and double bed. All four of the little dogs vied for space on the cot with Chris. The little guy giggled with delight at their antics.

"Time to settle down now. No more playing or I'll take the dogs and put them in the kitchen."

Chris lay back, scowled, and pulled the covers up to his chin. "You're a mean daddy."

Chet smiled. "I know. I'll work on getting better at it starting tomorrow." He kissed Chris's blond curls, patted the dogs and turned out the lights.

Millie stood when he returned to the living room. "I have to get on home, Chester. You're dropping Christian off on Monday morning?"

"Yeah, thanks Mom. We've got two funerals and a viewing on Monday."

Millie grimaced.

He kissed her. "Get that look off your face. I love my work. Live with it."

He walked her to her car.

Millie unlocked the door, dropped her purse on the passenger seat and faced Chet. "That young man's in love with Mariska, Chester, but I suppose you already know that."

Chet sucked his teeth and nodded. "Ain't life interesting?" He kissed her goodbye then watched as she pulled away.

Back in the house, he settled on the couch with a Vince Flynn thriller and waited for Risky's call.

Chapter Thirty-Three

Dave Williston's room, American Clinic

Tears ran from Risky's eyes when her father asked the inevitable question. Where was her mother? Was she okay? When could he see her? He didn't ask where he was, or what Risky was doing there. All he cared about was the woman who'd tried to kill him.

"Daddy, she was arrested when the police ambulance came to rescue you at Nadia's apartment. She's in the Lukyanivka Detention Center."

She leaned close to hear Dave's voice, no more than a whisper. "We have to get her released, Mariska. It's a terrible place."

"We can't, Daddy. All requests from the American Embassy have been turned down. They have no jurisdiction. She's a Ukrainian citizen."

Her tears increased when Dave's devastated and damaged face crumpled with emotional pain. A tear trail ran from the corner of his eye to his ear. She dabbed at it with a tissue. "Daddy, I love you so much. You have to get well so I can take you home."

"I can't leave her there. She'll die in there."

Risky sobbed. "Daddy she nearly killed you. She tried to kill her sister. You have to give up. You can't save her any longer." She was sure her pleas would fall on deaf ears.

Dave closed his eyes. Tears continued to leak from them, but he didn't speak. After a while, his steady breathing told Risky he slept again.

She stayed by his bedside until Anita came to relieve her, so she could make her call to Chet. She stepped outside the hospital, and the driver of the hotel car opened the door for her. She and Anita had been warned by the American Embassy not to go wandering around the streets of Kiev without an escort, or at the very least, her Aunt Nadia.

The city of Kiev, a mixture of ancient and modern, bustled around her and seemed as safe as Los Angeles. Then she smiled ruefully with the knowledge that she wouldn't think of wandering some of the L.A. neighborhood streets alone either.

Chet answered on the first ring. Noon in Kiev, so it was about 10:00 p.m. in Simi Valley. "Hello, doll, how are you holding up?"

Her heart warmed at the sound of his voice. "I'm hanging in there, Digger. Daddy woke up today."

"That's great news! Did the doctors give you a hint when he'd be able to travel? I can imagine it would be very stressful for him — the long trip."

"Among his passport and documents we found a travel health insurance policy which includes emergency medical evacuation by air ambulance." She chuckled. "Daddy never forgot his Boy Scout creed: Always be prepared."

"I'll be damned. Will you and Anita be able to accompany him?"

"Anita plans to head home in a couple of days. I've accepted Nadia's plea to stay in her apartment until Daddy and I leave."

"Is that wise?"

"She's a sweet and gentle woman, Digger. Nothing like my mother. There's a very strong physical resemblance, of course. Anita's going to send you some photos from her smart phone later today. You'll be surprised how much I resemble Nadia."

"Bobby's been nervous as a caged cat. Does he know she's returning early?"

"I think so, but you can tell him. The travel office at the Radisson will email her flight itinerary to him tomorrow."

"How are you going to communicate with Nadia? She doesn't speak English."

"She has a neighbor who worked as a translator at the NATO liaison office in Kiev. She's happy to sharpen up her English for Nadia and me. When she's not around, we'll use sign language. It works pretty well, in fact."

"I really miss you, doll. I can't wait to have you in my arms again. Oh, Chris made me promise to tell you that he's taking very good care of all your dogs."

She pictured Chris in her mind's eye and smiled. "How is the little guy?"

"He's coming out of his shell more every day. Been testing the limits of what he can get away with. I had to be a mean daddy and scold him when he gave Mom a hard time a couple of days ago."

She laughed. "Ah, the joy of being a parent."

"He's a good kid, and a very smart kid at that."

"Chet, I have to get something to eat, and then go to the embassy. There's paperwork that must be completed before Daddy and I can leave. They need copies of the police reports, and a statement from him as soon as he's strong enough."

"What a hassle. Has he told you anything?"

"No." Her voice caught. "Chet, the first words he spoke to me were questions and concerns about Anya. It broke my heart to tell him she was in jail. He just can't give up on her."

"Speaking of not giving up, Terry Redmond came over today looking for you. He asked me if we were living together. For a minute there, I thought he might want to take me apart. I'm telling you, doll, I'll fight him anyway I have to, to keep you with *me*."

She went silent. Terry Redmond hadn't entered her mind. Being pulled in so many directions, she couldn't think about Terry or Chet. Her father was the most important man in her life, and would be until he got well again.

"Mariska?"

"I'm here. Chet, I can't think clearly right now, except for my —"

"I know. I had to tell you, that's all."

"Good night, Digger."

"Good night, doll. I love you."

* * * *

Monday, after he buttoned up the funeral home, and before he went to retrieve Chris, Chet drove to Risky's house to feed the dogs and take the big boys for a run.

Following the same loop Risky usually took, he nodded to Oscar, Edgar, whatever his name, when he passed the house, but didn't slow down. On his second pass, the old man was standing at the front gate.

"Hey, you! Them ain't your dogs. Where's my little gal?"

Chet stopped and grinned when Harley and Shep stood on their hind legs in front of the old man, begging to be petted. He bent with hands on his knees to catch a breath. "I thought she was my little gal."

"Don't be a smart aleck."

"Sorry, can't help it."

"So, where is she?"

"I strangled her and buried her in the yard. I couldn't stand the fact she was in love with you."

Edgar made a sour face and flapped his hand dismissively. "You goldurned hippies is all the same."

"Look Ed—"

"That's Ed-gar, hippie. So where is she?"

"Look, I'm short on time, Ed-gar. I have to pick up my son. If you'd like to come by Mariska's house in a couple of hours, I'll explain everything."

"How do I know you won't strangle me and bury me in the yard?"

Chet resumed jogging and yelled over his shoulder, "I guess you'll just have to take your chances, Ed."

* * * *

Chet cleared the kitchen table and set a cup of coffee in front of Edgar. The old man listened carefully to Chris's long explanation of why soldiers were braver than Marines, even though his Gramma's dead husband was a Marine, and she said Marines were soldiers.

Chet patted Chris on the shoulder. "Okay, Private Jensen. Round up your troops and put them in their hut. Time to hit the shower then your bunk. Reveille at oh-seven-hundred."

Chris shot an eye-rolling glance at Edgar. "Whisky doesn't have a real shower. She has a funny old tub and a spray thing."

"You get along like your daddy said, sonny. Us senior officers have some top secret strategic plannin' to do."

Before long Chet rejoined the old man, topped off his coffee, and poured himself a cup. "He's down for the night. Four dogs are sharing his bed."

"He reminds me of my son, Oscar, at that age. Too smart for his own britches."

Chet smiled, and sipped coffee. "I won't deny he's a challenge. I love him so much it scares me."

"So, what's happenin' with my little gal?"

Chet told Edgar as much as he felt Risky would want him to know about the incident with her parents. He and Chris would stay at her place until she came home then they'd move back to his apartment in town.

He noticed the old man rubbing his knee. "How's the knee. Still painful?"

"Damn doctors, got me all messed up. Gotta wear a brace, but at least I can make it around on my own. Had to get away from Oz and the daughter-in-law quick as I could. That woman hovers over me so much you'd think I was addlepated."

Chet nodded. "You're a lucky man, Ed." He smiled inwardly as Edgar scowled at the nickname.

"You got honorable intentions with my little gal?"

Chet grinned. "Hell, no."

"You got yourself some competition in the form o' that doctor feller. I saw how cozy they was when I was in the hospital."

"Yep." Chet sighed. "I got my work cut out for me."

"What business you in? That makes a lot o' difference to women. Them're calculatin' creatures."

"I'm an undertaker. I own Jensen and Jensen."

"Ha. Won't be long before I'll be one of your customers, I suspect. Good luck with the little lady on that one. It don't stack up well to doctorin.'"

"Tell me something I don't know, genius."

Edgar got to his feet with a scoffing snort. "I gotta get on home. You tell my hippie girl I come to ask after her."

"I'll do that." Chet stood and put the empty cups on the sink. "Watch those front steps of yours, Ed."

"Mind your own business." But Ed wore a wry smile on his weathered face when Chet walked him to his car.

Tiptoeing into the bedroom, Chet gazed at his innocent son, and Risky's dogs piled on the small cot. He chuckled and shook his head at the memory of Christian's untimely interruption of his lovemaking plans with Mariska. Like she said, his life would never be the same again.

After washing the dishes and cleaning up the kitchen, he went to the dog run to see if Harley, Shep and the orphans were settled for the night. They all slept in a big wooden doghouse that Bobby built years earlier.

Bobby counted the hours until Anita's return, as if they hadn't been together for two years before they got married. Bob was a different man. In spite of the fact he sent her off with Risky, Chet knew he worried about her precious cargo.

Back inside the quiet old house, Chet's heavy chest weighed him down with loneliness. Risky wouldn't be checking in tonight. He picked up the Flynn novel, but couldn't concentrate. He needed a strategy for Terry Redmond. And he needed it before Mariska got home.

* * * *

Nadia's Apartment, three evenings later.

Mariska racked her brain to think of a polite way to ask Nadia to turn off the endless loop of classical Russian composers, Mussogorsky, Tchaikovsky, Borodin, Sokolov, and now Rachmaninoff. The music evoked horrible memories of her childhood, but Nadia had no way to know.

Her mother played the Russian composers at window rattling volume, day in and day out when she was home from *the place*. It was as if she'd been deprived of her precious music, and had to soak up as much as she could before her next crisis.

Anya never accepted the fact that Mariska had no desire to take ballet classes. All Risky really wanted was to ride her bike, *out-boy* Bobby, and play with her dogs. Convinced it was the filthy dogs that kept her daughter from becoming a ballerina, she schemed constantly to rid them from Mariska's life.

Oh, for some Vince Gill, Garth Brooks, Hootie and the Blowfish, or even Daddy's beloved Beatles. Anything but Russian music. Please! No more.

Nadia rhapsodized over the finish of Rachmaninoff's Third Piano Concerto. She placed her hand over her heart. "You like?" She sighed. "So beautiful."

Risky hadn't the heart to do other than smile and nod. She stood, yawned, rubbed her eyes to mime sleepiness, and pointed to the bedroom.

Crawling under a mountain of goose down comforters, she dragged a pillow over her head and prayed for sleep. Instead, her mind swirled with disjointed visions of Terry, Chet, her dogs, her father, and robbed her of the rest she so desperately needed. Tomorrow evening she and her dad would board the air ambulance for the long trip to California, with a layover in New York.

Chapter Thirty-Four

Simi Valley Hospital

Risky peered out the back windows. Terry waited at the rear entrance of the hospital as the ambulance carrying her and her father backed toward the doors.

The moment she stepped out, he embraced her, and murmured concern and apologies for her ordeal. He accompanied Dave's gurney to ICU and stood by until he was settled.

"Mariska, Dave's physician is reviewing the records sent by the American Medical Center in Kiev. Your father's asleep now. Would you come to the cafeteria with me? We could have a cup of coffee and catch up."

She sighed. "I'd like to, Terry, but I'm bone tired. I need to go home and get some sleep so I can come back this evening and sit with Daddy."

"I understand completely. I'll be off shift by then. If you don't mind, I'll look in on you and your dad later."

Risky's heart ached at the gray color her dad had taken on during the long trip back. He didn't look good at all, and hadn't said much during the brief periods when lucid. "No, I don't mind. Maybe we'll have a chance to talk then."

She turned at the sound of Bobby's voice.

"There you are, cuz. I made Anita stay home, but I'll stay here with you as long as you need me." He crushed her in a strong hug.

In his sympathetic embrace, her ability to hold it together crumbled. She sobbed against his shoulder.

He took his car keys from his pocket. "Here, brat, take my car and go home. You look like shit."

"I can always count on you to flatter me, Bobby." She wiped her eyes with the heels of her hands. "If Chet's still there, I'll have him drive your car back. The two of you can figure out the logistics after that."

She looked around for Terry, but didn't see him. Maybe he'd gone back to the ER. She'd feel more like talking to him later. "Bobby, call me if there's any change, right? I probably won't be able to sleep, so if you think I should be here, call."

"Will do. Now get going." He placed his hands on her shoulders and gave her a gentle shove toward the door. "Don't worry about the car. Anita will pick me up."

Bobby was as steady and dependable as a big brother. He teased her unmercifully, but he always had her back. Love for him swelled in her chest and tears clogged her throat.

God, she was so tired.

* * * *

When she pulled into her driveway, Edgar's truck was parked off to one side. He stepped out and waited for her.

Eyes wide with surprise she approached him. "Hello, Edgar. What are you doing here?"

He opened his arms and hugged her. "How's my gal? I come to see how your daddy was doing, and if you needed anything."

Risky rewarded him with a kiss on the cheek and a smile. "Careful there, you're in danger of losing your grouch reputation."

"Aw heck, that was gettin' old anyhow, don't you think?"

She took his hand. "Come around back with me. I need to say hello to my babies before I go inside."

Edgar hobbled alongside her. The dogs saw her approach and went nuts with joy. "What a racket! I see you got two new ones."

"They're temporary. My boss is trying to place them in good homes." She opened the gate to the dog run, and a rush of pleasure washed over her at the sight of their loyal, loving expressions of happiness. "Come here, babies. Mama's home."

Once they'd all managed to be touched by her, they raced around with excitement. Risky straightened up. "I didn't see Chet's car. Was he here when you arrived?"

"Him and the boy was just leavin'. He said to tell you he'd wait for your call so's he'd know when you had time to see him."

She took his arm. "Come inside. Have a cup of tea with me. It's great to see a friendly face after all this time."

"Friendly? Looks like I lost my touch already." He patted her hand at his elbow and followed her inside.

Her house sparkled. It looked like an entire cleaning crew had been washing and polishing for days. There was no sign whatsoever that Chet or Chris had been there for almost ten days. A feeling of loneliness and loss brought a lump to her throat.

Hours later, the sound of the cell phone in her pocket startled her into consciousness. After Edgar, left she'd fallen asleep sitting up on the couch. Her heart thumped with fear as she fumbled to find the Talk button.

"What?"

Bobby's voice sounded grim. "I think you'd better get over here, babe. Uncle Dave is asking for you."

"I'm on my way." Her heart pounded so hard her chest ached.

* * * *

Risky arrived at the hospital and ran to her dad's room. Anita had joined Bobby to wait for her. Unshed tears sparkled in her eyes when she reached for Risky's hand.

"Is he ...?" Please, God, no, please, she prayed.

"He's awake. He wants to talk to you."

She hurried to her father's bedside. His lips were blue, his color grayer than before. Placing her hand softly on his cold cheek, she leaned close. "Daddy?"

Dave's eyelids fluttered. "Is that you, my beautiful girl?"

She smiled through tears. "If you mean Mariska Williston then yes, Daddy, it's me." She gripped his hand and her heart squeezed when he didn't press back.

"Mariska, I have some things to tell you. Please listen. My will, deeds, and other important papers are in the safe at the warehouse. Bobby has access to everything."

Shaking her head hard, she protested, "Oh, Daddy, we don't need to talk about that now. You're going to be well soon and ..."

"No, sweetheart, listen to me. I want to apologize to you for any unhappiness in your childhood. I know I neglected you because of the years I tried to help your mother."

His words stabbed painfully in her heart. "No! Daddy! You have nothing to ..."

"Hush, Mariska. Listen. It's important to me that you know I realized what I was doing, but I couldn't stop. I hope you'll forgive me. I love you so much. I'm so proud of the woman you've become."

Risky dissolved in tears. She kissed her father and rested her forehead against his. "Daddy, I love you, please don't leave me yet. Please. I forgive you for anything you think you did wrong. But you didn't, Daddy, you didn't do anything wrong!"

"I'm very tired, baby girl. I need to sleep for a while. Stay here with me. I'll be right back."

But he didn't come right back. He smiled when she nodded then closed his eyes, and he was gone.

In a panic, she shook him. "Daddy! Daddy! Help, please, somebody help!"

A man's hands gripped her shoulders. "Step back, give them room to work." A nurse and a doctor rushed past her.

Risky struggled. "No! Daddy!"

"Mariska, honey, they're doing whatever they can. Step outside with me for a minute."

The man who led her from the room was Terry. She didn't know he'd been standing there in the doorway of her dad's room. "Terry, Daddy's ..." She put her arms around his waist, sobbed, and dropped her head on his shoulder.

Bobby and Anita hovered, offered murmuring reassurances then Anita took her hand, and led her to a chair.

The horrible sound of the heart monitor flat line alarm screamed endlessly in her head. Nurses rushed in and out of the room. Finally, someone turned it off. The silence was deafening. Risky's heart sank. She raised her head to see Terry talking to the attending physician.

He glanced at her, a stricken look in his eyes. Daddy was dead. Nobody had to tell her. Daddy was gone.

* * * *

It was very dark. A chilly breeze whispered through the canopy of the old eucalyptus. Risky lay on her back and stared at the sky, all the dogs clustered around her on the cold, damp grass. She couldn't remember how long she'd been lying there with them.

Bobby and Anita had protested when she begged them to go home and leave her alone. She needed to be alone. Their sympathy and compassion an oppressive weight she couldn't bear a minute longer. Finally, they left.

Going through the motions of feeding her babies then unpacking her suitcase, she stumbled about in a timeless daze. How long had she been lying on the grass? Abandonment lay heavy in her stomach and chest. Empty, she was ... so ... empty.

Shep licked her face and pawed her chest. His nervous whine woke her from a black well of sleep. A sharp pain in her chest startled her as it all came back. She sat up and stared into the cold fog of morning. Daddy, her daddy was gone.

A torrent of icy hatred for Anya so nauseated her, she could barely summon the strength to struggle to her feet. Stumbling to the back door, she fell to her knees and vomited on the cement path. Again, and again, until there was nothing more. Then again.

Her dogs circled nervously around her. Their distressed whines added to her sadness. She tried to placate them with a few words. On her feet, she fought with the garden hose while washing away the mess she'd made. Bending forward she doused her head with the shockingly cold water then flung it aside and turned off the faucet.

Run, she needed to run. A long, hard run would help her think, but as soon as she reached Edgar's house she tore up his front path, onto his porch and smacked her hand on the door.

The old man yanked the door open and stepped out. "What's wrong, little gal?" He opened his arms. "Come in here."

Through wrenching sobs she cried, "My daddy died, Ed. He died. I don't know what to do. What should I do?" She made a vicious swipe at her damp hair, pushed it back.

He tugged her hand and led her to his sofa. "You set yourself down in here beside me and we'll talk about it. You just go on and cry all you want. It'll make you feel better." He picked up a box of tissues from the side table and placed them in her lap. "You got to do it, child."

Through a wad of them she pleaded, "Please don't tell me everything is going to be all right, because it isn't."

He rubbed her back. "No, I ain't going to tell you that. Things ain't going to be all right, not for a good while. We both know that."

Once she'd calmed a bit she asked him if he knew the details of what had happened to her father in Kiev.

"That good lookin' undertaker feller told me he got hurt real bad in some kind of altercation. That's all he said."

Risky filled him in on the details. Ed shook his head and patted her hand during her broken narration. Other than a few grunts of sympathy, he let her talk without interruption.

She slammed her hands against her knees. "I hate her! I hope they hang her. He was so good to her. She murdered him, Edgar. That's not right, that's just not right."

He nodded. "I can see how's you'd feel that way, but I don't think your daddy would want you to agonize over it. Whatever happens to her is in the hands of them police over there. She's never gittin' back in your life, little gal."

Risky dropped her head in her hands then gave him a wobbly smile. "I have to go home. There has to be plenty of things I need to do."

He stood. "Come in the kitchen. I have some biscuits in the oven. I'll scramble up some eggs. You need to eat."

Without protest, she followed him and sat at the kitchen table. He set a steaming mug of coffee in front of her. She took a tentative sip.

"Ugh. This stuff would take paint off."

"Shut your trap and drink it. It's good for ya." He popped a light smack on the back of her head. "Show some respect for you elders."

Risky smiled and nodded. "You're back in form Ed-gar."

Chapter Thirty-Five

An hour later

Chet paced in agitated loops around Mariska's front yard. Where in hell was she? Bobby hadn't seen her since she left the hospital in his car last night. Anita drove Bob here to pick the car up later, but because the house was dark, they assumed she was sleeping, and left.

Risky's dusty SUV stood in the driveway, her kitchen door wasn't locked. There was no sign of her. All the dogs, including the little ones, were in the dog run. They wagged their tails when he walked through the back yard, by now a familiar figure around the place. They mostly ignored him.

He strolled to the end of the driveway and peered down Box Canyon Road in both directions. As he turned to go back to his car, he spotted her jogging from the direction of Edgar's place. Chet hadn't thought to go by there. As far as he knew, the old man was back with his son up in Bishop.

Unaware of his presence she pounded in his direction, her eyes focused on the road ahead of her. Her short black hair stuck out in all directions, flapping in the breeze. She raised her head and stopped.

Chet stepped out on the road and walked in her direction. She watched him, and then hands on hips, continued forward at a slow pace.

He raised his hands. "Where in hell have you been, doll? We've all been looking for you."

"You look like you're mad at me, Digger." She wiped the sweat off her forehead with her arm and shaded her eyes.

He shook his head regretting his angry words, and attributed them to worry. "No, just anxious when we couldn't find you." He embraced her, kissed the top of her head. "You okay?"

"No." Her chest heaved. "I don't know what I'm going to do without

Daddy."

He slung a long arm around her shoulders. "Come on, let's get you home. You need to call Bob. He's frantic."

She put her arm around his waist and pulled him closer. "I'm so sick of crying, Digger. I feel like I'm sleepwalking through a nightmare."

Her distress brought acid to his throat. "I'm really sorry, honey. I know what it's like to lose your dad. It takes a while for reality to set in." Chet knew from experience that words of sympathy only brought on new waves of sadness and despair. He'd let her do the talking.

She tilted her head to his shoulder. "I hate this reality. It sucks."

"Yes."

"Life totally stinks sometimes, doesn't it, Digger?" She stopped walking and turned to stand in front of him. "You got a kiss to spare?"

"All you want." He kissed her with tenderness, grateful to have her back in his arms. Heart thudding, he lowered his cheek to her head. "Anytime."

A rusty pickup slowed as it passed them. The driver shouted, "Get a room!" grinned and sped off.

Risky's ragged chuckle warmed his heart. "You know that guy?"

"Yeah, Clint, my neighbor." She pointed to the place just beyond her house.

"Looks like a junkyard."

"Please. He's a collector of rare and valuable antiques." She smiled into his eyes. "Anybody can see that."

He kissed her nose. "I stand corrected."

"How's the little guy?"

"He's been worried about you ever since you left. I think he was afraid you'd never come back, like Noreen."

Stricken, she said, "Oh, the poor little guy. Where is he? Can we go see him now?"

He smiled and jingled his car keys. "Absolutely, doll, he's at Mom's, but first you should call Bobby and lock up the house."

"Yeah, I need a shower. I'll make it fast. You let Bobby know I'm okay while I do that then we can leave. Is it a plan?"

"It's a plan." He smacked her on the bottom. "Get a move on." He thought it best not to mention that he would be picking up Dave's body from the hospital morgue late in the evening.

* * * *

Risky entered Millie's house ahead of Chet when he opened the door without knocking. "Hello? Anybody home?"

Chris and Slick bounded into the entry hall. "Whisky! Whisky's home." He grabbed her around the waist. Slick couldn't get traction on the tile floor and slid into her legs. He scrambled with excitement.

Hugging Chris and patting Slick's head, she laughed. "Wow. It looks like I was missed." She bent down until her face was even with Chris's. "How've you been, handsome?"

His rosy face and big blue eyes brought a clog of unshed tears to her throat. She wouldn't cry though, she'd cried enough. She hugged the little boy. He took her hand and pulled her through the house and out the back door.

Millie smiled and patted her back as she passed. Risky could tell Millie couldn't say anything. She just pressed her lips together and nodded. That was fine. That was good. Words weren't necessary.

Christian showed her his big battle. He'd set up his soldiers behind mounds of dirt and rocks in one of Millie's flowerbeds. He'd even dug a river and built a bridge of twigs across the widest part. Even though no water flowed in the river, she marveled at his rich imagination and endless explanation of every part of the scene.

"These are the bad guys. The good guys are here."

Chet carried over some lawn chairs then a small table, where Millie set a tray with sandwiches and steaming mugs of hot chocolate. They chatted and laughed during lunch.

Later Mariska couldn't remember what they'd talked about, but it wasn't important. They'd all been together, and the love warmed her, relaxed her and eased her pain.

* * * *

Chet's cell phone sounded off. He answered and walked away from them to talk. When he returned he carried Chris to the guest room. "Time for a nap, buddy."

Chris scowled and stiffened. "No, I want to stay with Whisky."

"You'll see her again soon."

Reluctantly accepting the inevitable, Chris yawned and petted Slick. "Is Whisky going away again, Daddy?"

Chet brushed sweaty curls from his son's face. "I don't think so, but sometimes people leave for a time because somebody needs them, or something needs their attention. It's usually nothing to worry about it."

Christian's chin wobbled. "Is my mama ever coming back?"

Drawing a deep breath, Chet shook his head. "No, Christian, she can't come back." He tapped the little boy's chest. "But she'll always be with you. Right here. She'll always love you."

Chris rolled over and faced the wall. Chet pulled the blanket over both of them. "I'll see both my little buddies later." He tilted the blinds to darken the room then rejoined Mariska and his mother.

"Mariska, that was Bobby on the phone. They'd like to meet with us at my place. He wants to talk to you about some instructions your dad left with him before the trip to Ukraine." His stomach churned at her stark expression. "It shouldn't take long."

Millie stood and piled the empty plates and cups on the tray. "You two go on. I'll watch Christian until you come for him, Chester." She put her arm around Risky. "I'm so sorry for your loss, Mariska. Please call me or drop by if you ever want to talk."

Risky nodded mutely. Returned Millie's hug and took Chet's proffered hand. "I'm okay. Let's go."

As they were about to get in Chet's car, he hesitated. "Wait. I want to show you something. It'll only take a couple of minutes."

"What is it?"

"Walk down the street with me." A long half block along Millie's street he stopped in front of a sprawling California Ranch Style house. He led her to the side gate and opened it.

"What are you doing?"

"You'll see." They walked along the side of the house to the open back yard. Beyond the expanse of grass, a long dog run took up an entire side, surrounded by chain link fence. Avocado trees were planted across the back. On the side where they stood, several fruit trees grew along the block wall, separating them from the neighbors.

"Nice, isn't it?" He swept his arm in an arc. "It's at least half an acre, not counting where the house sits. The house is three thousand square feet and has four bedrooms. Do you like it?"

"It's beautiful. Whose house is this, Digger?"

"Soon as escrow closes at the end of the month, it'll be mine." Her brave smile tickled him.

She gasped. "You bought this house? Chris is going to love it here. He can walk to his gramma's. Slick will be in heaven in all this grass." She squeezed his hand. "I didn't know you were shopping for a house."

He chuckled and shrugged. "My place is too small to tolerate much longer. I hadn't begun looking for a bigger place when Millie told me her neighbors were putting this on the market. It fell right in my lap."

She had a faint twinkle in her eye when she poked her finger in his chest. "A few weeks too late to keep Chris from walking in on us, huh?"

"That's not likely to happen again, doll." He kissed her. "We should go.

Bobby and Anita are waiting."

Her mood changed abruptly, and her shoulders stiffened. She pressed her lips together.

"I know, doll. We'll make it as easy as we can."

He drove the short distance to Jensen and Jensen. Risky dropped her head on the backrest and stared out the passenger window. Every now and then, she'd brush a tear from her cheek. He hated to see her suffering, but there wasn't much he could do about it.

He parked the car and led her to the back door of the funeral home. She stopped and pulled away from him. "No. No, Chet. I'm not going in there."

He took her hand again. "Bobby and Anita are waiting in my office. This won't take long. It'll be okay."

"No!" She yanked her hand free. "I can't go in there. I won't."

He reached in his pocket for his keys. "Okay, you don't have to. We'll talk upstairs. Take my keys and go on up. I'll have them join us there." Hands on her shoulders, he brushed a kiss on her forehead. "All right?"

Risky didn't answer. She took his keys and climbed the stairs. He stood for a moment and watched her before he proceeded inside the mortuary.

* * * *

Mariska opened the door to Chet's apartment and went directly to his bathroom. She stood leaning against his sink, her hands gripping the sides, eyes closed tight against a threatening flood of tears. When would it stop hurting so much? Why couldn't she do the simplest thing, sit with Bobby and plan her dad's funeral? Daddy wasn't downstairs. He couldn't be there yet. Chet would have told her.

She heard Bobby's voice when he entered the apartment with Chet and Anita. Her hands overflowing with cold water, she splashed her face again and again. Gritting her teeth in an attempt to control her turmoil, she pulled one of Chet's precisely folded towels from the bar and buried her face in it.

Her eyes seemed too big for her face. She stared at her reflection, her irises so dark she couldn't see the pupils. Spider webs of red marred the white. Dark puffy smudges beneath emphasized her sharp cheekbones. She looked like a terminal cancer patient. God! She was a mess.

Chapter Thirty-Six

Risky took a deep breath, ran her fingers through her hair then joined the others in the living room.

Anita patted the spot next to her on the couch and took her hand when she sat. "We'll get through this fast, honey. Bobby has everything sorted out."

Risky took another deep breath. "Thanks, Bobby. I'm sorry I'm such a wuss. You and Anita have gone way beyond for me. I appreciate it."

"Don't worry about it, babe. That's what family is for."

That was true, but what had she ever done to help Bobby? She'd behaved like a jerk at his dad's funeral, had always expected him to be there for her, and what did he get in return? Damn little.

Chet set a tray with four bottles of water on the coffee table. He pushed a box of tissues in her direction.

"Dave came to me before they left for Ukraine. He arranged everything. All you and Bobby have to do is decide on details."

She raised her eyes and directed her gaze to Chet. "Are you ... did he want you ...?" Hands icy, her stomach threatened to revolt. Chet would do whatever undertakers do—for Daddy? He gazed at her with smoky compassionate eyes.

Bobby raised a hand. "Uncle Dave was very specific about that, Risky. It's spelled out right here." He held up a small sheaf of papers.

Chet stood. "Perhaps I should bow out of the conversation for now. I think you'd be more comfortable with family only." He strode to the door. "I'll be in my office."

When the door closed, a wrenching sob shook Risky. Anita moved closer and put an arm around her shoulder. The sound of Chet's footsteps grew faint as he descended the stairs. "I didn't want him to leave, but I never thought ... I don't know what I thought.

"For a while I forgot what he is. I love him, but I can't be ... I can't stand what he does. I feel like Daddy's death means I'll lose Chet too."

"Look." Bobby pointed a finger at her. "I'm not going to baby you anymore. You have some choices to make, starting now." He picked up a file folder, and held it in front of her face.

Anita shifted uncomfortably. "Bob, you don't need to be so —"

"Yes, babe, I do." He set the folder down and turned over a few pages. "You listen up, Risky. We *are* going to sort this out, and we *are* going to honor Uncle Dave's wishes no matter what hang-ups you have. Do you understand me?"

He had every right to speak to her that way. It was time she faced her fear of funerals. "Yes. Go ahead." She lowered her elbows to her knees and rested her head on her hands.

Bobby proceeded to read Daddy's instructions. Dave wanted to protect her, like he always had, by arranging his own funeral, to spare her that painful responsibility. He specifically chose Jensen and Jensen and pre-paid everything, including a small reception for friends and family following the service, if Mariska approved.

Dave made the same arrangements for his wife. He accepted Mariska's feelings about her mother, but he loved Anya and wanted her funeral to be handled with dignity and respect, if he weren't there to arrange it. He specified Chet to personally carry out his wishes.

"Are you listening?"

She raised her eyes and sat straight. "Yes." She'd get through this. She owed Bobby, and she owed her dad.

Bobby picked up another paper. "This is his life insurance policy. It's in the amount of five hundred thousand dollars. The beneficiaries are you and the company, in equal parts. Dave owed a large debt to the company, and he didn't want you to lose your small share of stock because of it."

Risky shook her head. "I didn't know that."

"Of course you didn't. He kept everything from you. We can discuss some other time whether or not I think that was a good idea."

"He used to joke with me," Risky murmured, "and say he was worth more dead than alive. He probably wanted to tell me more, but didn't."

Anita hugged her. "He loved you so much."

Risky nodded. "He loved Anya, too. He said he couldn't explain it. She was a vampire, sucking the emotional and financial life out of him. No wonder he owed money to the company." She gazed at Bobby. "Is the insurance enough to pay what he owed?"

"Almost. I'll write off the rest."

"No, Bobby. I'll pay it."

"You don't have to."

"I'll pay it, Bobby!" A rush of anger filled her. Her daddy, the man she loved more than any person in the world, had been a fool about Anya. Risky would pay the debt. That was the least she could do with the insurance proceeds.

"That's up to you. It'll take about half your insurance payout to clear it."

"Good. Fine. That's what we'll do."

"Should I continue?"

"Yes." Strength she didn't know she had filled her. "Tell me everything, Bobby. No more secrets. I'm entitled to know, and I want to do as Daddy wished."

He smiled and reached over to pat her knee. "Good girl."

Daddy left the family home to her, free and clear. He told Bobby she'd probably want to sell it, and that was okay with him. He also left her a large parcel of property at the edge of town, zoned in a way that would allow her to construct the dog rescue facility of which she'd always dreamed. Finding a way to finance it would be her problem.

When Bob read that part of Dave's instructions, she burst into a new round of tears. He put the file down. "Okay, we'll take a little break, then I'll ask Digger to come back, and we'll finalize the funeral. Are you ready to handle that?"

Risky nodded, scrubbed her eyes and blew her nose. "Time I grew up, huh?"

"Fraid so, Dog Breath. Happens to all of us." He stood and stepped around the coffee table. "Give us a hug."

A few minutes later Chet rejoined them. "Look, Mariska, I have a trusted employee who is more than capable of handling everything if you don't want me to."

"No, it's okay. Daddy wanted you. I'm not going against his wishes." She wobbled a smile. "I'm fine." She wasn't fine, really. The cold reality of Chet's occupation turned her stomach. "Bobby and Anita will take me home."

Chet cocked his head. "Would you like me to come over later?"

"No. I want to be alone for a while. I need to be alone." She dodged the hand he was about to place on her shoulder. He dropped it, and deep hurt filled his eyes.

"We'll talk later then."

"Yes." She avoided further eye contact with him, and picked up her sweater. "Let's go, Bobby."

* * * *

Just before midnight, Risky heard a knock on her door. Her heart squeezed. It had to be Chet. She was glad he came. She loved him. They'd find some way to iron out any difficulties that would keep them apart.

She pulled the door open. "Terry?" Her heart sank.

"Hello Mariska, I hope it's okay for me to be here."

She reached for his hand and tugged him inside. "Of course, Terry, I'm happy to see you." Really? Was she happy to see him, or did his presence further complicate things?

"Come in."

"Mariska." He pulled her into a hug. "I missed you so much, and I'm so sorry about what's happened. I was hoping you'd let me stay here tonight."

She stiffened and pushed back from him. "Terry, I don't want to ... I can't even think of ..."

No! No, that's not what I meant. I want to be with you. That's all. I was hoping I could offer you a friendly shoulder to lean on."

A hot blush flared in her face and neck. She hugged him. "Oh, Terry, you're such a good man. Yes, I'd like you to be here. I don't know how much longer I can stay awake though, I'm totally numb with jet lag, and the rest of it."

"I know, sweetheart." He followed her to the couch. "We don't need to talk. If you have to fall asleep, go ahead. I just want to hold you."

Terry, such a wonderful guy. She'd missed him, missed his sweet ways and his warm sense of humor. But as soon as he'd left town she'd jumped into bed with Chet. What had she been thinking? Terry'd made it plain how he felt about her. He'd trusted her.

Disgusted with herself, she sighed. She should be with Terry, not Chet. Terry was safe. He didn't have that air of danger and risk she always felt with Chet. He didn't fire her with lust the way Chet did, but she didn't need the emotional roller coaster she was on every time she and Chet, and now Christian, were together. No. She wanted a calm, steady, predictable man like Daddy, like Terry.

Resting her head against Terry's shoulder, she sighed, a sense of relief filled her. Relaxing for the first time in days because of Terry's warm steadiness, she smiled and rested her hand on his cheek. "I've missed you."

He smiled back. "Me too. I'm so glad to be here with you, Mariska." His hand rubbed up and down her arm as he pulled her close.

When she could no longer keep her eyes open, she struggled to stand. "I have to sleep, Terry. Would you lie down with me?"

He put his arms around her and grinned. "I'd love to. No funny stuff, I promise."

"I trust you." And she did trust him. She'd always known that he was a man to be trusted. "Come on then."

Terry reclined on her bed while she went to the bathroom to brush her teeth and put on her pajamas. When she returned to the bedroom, he reached across the bed and flipped the covers back so she could slide in. He lay on top of the blankets.

She turned on her side as he dropped the covers over her and snuggled against him. Terry rolled to his side and put his arm across her. He raised his head and kissed her cheek. "Good night, sweetheart."

* * * *

The next morning after Terry left, Risky prepared to take the dogs for a run. The phone rang. It was Chet. She let it go to voicemail.

He called again around mid-day. "I'm just checking to see if you're okay, doll. Let me know."

She didn't answer. Didn't return his call. He didn't call again.

Chapter Thirty-Seven

David Williston's Funeral

Chet hovered at the edge of the chapel. Constantly checking to make sure everything went as planned. Mariska sat in the front row with Redmond, his arm around her shoulders. He hadn't spoken to her since she left his apartment two nights ago. She hadn't returned his calls. Bobby had been his only contact since then.

When she entered the chapel, she glanced in his direction then quickly looked away. Redmond held her hand, and helped her to her seat next to Bobby and Anita. Anita pressed her lips together and barely shook her head when Chet made eye contact with her.

The ceremony was simple. An old friend of Dave's delivered the eulogy. Bobby and another friend spoke briefly. Mariska sat like a stone during the service, never raising her eyes. At the conclusion, Dave's favorite George Harrison song, All Things Must Pass, played softly in the background.

That was the first time Chet detected an emotional reaction from Mariska. She pressed her hands to her lips and rested her head on Redmond's shoulder.

Bobby hung back as the other's left. He shook Chet's hand. "I don't know what to say, Digger. She's barely said two words to me or Anita the past two days."

Emptiness filled every corner of Chet's mind and body. "If you don't mind, I'll pass on the reception. It'll be awkward. Your house and—you know?"

Bobby shoved his hands in his pockets. "Sure. I'm glad Uncle Dave didn't want a graveside service. You did a great job." He looked around the chapel, pointed. "With all this. Thanks, Chet."

"That's my job." Indeed. His job, his chosen profession. The job he found rewarding and satisfying. The very thing Mariska couldn't seem to accept.

Bobby gripped his arm. "Look, man. Give her some time."

Chet shook his head. "I don't know, Bob." He rubbed his forehead. "I gotta go." He turned on his heel and walked through the chapel and out the back entrance to his office. He had work to do. Another funeral this evening would take up most of the rest of his day.

First, though, he'd go to Millie's house and spend some time with his son.

* * * *

Risky was relieved Chet didn't appear at the reception. Anita had hired a local caterer to ready their condo, while they attended the funeral.

Terry stayed at her side. They'd spent many hours together since he showed up at her front door. He patted her arm. "I'll help Bobby at the bar. You okay?"

She smiled a smile that felt foreign on her face. "Sure. I'm fine. I need to talk to some of Daddy's friends. You go help Bobby."

Anita approached her then pulled her aside. "What's going on, Risky?"

"What do you mean?" Anita's meaning was clear, but she didn't want to have a conversation about it. Not now.

Anita gazed directly into her eyes and shook her head. "Okay, forget it." She turned and walked away.

Anita had been her best girlfriend, her only girlfriend really, for the past four years. They met at the vet when Anita carried in an abandoned puppy. She hadn't known what to do with the poor little thing. He was sick and hungry.

Risky assured her they'd take good care of him and find him a home when he got well enough to be adopted. Anita wrote down her phone number, and asked Risky to call and let her know how he was doing.

Three days later Risky did just that. She told her the pup had improved, was eating the kennel food, and wagged his tail when she checked on him. Anita asked her if she'd like to have a cup of coffee or a drink after work, and Risky accepted.

They hit it off immediately and couldn't have been more different.

Anita had long, straight, light brown hair, and an oval face complementing her sweetly rounded, softly feminine figure. A good six inches shorter than Mariska, her sunny personality never failed to evoke laughter and warmth. Qualities foreign to Risky.

Risky introduced her to Bobby not long after that. He'd been complaining about the lack of quality women in his sphere. Risky warned him to be nice, because if he did anything to hurt her friend, she'd beat the piss out of him. Not that she could, but he got the message.

All these years Risky had been able to tell Anita anything. But now she chose not to explain or justify her rebuff of Chet. Bobby told her it was time to grow up. She intended to do just that, and Digger Jensen didn't fit into her grownup plans. He represented powerful emotional turmoil, and she didn't need that in her life anymore.

Terry had what she needed. Strength, steadiness, quiet conversation, gentle loving. Yes, they slept together again last night, and this time she invited him make love to her. Sweet lovemaking. Slow, tender and warm, kind and considerate.

Terry would provide the life she wanted. A life without turmoil and drama.

He asked her to marry him this morning. He apologized for the bad timing. He loved her, wanted to marry her, have a family with her. He promised he'd always work hard to make life good for them.

She admired his job. He was in the business of saving lives, not the — no, she wouldn't go there. She never had to think about that again. About Chet again.

She loved Terry. She did. Not with the uncontrollable fire she experienced with Chet, but that was destined to be fleeting. That kind of mindless burning passion wouldn't last.

She told Terry she needed time, but she'd made up her mind. She'd marry him. The sooner the better.

* * * *

Same night, 9:00 p.m.

Chet inserted his key in Millie's door and entered quietly. Light came from the kitchen, and muted music played on the stereo in the living room. He went to the kitchen first.

"Sweetheart, you're here." Millie looked up and smiled. "Oh dear, I can see it's been one of those days. Sit down and I'll make you a drink. I could use one myself after chasing my grandson all afternoon and evening. He's only been asleep for an hour."

She kissed his cheek, opened the cupboard, took two highball glasses and set them on the counter. "Maker's Mark and soda, right? I'll join you."

Chet took off his jacket. He groaned, stretched then sat on one of the kitchen chairs. He smiled when his mother set the drink in front of him. "Thanks, Mom, just the ticket." He took a swallow of the mellow Kentucky bourbon. "You've been a godsend for me with Chris."

She put a slender, manicured hand on his. "What's wrong, honey? I always know when something is bothering you. Is it Mariska Williston?"

He sighed, shrugged and took another sip. "Yeah." He held the glass aloft. "Whisky."

"Tell me."

Chet related the events of the past two days, from the meeting in his apartment to the conclusion of Dave's funeral.

"Well, that doesn't necessarily mean what you think it does, Chester. Her father died under awful circumstances. It's been very hard for her. Give her time."

He scoffed. "That's what Bobby said, but I could see it in her eyes, the turning away. She's back with Redmond. I'm history."

Millie sniffed. "Terry Redmond is certainly a fine young man, Chester, but any woman would be a fool to choose him over you."

Chet smiled through his sadness. "You couldn't be a little prejudiced could you, Mil?"

She smiled and squeezed his hand. "Maybe, but I've always been a good judge of men. I don't like those mother's who're always handing out unsolicited advice to their kids, but don't give up, Chester. I think you should relax and let things happen naturally. It's for Mariska to work out. You can't be sure what she'll do this early on."

They finished their drinks in silence. He'd always been comfortable with their long silences. On so many occasions over the years, words were unnecessary between them.

He carried their glasses to the sink. "Time to get Chris home."

"Okay, honey. His things are in the entry hall."

"I may close escrow on my house tomorrow afternoon. They said they'd call me in the morning."

"Oh, Chester. The school called. They can take Christian starting Monday. He's very excited. I'm sure he'll be babbling about it in the morning."

"If I close the house deal, let's the three of us go out and celebrate tomorrow."

"I'd love to."

A well of love filled Chet's heart when he lifted his sleeping child and carried him to his car, and then up the two flights of stairs, with Slick trotting ahead of them. He'd have a new perspective after a good night's sleep.

Chapter Thirty-Eight

Risky's house, One Week Later

Risky handed the pillowcase full of clothes for the dry cleaner to Terry. "I really appreciate you dropping these off on your way to work. After the reading of Daddy's will, Anita's going to our old house with me to do the real estate listing. I'm so swamped."

"No problem. It's on my way." He kissed her cheek then stopped, dropped the pillowcase, and took her in his arms for a proper kiss. "I'm working late tonight, sweetheart."

She smiled and patted his cheek. "I remember. Use your key to let yourself in if I've already gone to bed."

As soon as Terry left, she made the bed and dressed. The dogs would have to wait for their run until this evening. She'd promised Dr. Larry she'd return to work today.

The last person she expected to see when she left the lawyer's office to meet Anita was Chet's mother. Millie Jensen and a gentleman with white hair were waiting for the elevator when Mariska stepped out.

"Mariska, how are you?" She turned to the man. "Jim, do you mind? I'll meet you upstairs in a few minutes."

The man smiled. "Not at all, my dear." He tipped his head to Risky and stepped in the elevator. The doors closed.

Risky swallowed. "I'm doing fine."

"I'm so sorry about the loss of your father. I can only imagine what you've been through this past month."

"Yes, well, uh, how's Chris? Did he start school?"

"Yesterday." Millie smiled. "He was so excited when Chester picked him up after work. He couldn't stop talking, and he couldn't wait to go back this morning."

Risky waved her hand. "Uh, what are you doing ... here?

"Chester closed on the house this morning. I came with his CPA to pick up some papers for him. Jim is my lunch date."

"I'm sorry. It's really none of my business."

"Nonsense. The real estate transaction will be listed in the business notices of the paper tomorrow. Public information."

"I'm late, Millie. It was so nice to see you." Risky took a few backward steps. "Bye."

"Let's have lunch sometime, Mariska."

"Oh, sure." Risky didn't miss the look of confusion and regret in Millie's expression. "Bye."

It was inevitable that she'd bump into Millie or Chet now and then. Bobby and Chet were best friends. They spent a lot of time together. She'd have to learn how to handle herself in these awkward situations.

Anita's car was parked in front of the house when she arrived, but Risky didn't see her, so she walked around to the back of the house. Anita, a hand shading her eyes from the sun's glare, studied the old peach tree near the back bedroom window.

"Anita, sorry I'm late."

"You're not. I got here early."

"Why are you staring at the tree?"

"It's too close to the house. Probably be a good idea to take it down. I see a lot of dead branches." She pointed to limbs in the center of the canopy.

"Gosh, it's so beautiful in spring when it blooms. It'd be a shame to cut it down, but you're probably right. It hasn't had any good fruit on it for years."

"I know you're in a hurry, so I'll get right down to business. I've contacted a surveyor to stake out the property lines, and a home inspection service to do a report in advance of the listing. You'll have to do that anyway, so let's get it out of the way. I recommend you purchase a one-year policy on the appliances. It's an added value for buyers."

"Daddy replaced the stove and refrigerator last year. They might still be on warranty."

"It's easier to have the policy. They're inexpensive, and it relieves you of any hassle."

Anita was all business. There'd been tension between them since the day of Daddy's funeral. Familiar warmth and easiness between them was missing. It hurt. Risky decided to ignore it and act as if everything was fine.

Anita checked a couple of boxes on her listing form. "I know you have to get to work. What are you planning to do with the contents of the house? The furniture, your dad's personal property?"

Risky's stomach churned. "I haven't been in the house."

Anita pressed her lips together and shook her head. "You can leave the furniture in place until after the sale, but you really have to clear out Uncle Dave's clothing and personal possessions, Mariska."

Anita never called her Mariska unless she had a bug up her butt. It was time to clear the air.

"I'll do it, okay? I'm not scheduled to work Saturday. I'll do it then." She crossed her arms. "Go ahead and tell me what's on your mind, Anita. You're ready to boil over."

Anita took a breath, started to speak, changed her mind and stared across the yard past Risky's ear. "Look, it's none of my business."

"Right. It's none of your business, but we're friends, so spit it out. Or maybe I'll just save you the time. I'm going to marry Terry Redmond."

Anita's eyes goggled. "You're what! When did this happen? Does Bobby know? Does Chet know? When were you planning to drop this bombshell?"

Unexpected tears clogged her throat. "I didn't say anything because I haven't actually said yes to Terry. But I will. I am. He loves me."

Anita dropped her clipboard on the grass and put her arms around her. "Oh, honey, are you sure? Why the rush to this decision? Everything is in such turmoil for you right now. Shouldn't you wait and give it more time?"

Risky dragged in several shuddering breaths before she could answer. "Anita, I'm so unhappy and so conflicted. I love Chet, but I could never marry him."

"For heaven's sake, why? He's crazy about you."

A full-throated bawl prevented her from answering. She sat on the grass with a plop and put her head between her raised knees. Anita sat next to her and rubbed her shoulder. "Go ahead and cry."

Risky gasped. "I didn't know there were this many tears in the whole world. When will it stop?"

"I don't know. Just let them out."

After several moments, Risky raised her head. "Anita, promise me something."

"Anything. Tell me."

"No matter how awful I am, please keep being my friend."

Anita's chuckle was soft. "Wow. That's a tall order, but I'll do my best. Now tell me, why can't you marry Chet Jensen?"

"For one thing he hasn't asked me." Risky rubbed her eyes with the heels of her hands. She probably smeared black mascara all over her cheeks, but she didn't care. "Anyway, he's an undertaker."

"And?"

"And, that's it. It creeps me out. I don't know how he can do what he does. We talked about it a long time ago. He even made a joke and we laughed about it, but I just can't accept it."

"Risky, being an undertaker isn't who Digger *is*, it's what he *does*."

"I know, but ..."

"His job is just as essential as Terry's. He performs a great service in his special dignified way. He helps people, Risky, during the worst times in their lives. You know that firsthand."

She rolled her head, rubbed her eyes again and nodded. "Yes, I know all that."

"Do you love Terry?"

"Yes."

"Are you *in* love with him? I know you're in love with Chet. It's all over you every time you look at him."

"I'll get over it."

"Oh, honey, that's so sad. Are you sure? Are you being fair to either of those great guys? Think about it."

That's what she did all afternoon at work. Think about it. She visualized a list. Terry headed one column and Chet the other. When she was absolutely sure she had it all figured out the doubts would creep in, and she'd start rationalizing all over again.

When she got home, she changed clothes, fed her three babies, and laced up her Mizunos. They ran way up the road, further than usual, before she headed back. At Edgar's she opened the gate, led the dogs to his front porch and looped their leashes over the railing.

Edgar must have heard her approach because he had the door open by the time she finished. "Hello, little gal. You had supper?"

She shook her head.

"No? I didn't think so, come on in."

She smiled and kissed him on the cheek. "What are we having?"

"Rabbit stew."

She felt the color drain from her face. "What! Rabbit?"

"It's chicken, but what difference does it make, hippie girl? Somethin' got killed and we're eatin' it."

"I know, but rabbits are so—"

"—cute? And chickens aren't? Think about it."

He had a point. She had to admit it. At least he hadn't said he was serving dog. "Edgar, you're a devil. You get off teasing and provoking me."

"What else is a useless old man supposed to do for entertainment?" He chuckled and dished up the stew. "Lookie here. I put old-fashioned dumplings on top. Used my mother's recipe from the Basque country."

She took a deep sniff. "It smells wonderful. I'm starving."

"Dig in then, before it gets cold." He sat down and patted her hand. "I'm sure sorry for your daddy's death, and your troubles. You come and talk to me anytime you take a notion to, you hear?"

"You may live to regret that." She took a big bite and smiled through chipmunk cheeks.

They ate in silence for several minutes. Risky studied the old man, his unruly mop of gray hair, wild eyebrows and ruddy cheeks. She imagined him as the handsome cowboy of his youth. He had the sturdy body and work worn hands of a man who'd labored long and hard.

"I love you, Edgar." She directed her gaze at him.

He raised his head and shook it. "Forget it, I ain't marryin' ya. I'm too old."

She dropped her fork as an explosion of laughter engulfed her. God, it felt so good. She hadn't laughed so hard in weeks.

Edgar winked. "You're goin' to be fine, little gal."

They sat on his porch and sipped coffee after supper. The dogs competed for Ed's attention. It warmed her heart to see him mumbling nonsense while he patted their heads.

All those years he played the grouch card, and he was nothing but an old softy.

"You and them damn dogs get in my truck. You ain't walking down this road. It's too dark. No moon. Yahoos is always driving too fast." He stood and took their cups. "I'll get my keys."

Risky got the dogs settled in the back of the pickup then opened the passenger door. Edgar's porch light winked on when he stepped out to lock his door. She hadn't noticed until now that he seemed to be walking better.

"How's the knee, Ed?"

"Ed-gar, smart aleck. It's better. No thanks to them butchers at the hospital. Arrest 'em all, that's what I say. String 'em up."

She snapped her seat belt and giggled.

When they pulled into her driveway, they saw Terry's car parked near the house.

"Speaking of butchers—looks like your doctor feller's here. You keepin' company with him?"

"Um hum."

"What about that good-looking man and his boy that was taking care of the place while you was gone?"

She leaned across the seat and kissed his cheek. "Thanks for the delicious stew and the ride home, Ed. I'll see you later." She stepped out of the truck and called the dogs.

Terry stood when she walked in the kitchen through the back door. "Who was that?"

"Edgar. He fed me and dropped me off. He wouldn't let me and the dogs venture out on the dark road. When did you get here?"

"Just a few minutes ago."

"Have you had dinner?"

He shook his head. "I'll rustle up something."

She detected tension in his voice. "Is something wrong?"

"You tell me. I'm not sure. There was a man's white dress shirt in the things I took to the cleaner's. Care to explain?"

No. She didn't care to explain. Her cheeks flushed with unwelcome heat. "Explain? I'm not sure I like your tone, Terry."

He remained silent. His face immobile except for a small tic of one eyebrow.

She threw up her hands. "Oh, for heaven's sake, it's Chet Jensen's shirt. I borrowed it from him because I got something spilled on me when we took Chris to Disneyland for his birthday. Happy?"

Nice, Risky. Nice beginning. Lie to him. A great way to start a marriage. Disgusted with herself because the lie rolled off her tongue so easily, she regretted her snotty attitude.

"Look, Terry, I'm sorry. I'm just tired."

He stood and embraced her. "I'm sorry too, sweetheart. I'm jealous of Jensen, I admit it. It's your history with him." He smiled and kissed her nose. "Forgive me?"

About to deny that she had any history with Chet, she stopped herself before she piled on another lie. She wouldn't do that again. She'd never lie to Terry again. Her mother lived in a world of lies and deceit. She refused to be like Anya. "Yes, I forgive you." She stroked his chest. "Want to take a shower?"

His handsome face broke into a broad grin. His eyes sparkled. "I thought you'd never ask."

Their lovemaking that night had a desperate quality to it. Terry seemed as if he were trying to prove something to her, to himself. She responded with deliberate enthusiasm and warmth. He deserved it. A good man, he deserved her to love him and only him. Otherwise, why were they together? Here. In her bed.

The next morning he asked her again if she would marry him.

Chapter Thirty-Nine

Two days later Risky picked up Chet's shirt from the cleaners. She drove to Jensen and Jensen and parked in front. It wasn't five yet, so he was probably still in the mortuary. She took a breath to calm her nerves. Paused a couple of seconds then stepped out of her car.

A faint chime sounded when she entered. She didn't remember hearing it the last time, actually the first time, when she delivered Beau's ashes so long ago.

The same old gentlemen approached her. "Hello, again, Miss Williston. What may I do for you?"

Her lips formed a trembling smile. "Is Chet Jensen in?"

"Yes, you can just catch him." He pointed down the hall. "He's preparing to pick up his son from school. His office is the last door on the left."

She steeled herself to keep from running. She had to talk to Chet, but dreaded it, dreaded being in this place again. She never expected to return here after Daddy's funeral.

She tapped on the door. "Chet?" A chair squeaked, and footsteps approached the door. The next second he stood before her, eyes shining, smiling.

Oh, God.

"Doll! I'm so glad to see you. Come in. I have to leave in a minute to pick up Chris. He's been asking for you. Would you like to go with me?"

Relieved when he didn't embrace her, she nodded. "Um, sure. I came to return your shirt, but I'd love to see him."

He pulled his suit jacket off the coat rack by the door, took the shirt hanger from her and hung it on the same hook. "Great. We'll go out this way, my car's out back."

She stopped, thought of taking her own car, but decided that was silly. They'd pick Chris up from school and return here. The entire thing would take no more than half an hour. "Okay." She followed him to the back exit.

Risky was too tense to engage Chet in small talk on the short five minute drive. He seemed to feel the same. It was a relief when they arrived at the preschool. Chet told her he'd only be a minute or two.

Chris bounced with excitement when he saw her in the car. "Whisky, Whisky, look what I made." He held a finger painting and pressed it against the car window.

Chet opened the back door of the car. "Come on, son. You can show Risky the painting when I get you buckled in."

He handed the picture to Risky, lifted Chris and plopped him into his car seat.

Risky twisted so she could see his face. "Oh, Chris this is beautiful. I see the sun and the trees." She pointed to four stick figures." Who are these people?"

Eyes wide, he pointed. "Me, you, Daddy, and Gramma, and that's Slick." His head bounced like a bobble-head doll.

Smiling, she blinked back tears.

He chattered the short distance back to Chet's apartment. She laughed at his description of the teacher and told her, in great detail, the entire day's activities.

Chet pulled into his parking space. He looked into her eyes. "Stay here for a minute, please." He opened the back door and helped Chris out of the car. He handed him a key. "This is the key to the door. Remember, I taught you how to put it in the lock this way? Go on up and get your dog. He probably has to pee by now."

Chris trudged up the stairs. Chet opened Risky's door and drew her into his arms.

She returned his hug, but her breath was short and her spine painfully stiff. She longed to be in Digger's arms, but then—not.

He contemplated her. "How are you, doll? Is everything okay? I've been concerned."

"Chet I have to tell you something."

She pushed back from him and blurted it out, "I'm going to marry Terry."

He went still, looked like he'd been slapped in the face. His eyes glittered with an iciness she'd never seen. "Congratulations. I hope you'll be very happy."

Her chest hurt. "Chet, I'd like to explain."

"What's to explain? You're marrying Redmond. You love him. You don't love me."

His words stabbed right into her heart. "It's not that simple."

"What then? You do love me. You don't love Terry, but you're marrying him all the same?"

Oh, God.

She choked down a clog of tears in her throat. "Yes, I do love you, Digger, but I could never marry you. You don't understand. I just can't accept what you do for a living. If there was any way that you could ..."

Anger flared in his eyes. "Could what? Change my career, maybe my whole life?" He shook his head, his lips twisted with disgust. "Try this on for size. I love you, Mariska, I'd marry you if you'd promise to never rescue another dog, quit your job at the vet's, and bring some order and discipline into your life."

His irate words slammed her. She had no response.

Chris descended the stairs with Slick and led him to some bushes.

Chet's jaw muscles twitched. "I'm sure you have someplace else to be, Ms. Williston." He turned his back on her and watched Chris.

Frozen in place for several seconds, she raised her hands to her face and shuddered then snatched her purse off the seat of Chet's Lincoln. She walked, nearly ran, to the far side of the building.

She heard Chris's plaintive question. "Where's Whisky going, Daddy?"

All the way home, she sobbed. Why was it so hard to leave Chet? She loved him, and Chris too, but that whole scenario was too complicated, too full of emotional risk. She was sick of emotional upheaval after living with it all her life.

Terry would give her a good life. He accepted her as she was, no questions asked. He loved her. But Chet loved her too, and Chris loved her. She was on the fast track to hurting all of them including Bobby and Anita. But she had to think of herself. Marrying Terry was best for her.

Terry's car wasn't there when she got home. Limp with relief, she went inside the house, fed the little dogs, and took a hot shower. As hot as she could bear. She stood under the water until it cooled. How long had she stood there to have gone through thirty gallons of hot water?

She should have felt better, but she re-played Chet's words over and over. Each time, every word stabbed her in the belly. She dumped her cinnamon hair rinse down the drain. Sick to her stomach, she turned off the water. What was left of the cinnamon scented body cream went into the wastebasket with a vicious bang.

"Mariska? You in there?"

"Terry?" Her hand went to her throat. "Yes, I'll be out in a minute." She yanked a towel off the bar, wrapped it around her body, and slumped on the toilet seat, hands shaking. Sweat mixed with the water droplets growing chilly on her skin. The bathroom walls and mirror were blanketed with a layer of moisture. She stepped back in the tub and reached to open the small high window.

"I brought dinner, sweetheart. I was hoping to beat you here and have it all set out."

God, the man was so sweet and thoughtful. She swallowed the acid rising in her throat. "Thanks honey. I'll be right there." She dried off and put on her Harry Potter peejays.

* * * *

Terry jumped up from the table, all smiles, brown eyes dancing, when she entered the kitchen. "There you are." He put his arms around her and gave her a crushing hug. "I miss you every minute we're not together."

Because she couldn't honestly say the same, and wouldn't break her vow never to lie to him again, she put her arms around his neck and kissed him. She wrinkled her nose. "What smells so good?"

"Chinese. I hope you like it."

"I love Chinese." At least that was true.

* * * *

After dinner, she went outside to feed the big dogs while Terry cleaned up the table, and washed the few dishes they'd used. She came back inside and saw he'd pulled on a sweatshirt over plaid pajama bottoms, and was sliding a DVD into the slot on the player.

"You got a movie? What is it?"

"Dear John. Do you like Nicholas Sparks?" He sat on the couch and patted the cushion next to him.

Great, just what she needed, a Nicholas Sparks tearjerker starring, to-die-for, Channing Tatum. Once she got started sobbing she wouldn't be able to stop. "Yes, I love Nicholas Sparks." Oh, damn, damn, damn. Not exactly a lie, but not the whole truth either.

"Good. We can watch it and cuddle while we cry. When we take a break I'll make some popcorn."

She cocked her head and smiled. "Do you cry at movies, Dr. Redmond?"

"Oh, God, yes, Ms. Williston, I'm a real sob sister." He grinned and held up a box of Kleenex. "You gonna throw me out?"

How lucky could a girl be? A handsome, sexy, macho guy who cries when watching chick flicks? She sighed with relief. He wouldn't think her tears were anything but a reaction to the movie. "Nah." She pushed her three babies out of the way and sat next to him. "You can stay."

They only made it halfway through the movie. Their necking got super heated, and Terry had his hands under her pajama top. Without interrupting the kiss, he pushed the dogs off the couch and lowered Risky to her back. Grinning, he slipped off her pajama bottoms and pushed his out of the way.

"My God, Mariska, I can't keep my hands off you." He lifted her leg and brushed a kiss on the side of her knee.

The kiss and his hands were very nice. Everything about him was very nice. She should be crazy about him. She wanted to be crazy about him. "Terry?" she mumbled against his mouth, and stopped when he moved between her legs.

He pushed back so he could see her face. "What? Am I hurting you?"

She shook her head. "No I wanted to ... to tell you something."

He chuckled. "Now? Can't it wait?"

"No. Terry, I have to tell you right now." She caressed his cheek. "You asked me to marry you. Yes, I want to marry you." There. That wasn't too hard. She said it.

He let out a whoop and kissed her hard. "When?"

"Tomorrow?"

"Can't, I have to work tomorrow."

"Oh, yeah, me too."

"I've got four days off starting day after tomorrow. Want to drive my Pontiac to Vegas?"

"Yes, and Terry, I want to have kids right away."

"I'm a happy man, sweetheart." He kissed her eyelids then her nose and her chin. "I'm also a doctor. I know how everything works. Shall we start that project tonight?"

Her heart thundered. "Yes. Tonight. Now."

* * * *

She lay awake staring at the ceiling. Terry slept beside her like a corpse. He earned it. Wow, did he earn it. She wanted to get pregnant right away, and he did everything he could to make sure it happened. Twice. She told him she'd been off the pill since her trip to Ukraine. Condoms never left the drawer.

He rolled over, woke up, grinned at her, and they did it again. Her wish was Terry's command.

* * * *

211

Chet's Apartment

Chet called Millie and told her he and Chris couldn't make it for dinner that evening. He had a bad headache, and wanted to stay home and kick back.

"I'm sorry, sweetheart. I'll tell you what. I invited Jim Fowler over for dinner on Saturday evening. Why don't you and Christian join us?"

"I don't want to horn in on your date, Mil."

"Don't be silly. It's Jim. We've known him for years. He's like family."

"I don't think Jim sees it that way. I can tell when he looks at you, Mom. He's dying to get you in bed."

His mother's laughter always evoked a smile, no matter what kind of mood he was in and tonight it was black.

"Chester. I may at some point invite Jim to sleep with me, but he'll have to earn it, and he's not quite there."

He pictured her beautiful face. "Well, when Jim does 'get there' I doubt there'll be much sleep happening."

"I certainly hope not. Now, you take something for that headache get to bed early."

No problem following those orders. It looked like getting to bed early, and alone, would happen at his place for a long time to come.

Heartbroken, angry, and puzzled, he prepared dinner for himself and Chris. He'd thought Risky'd finally accepted what he did for a living. What happened? It hadn't come up in a long time. Everything changed when she returned from Kiev.

Did they really have that brief, steamy, uninhibited love affair, or was it his imagination? He sure as hell thought it was real. Right up until he put her on that airplane, he had zero doubts about their future.

Mariska Williston was the only woman he'd fallen flat on his ass in love with since Noreen. She had no similarities to Noreen, or any other woman he'd ever known, for that matter. The instant he'd laid his hand on her shoulder at Jack Williston's funeral, she'd enchanted him.

Why was he so bewitched? Could it be because she was the most unconventional, disorganized, maddening, strangely beautiful, sexy and bizarre female he'd ever encountered?

The woman should have come with a caution label tattooed on her forehead. Warning:

Use with extreme caution. Use only as directed, but you may be sorry even if you do. Don't drive or operate machinery until four hours after use. Repeated use may cause loss of vision; dangerous levels of sexual desire; loss of motor skills; the inability to think clearly.

He may have felt this crappy at some point in the past, but he sure as hell couldn't remember when. His ability to attract women effortlessly was more a curse than a blessing. He could have a different woman in his bed every week if he wanted to play that game. But he didn't. Hadn't for a long time.

The only two women he'd ever truly loved were lost to him.

Hot fat spattered on his hand when he turned over the eggs. "Shit! Shit! Shit!" He dropped the spatula and stuck his hand under cold water.

From the corner of his eye, he saw Chris look up from his art project, staring at him with disapproving eyes.

"That's a bad word, Daddy. Wash your mouth with soap."

Chet turned off the tap, gripped the edge of the sink and laughed. He touched his precious little boy. "If I apologize for saying it, can I skip the soap this time?"

Chris considered the request with a sober expression. He put his elbow on the table and rested his cheek on his hand while he thought about it. "Okay. This wunst."

Chapter Forty

Veterinary Clinic, two days later.

Updating the new lost-and-found page on the clinic's website, Risky's concentration fractured when her cell phone rang. "Hello?"

"Risky, it's Anita."

Oh, God, Chet must have told Bobby what happened.

"Risky, are you there?"

How would she explain? "Yes, sorry, I'm working on the computer. I lost my concentration for a few seconds."

"I have an offer on Uncle Dave's house. It's on the low side, but I'm pretty sure we can hold out for a higher price. The buyers want to meet us at the property this afternoon. When do you get off work today?"

She'd forgotten about the real estate listing on Daddy's house. Anita wasn't calling because she knew anything about her and Chet. What a relief. "I get off at three thirty. Is that too late?"

"No, that's perfect. Still plenty of daylight left. I'm pretty sure they're serious buyers. They want to inspect outside as well as inside of the property."

"Great. I'll meet you there around three forty."

"Good. I'll tell them to come at four. That'll give us a chance to talk before they get there. Bye, gotta run."

"Anita? Do you ...?" She'd already disconnected. Risky was left to worry for the next few hours. What did Anita want to talk about? One way or the other her friend would be royally pissed that she hadn't mentioned her world-changing decision to marry Terry Redmond. Best friends shared that kind of information.

The fact that she hadn't told Anita the very next morning brought on a nasty headache when she went back to the computer screen. She should have confided in her. God, she was such a coward. If accepting Terry's proposal was the right thing to do, she'd have been on the phone as soon as he left for work, anxious to share the happy news.

The front office clerk stuck her head around the door. "Good news. The owner of one of those strays just came in, all excited to get her furry friend back. Would you come up front and talk to her?"

That was a bit of happy news. "Sure. Do you know which one?"

"The scruffy little mongrel we named Orfink. She put her finger right on his picture and broke out crying."

Bless all the dog lovers in the world. There was nothing happier than reuniting them with their lost pets.

Risky followed the clerk to the front of the clinic.

The sweet looking blue-haired lady had the photo in her hands, and talked to the younger woman with her.

"Hi, I'm Mariska Williston. I have your dog at my house."

"Oh, God bless your heart. I'd almost lost hope of finding Sugar Angel after all this time." Tears of happiness sparkled in her eyes.

Sugar Angel? Risky and the clerk exchanged secret glances. Buster, maybe, but Sugar Angel?

"If you'll wait here for about half an hour, I'll go get him. Is that okay?"

"Oh, my dear, take as long as you need. I'm so thrilled to find my little darling. I'm happy to wait."

The younger woman put her arm around the old lady. "I'm glad you found him, Mom, but why don't we go to the drugstore to pick up your prescription then come back?"

"Oh, of course, that's the sensible thing to do. Then we can take Sugar right on home."

Risky smiled and pulled keys from her pocket. "Good. I'll see you back here about two then?" She turned to the clerk. "Tell Dr. Larry where I went, okay?"

* * * *

Shocked to see Terry leaving her front door when she pulled in, she rolled down her window and waved. "Terry, what are you doing here in the middle of the day? Are you okay?"

"Dammit, Mariska, you're spoiling my surprise. Do you have to go in the house?" His hands on top of his head, he looked as disappointed as a small child who'd been told there was no Easter Bunny.

He was so cute. She had to smile. A surprise, he was planning a surprise for her. She stepped out of her car and gave him a hug. "No, I don't have to go in the house. You're not going to cry are you?" She poked him in the chest. What a sweet man. She was so lucky.

He flashed a dazzling, happy smile. "No. I'm not going to cry, you goldurned hippie, you. What are you doing here?"

"Orfink's mama showed up at the vet's and wants her baby back. I came to get him."

Terry glanced at the dog run. "Which one is he?"

"That pug-ugly little ragbag who's always harassing poor Shep." She pointed, and laughed. "See? He won't leave the old guy alone."

Terry followed her to the dog run. She pulled a kennel leash from her back pocket before she opened the gate. "Come, Sugar Angel. Your mama wants you to come home."

Terry snorted. "Sugar Angel?"

She looped the leash over the dog's head and nodded. "Yep. Believe it or not that's Orfink's real name."

"That mutt has a mug only a mother could love." He walked back to her SUV and opened the passenger door. "Up you go, Sugar Angel. Your mother awaits."

He kissed Risky. "Speaking of mother ... any morning sickness, dizziness, other hopeful symptoms?"

She kissed him back and shook her head. "Not yet."

"I see I have work to do."

"Oh, yes, you do." She pushed back from him. "I gotta get back. I'll be a little late. Anita and I are meeting a potential buyer at Daddy's house."

"Good." He smacked her bottom when she turned to get back in the car. "Do not — I repeat — do not walk through that front door before five."

She winked. "I promise," and blew him a kiss. What a prince. In every way, almost, but definitely more than enough.

Stop rationalizing, Mariska!

At three-forty on the dot, she pulled in the driveway behind Anita's Escalade. To see that bitty girl drive the monster car always made Risky smile. It used to be Bobby's, but he insisted she drive it because of her 'condition.' He took her Corolla back and forth to the warehouse.

"Hi." Anita hugged her. "My instincts say we have serious buyers. First he came alone then he brought his wife to see it the same afternoon, now they're coming back together."

"Sounds promising." Risky turned and stared at the house. She had many happy memories, and so many horrible ones associated with her childhood home.

Galahad, her puppy, had grown up happy and robust during the two years

Anya was gone, after she threatened to kill him by pushing him in the garbage disposal. Talk about a roller coaster. Ugh. Her stomach churned at the memory.

It's a wonder she didn't grow up totally tweaked. If it weren't for Daddy, she couldn't imagine what would have happened to her.

They walked around the side and Risky stopped. She pointed to the back of the yard bordering on Bobby's childhood home. "When did that happen?"

"The block wall?" Anita shook her head and snorted with disgust. "Just went up in the past few days. Bobby's last stepmother had it constructed. She still lives over there. What a vindictive witch that one is. She's still pissed that Bobby got sole possession of the business."

"Gosh, it really looks out of place to me. She has that huge back lot. Why would she go to the expense of a concrete block wall? There was already a chain-link fence there."

Then she noticed something even more disturbing. "What happened to the old tree house? Bobby and I spent half our kid years up there. And the tree! It's gone."

"The bitch from hell told Bobby she always hated it, and now it was hers to take down."

An unexpected wave of nostalgia filled Risky with sadness. "I loved that old pepper tree and the tree house. It was my sanctuary too many times to count."

Anita put an arm around her waist. "The bad news is Bobby couldn't do anything about the tree, but the good news is he took the house apart and put it in storage. He plans to reconstruct it if we buy that old homestead on Tapo Canyon Road. The property has lots of big old trees."

"How long have you been waiting for that place?"

"Over a year." She sighed. "It's way too much for the elderly widow to take care of, but she can't bear to part with it yet. That's okay. We have plenty of time. In fact, Bobby offered to renovate the guesthouse. He told her she could stay on the property as long as she wanted."

Risky sighed and shook her head. "My cousin, your husband, is a God. How that ever happened with him having Uncle Jack for a father is a mystery."

Anita smiled. "A happy mystery though. I worship at his godly feet, but if you ever tell him that, I'll kill you." She turned at the sound of voices. "Oh, they're here. Let me do all the talking. I mean it."

"No problem." They walked to meet the smiling couple.

* * * *

An hour and a half later Anita and Risky shook hands with the new owners of the Williston residence. Risky gazed at her girlfriend with newfound admiration. "I can't believe you got them to come up another fifteen thousand dollars. When did you become such a super negotiator?"

Anita grinned and turned around. "Here." She pointed over her shoulder. "Pat me on the back. I deserve it." She wagged her hips for good measure.

Risky complied. "You sure do. I thought we were asking too much when you took the listing."

"Shows what you know. That's why I told you to let me do the talking. I happen to be good at this job. Anyway, I'm getting a nice fat commission, so it was money in my pocket too. Soon as I found out her parents were giving them the money for a cash deal, I knew how much wiggle room I had. "Let's go back inside and do the furniture inventory. You need to take another look at everything before I call the Goodwill truck. You may decide to keep something. I wish you'd change your mind and have an estate sale. You have some really nice furniture here."

Risky reached for the door. "No." She shook her head. "Too many bad memories." She put a hand over her heart. "I'll keep the good ones in here."

"Look, as long as you're giving it away do you mind if I take some of it? We could use some pieces to furnish the guest house on the property we're trying to buy."

"Take anything you want. I'm sure Bobby can find a place in the warehouse to store it. Take it all. Then you'll have plenty of time to decide what you need before the rest is donated."

They walked through the big old house. A tsunami of memories bombarded Risky. Her old bedroom overflowed with little-girl white furniture. A puffy cotton candy colored canopy over the bed matched the café curtains on the window. A fancy dollhouse Risky never had any interest in, gathered dust in the corner. It took Daddy years to accept she'd never be a girly girl.

Half hour later they returned to their cars. Anita grabbed her arm. "Oh, I almost forgot. Can you, Chet, and Chris come for dinner on Saturday? Bobby's dusting off his outdoor grill."

Her breath caught as a hot blush burned her cheeks and chest. "Uh, no, I can't. I'm going to Las Vegas for a couple of days."

Anita grinned and shook her finger. "Can't wait to gamble away the money you made on the house today?"

Now. She had to tell Anita right now. "Not exactly. I'm ... Terry Redmond and I ... we're getting married."

Shock and disbelief painted Anita's face. She jerked back like she'd dodged a blow. "You're ... you're ...?"

"Yes. I'm marrying Terry. We're leaving for Vegas in the morning. I know it might seem sudden, but ..."

Anita put her hands over her ears and drew in a shaky breath. "Sudden! Were you even planning to tell me? I can't believe what I'm hearing. Are you out of your mind? What about Digger? You told me you were in love with Digger."

Risky swallowed. "I like Digger a lot, but ..."

Anita glared. "You like him a lot? Cut the crap, Mariska. It's me, Anita, your best friend, remember? You're crazy for him. You told me what a breathtaking lover he is, how you admired the way he took to being a father. The first honest to God grown-up man you ever compared to your dad. What happened to 'I can't imagine life without him?' He went out and bought a house big enough for you and all your dogs. I can't believe I'm hearing this."

"I know all that. I did feel that way, but Terry loves me. He wants to marry me. He's a doctor. Chet's a ..."

Anita shook her head. Her lips twisted in an angry sneer. "A what, Mariska? God, how is it I never saw what a shallow twit you are?" She stepped in her car, stuck her head out the window and said, "Have a nice life. See you around." The window slid up, and Anita stared straight ahead.

Risky got in her car and backed up so Anita could get past. Brokenhearted, she watched as the black Escalade disappeared around the end of the block.

Chapter Forty-One

Past six when she parked in her driveway, Risky turned off the engine and stared at the old house. All the lights were on. Terry's shadow passed the kitchen window. A short flare of light flashed as he bent over the table. He must have been lighting candles.

His surprise. She remembered now. Sweet, wonderful Terry was making a surprise for her. She choked back threatening tears and shook her head. No. She would not cry. This was entirely her decision, and it was the right decision. She and Terry would have a nice life together.

She put a smile on her face and knocked on the kitchen window. "Can I come in, honey?"

"Be right there." He sounded so happy.

Terry threw open the front door. "Surprise! Close your eyes." He picked her up in his arms and carried her inside. "Keep 'em closed until I say it's okay to open them."

He set her on her feet. Put his hands on her shoulders and turned her around. "Okay, open."

Her living room bulged with flowers. Flowers on every surface. Champagne chilled in an ice bucket, and two of her best crystal glasses, fresh raspberries in the bottom of each, winked in the candlelight.

Her hands flew to her mouth. Tears pooled in her eyes when Terry stepped forward and embraced her, pulled her back against his chest. He kissed her neck. "I love you, Mariska. You make me so happy."

She turned in his arms. "Terry, honey, you're one in a million. Thank you so much. I'm so lucky." Yes, she was lucky. Overcome with emotion, she rested her head on his shoulder. "I'm lucky, lucky, lucky."

His kiss was so tender her lips trembled against his. He raised his head and grinned. "This isn't all." He opened the bedroom and the three small dogs scampered into the room. Each wore a big pink ribbon, and a small box dangled at their necks.

"What?" She reached out and fingered one of the boxes. "What is this?"

"Not yet. Sit down and I'll pour some champagne."

She sat and the dogs joined her on the couch, competing, as usual, to be closest to her face.

Terry handed her a glass of champagne. "To us, my darling." He sat next to her. "Now you can open the boxes. Brutus first." He untied the ribbon and dropped it in Mariska's lap.

Hands shaking, she slipped the ribbon off then pulled the smaller bow. She gasped at the beautiful diamond solitaire gleaming in a white satin nest. "Oh, Terry, it's so beautiful. Thank you so much."

He lifted the ring from the box and slipped it on her finger. It fit perfectly. Lifting her hand, he kissed her palm and pressed it against his cheek. "I'm so in love with you."

Oh, God.

She threw her arms around him, kissed him. "Terry, honey, you're wonderful." That was true. "I love you." That was also true. She did love him. Who couldn't love him?

His smile nearly melted her heart. He handed her the next box from Minnie's neck.

Tears escaped her lower lashes and slipped down her cheeks. The box held a beautiful, diamond encrusted wedding ring, made to match the solitaire.

He lifted it from the box and held it in the palm of his hand. "When I put this on your finger day after tomorrow, it will be one of the happiest days of my life."

He handed her the third box. "Now from Mickey." It contained his wedding ring, fashioned after hers. She gazed at him with love and gratitude in her heart. This truly wonderful man would be the one she'd spend the rest of her life with.

He kissed her softly. "I hope you're hungry. I made dinner."

Her eyes opened wide. "You can cook, too."

He grinned and sipped more champagne. "I left something on the bed for you. Why don't you change and meet me in the kitchen?"

On her bed, a beautiful Nordstrom's box waited. She opened it and gasped at the filmy, silk kimono and matching gown. Pressing the soft fabric to her cheek, she sighed at her marvelous good fortune.

When she entered the kitchen, Terry stared with admiration and love. "Wow. You are so beautiful."

Embarrassed at his raw gaze of pure lust, she blushed hotly. "Shouldn't I save this for, you know, Vegas?"

He shook his head slowly. "Nope. You won't have it on for long." He pulled out a chair. "Let's eat. You're going to need your strength."

The candles burned low as they finished eating, and then drank the last of the champagne. They hadn't talked much during dinner. Mostly they'd exchanged significant glances.

Terry stood and reached for her hand. "Let's make a baby."

* * * *

Early the next morning Terry loaded their bags in the back seat of the Pontiac. He met her at the door. "You ready, sweetheart?"

She nodded, and raised her face for a kiss. "Yes, lover man, I'm ready." He locked the front door. "Don't forget I have to drop my keys off with Ed."

"I guess he wasn't such a grouch after all." Terry grinned as he backed out of the driveway.

"Nah. It was all an act."

Terry waited in the car when she walked to Edgar's front door and knocked.

"Good morning, hippie girl. You and your sweetie on your way to Lost Wages?"

She held up the keys. "Yep." She kissed his cheek. "Thanks for taking care of my babies."

"I'm gonna bring them three little ones home with me after I feed 'em this evening. I don't like leavin' them out in your yard all night. Too many coyotes 'round these parts."

"You are an old softie, Ed." She held up her hand. "Sorry, Ed-gar."

He spotted the ring when she waved her hand. "I see things is moving right along with you and your doctor feller. You wouldn't be gettin' hitched up there by any chance?"

Risky grinned. "Bye, pops, see you Monday."

Terry squeezed her knee when she got in the car. "What were you talking about?"

"He asked me if we were gettin' hitched."

Terry chuckled. "What did you say?"

"Bye, pops, see you Monday."

"You're an awful tease, Mariska."

"Yeah, I know. Can't help it."

In Baker, they stopped for lunch, and Risky drove the rest of the way. She'd never been to Las Vegas and got so rattled when they got to town, that Terry laughed and asked her to pull over. He knew exactly where they were going.

When the valets opened the car doors for them, she overheard one say to Terry, "Bitchin' ride, man."

Terry'd booked a luxury suite at the Four Seasons. Risky had never been in such a luxurious hotel. She extended her arms and spun around in wonder while the bellman pointed out the features of their suite.

Terry joined her at the balcony, drawing her against him, his arms around her shoulders. He kissed her head, lowered his lips to her ear. "Tomorrow I'm going to carry you across that threshold as my wife."

She pressed against him and rested her head on his shoulder. A barely detectable chill went through her chest. She ignored it and kissed his jaw.

He tightened his embrace. "I booked a table for dinner, but we could eat here if you'd prefer, sweetheart."

"No, let's get dressed up and do the town tonight. Let's have a party." She turned, placed her hands on his cheeks and kissed him once, and then again.

"Your wish is my command. I'm your slave, if you haven't figured that out by now." He winked.

Her stomach cramped at the slave tease. So silly of her, why should she not want to hear that this great guy was her slave? It just didn't sit well really. She pushed it to the back of her mind. "Okay, let's do it."

He grinned. "Do it? Oh, I thought you wanted to go out on the town."

She smiled and smacked his chest. "Now look who the tease is."

After a whirlwind of dinner, entertainment and casino crawling, they returned to the hotel in the wee hours. Terry stopped at the concierge desk and ordered room service breakfast for the morning then booked a couple's massage in the spa after lunch.

Barely able to stay awake, Risky asked Terry if they could just cuddle when they went to bed.

He put his arm around her. "My thoughts exactly. Tomorrow's the big day."

The big day. The day she would marry Terry Redmond. This gentle, kind, great smelling man who held her so tenderly. Who drifted off to sleep in an instant, while she stared at the window, and the artificially bright night sky above Las Vegas.

Breakfast was leisurely and sumptuous. She enjoyed the artistic presentation even though she didn't have much of an appetite at ten the next morning.

After breakfast, they showered, put on the complimentary bathrobes and slippers, and took the elevator to the spa for their massage.

Terry reached across the space between their spa tables and held her hand.

"Your hand is cold, sweetheart."

"I got a little chill on the elevator. I'm fine."

The masseur working on Terry's back asked if they were enjoying their stay.

"Yes, we are. We're getting married this afternoon. This beautiful woman will be my wife in a few hours."

The attendants murmured congratulations.

The masseuse said, "You get a fifty percent discount at the spa as a wedding gift from the hotel. I'm glad you told us."

Risky raised her head and smiled as she withdrew her hand from Terry's. "I'm the lucky one." She was. Lucky. The lucky one. The sinking feeling in her stomach had to be the result of their late night and she hadn't had much breakfast.

* * * *

Terry got directions to the wedding chapel from the concierge while Risky paced in the lobby. She wore the same gray suit she'd worn to Bobby and Anita's wedding. It was the only suitable thing she had to wear to her own wedding. Everything else in her closet was either too casual or too bizarre.

Terry tipped the valet generously when he brought the tricked-out muscle car to the entrance. Once they were seated, Terry put his hand on her shoulder. "Soon as we can both manage some time off I want to take you to Seattle to meet my parents. They'll be crazy about you."

Tension rolled down her spine. His parents. He'd told her his dad bought the Pontiac for his graduation from medical school. Other than that she couldn't recall him mentioning his parents.

She gazed at him. "Did you come from Seattle?"

"Yep. Born and bred. My Dad's in upper management at Boeing. He's worked there for almost thirty years. Started out as an entry level aeronautical engineer."

"And your mother?" It seemed strange that he'd never talked about his parents.

"She's a hospital administrator."

"Do you have any brothers or sisters?" Why had she never asked him these questions? She was marrying him. She should have asked these questions.

"I have an older brother, Frank. He's a research scientist at Cal Tech." Terry smiled. "He's the real over- achiever. I'm the stupid child in the family." He chuckled. "At least that's what Frankie says."

"I don't think I like Frank." It was beyond silly for her to feel so offended, but come on, who would ever say such a thing about Terry?

"You'll like him. Everybody likes him. Even me." He glanced at the note in his hand. "I think we're here. Yes, I see the parking entrance."

He parked the car, rounded the back and opened her door. "You ready?"

Her knees went weak when she stood. "Yes, but I really have to pee first."

Terry put his hands on her cheeks. "You sure you're okay? You look pale, your cheeks are cold."

She pulled his hands away and stepped back. "I'm fine." A whopper, if she'd ever told one. "I mean, of course, I'm nervous. I never got married before." She doubted her smile looked very reassuring.

He put his arm around her shoulders. "Let's go inside, they were very clear about being on time. I bet they have a powder room right near the lobby."

Risky found the ladies room just off the lobby, as Terry predicted. She used the toilet then stared at her reflection in the mirror. "Come on, Risky, you can do this. You want to do this." She took a deep breath and refreshed her lipstick.

All of a sudden, she became aware of the piped-in music in the ladies room. Her breath caught, she clamped her hands over her ears when she heard the lyrics of the old blues song. "... and he'll be big and strong, the man I love."

She was engulfed by a wave of nausea, and couldn't get out of there fast enough.

One couple waited ahead of them. A smiling bride and groom exited the chapel, several laughing friends in their wake. The couple ahead of Risky and Terry entered the chapel.

A wave of dizziness made her grab Terry's arm. He squeezed her hand and leaned in to kiss her cheek. "We're next, sweetheart."

Oh, God.

The first few minutes inside the chapel were a nauseating blur. They stood before the minister. Terry took her hand.

"Will you, Terrance Fletcher Redmond, take Mariska Anastasia Williston to be your lawful wedded wife? Will you love her, cherish her, and cleave only unto her until death do you part?"

"I will." Terry slipped the wedding ring onto her finger. His sigh was like a sharp smack in her face.

"Will you, Mariska Anastasia Williston, take Terrance Fletcher Redmond to be your lawful wedded husband? Will you love him, cherish him, and cleave only unto him until death do you part?"

She couldn't answer. She'd lost the power of speech, and her knees shook.

Terry leaned closed and whispered, "Mariska?"

Unbidden, tears streamed down her cheeks. "I ... um ... I. No, I ... Terry ... I ... no."

The minister closed his book and stepped back. "I'll step out for a few minutes. Take your time."

"Mariska? What's going on? I don't understand."

"Terry, I'm sorry. I can't do this. I can't do this to you."

"Mariska, this is not funny."

"I know. I want to, Terry, but I can't. It's not fair to you."

His face was void of expression. "It's Jensen, isn't it?"

She couldn't answer and drew in a few ragged breaths. Her lips pressed tight, she looked away from him. She couldn't bear to look at him.

"It's always been Jensen, hasn't it?"

Instead of answering, she pulled off the rings, took his ring out of her pocket, and put them in his hand. Through a racking sob, she managed two words. "I'm sorry."

She fled the room. Left him standing there. Outside she flagged down a taxi and told the driver to take her to the bus station. Terry made no attempt to follow.

Ten hours later, she called Bobby. When he answered the phone, groggy voiced, she glanced at her watch. Two a.m.

"Bobby?" Sobs raked her chest.

"Risky? What's wrong? Are you hurt?"

"Bobby, please come and get me."

"I'm on my way. Where are you?"

"I'm at the Greyhound station in San Fernando."

"Jesus, I don't know where that is."

"It's on Rinaldi. Can you find it on Anita's GPS?"

"Sit tight, we'll be right there."

"No, Bobby. Just you, please."

Chapter Forty-Two

Two Weeks Later

Risky and Anita sat across from each other at the escrow office. The buyers were also present. The sale of her father's house closed. Anita handed her the bank draft without meeting her eyes. They were uncomfortable with each other.

"Anita?" Risky stood as the others filed from the room. "Wait, please."

Anita turned, but didn't answer, her face a mask of disappointment and pain.

"Anita, please. We have to find a way to make up. *I* have to find a way. I'm so ashamed and sorry for all the stupid mistakes I made, for taking advantage of you and Bobby."

Anita sighed and shook her head. "I don't know what to say. You're my husband's cousin. You're part of Bobby's life. But you didn't treat me like a friend, Risky."

"Can we sit down somewhere and talk? I'm trying to find a way to make it up to you, Bobby, Chet and Terry."

"Did you know Terry left Simi Valley Hospital? No?" Anita sighed and put her hands on her cheeks. "I didn't think so."

Risky slumped in a chair, crossed her arms on the table and dropped her head. Wrenching sobs ripped from her throat. She'd made a complete mess of her life, all their lives.

Anita sat next to her and rested her hand on her back. "Oh, Risky, don't cry anymore. It doesn't help. Not really. Come here." She tugged her into an embrace.

"I'm so sorry, so sorry. I don't know what to do. I got laid off from my job yesterday."

"What! Why?"

"I've taken too much time off. Dr. Larry said he might call me back in a few months, when Marcie takes maternity leave, but he didn't make any promises. I'm stumbling around like a drunk trying to figure out what to do."

Anita stood. "Okay, get up, come on. We're going to my house. We'll talk this out."

Risky's chest warmed with a small spark of hope.

* * * *

Bobby came home from work hours later. He walked in the living room, and Anita waved him off. "Have a beer, honey. We'll be through here in a few minutes. We're going to the Golden Dragon for dinner."

He shrugged, nodded and left them.

"I'm fine, Anita. I should go. You and Bobby have done enough."

Anita smiled. "I know, but that doesn't mean there's not more to do. I have a couple of ideas, but Bobby has to be part of the conversation. Go wash your face. You're a mess."

When she left the bathroom, Bobby and Anita were waiting by the front door. She noticed the modest swelling of her friend's abdomen. Anita was beginning to show.

Bobby jangled his keys. "Let's get a move on. I'm starved."

Over dinner, they discussed Anita's idea. Bobby finished off the last of his Tsingtao and motioned for the waiter to bring him another bottle.

"Look, Dog Breath, before you decide to embark on Anita's ambitious plan you need to sit down with a lawyer and a CPA. Develop a business plan with every income-expense scenario from the worst to the best. Then I suggest you take a hard look at the trail of wreckage in your personal life."

"But, Bobby can't you ...?"

"No, I can't. You're a big girl. Do it yourself. It's about time you stopped relying on me so much. I love you, cuz, but I can't be responsible for your decisions. I won't."

This was tough talk from Bobby. Tougher than Risky could remember. She'd really hurt Digger when she dumped him to embark on her loony plan to marry Terry. Bobby didn't say so, but he got caught in the backwash of that pain suffered by his best friend.

"I realize I'm not a baby, but all my life I've had you or Daddy to go to. Now I feel like an orphan."

Bob's smile was grim. "You are an orphan."

She pressed her lips together and sighed. "Yeah."

Anita passed the plate of pork-fried rice. "You still have family. You're not a total orphan. But, Bobby's right, you have to decide on this yourself."

"Okay, I'll contact an attorney and a CPA. Any recommendations or is that not allowed?"

Bobby pursed his lips and wrinkled his brow. "You can use the same attorney we use at the company, you know, the man who handled Uncle Dave's will. As to a CPA, hmm, the only one I know well enough to recommend is Jim Fowler. We do our accounting in-house, but Jim prepares our quarterly and year-end audits. You might want to get some other recommendations before you decide."

A sense of strength and resolve welled inside. She could do this. Yes, she could do this. "Jim Fowler, why is that name so familiar?"

"Maybe you met him at the warehouse? Maybe Uncle Dave mentioned his name?"

Risky shook her head. Curious and confused, she wracked her brain. Why did she know that name?

Bobby told her she'd have to form a corporation to protect herself from liability. She thought a not-for-profit enterprise would be the best. Nearly all the funds for ongoing daily operations would have to come from donations. She'd only take enough salary to live on.

* * * *

The next morning Risky contacted the lawyer. She made an appointment to discuss her plan. She asked the attorney if he had an opinion about Jim Fowler.

"Yes, I know Jim, good man. He has a blemish-free reputation in the community. You can't go wrong there. Why don't I see if he's available so we can all sit down together? That would be a more efficient way to tackle your proposal."

Risky agreed. Two days later, she arrived at the law offices a little early, but the receptionist showed her right in.

She and the attorney were enjoying a cup of coffee when the receptionist announced Mr. Fowler's arrival.

"Send him right in, Doris."

Risky turned when Fowler entered. She recognized him immediately. Her heart thumped.

"Jim, this is Mariska Williston."

Jim smiled and extended his hand. "I believe we met briefly, Ms. Williston. You're acquainted with Millie Jensen. We bumped into each other the day Chester Jensen's real estate transaction concluded."

Risky extended her suddenly cold hand. This was really awkward. What now? "Yes, I remember. Nice to see you again." Amazed at how the lie slipped off her tongue with such ease, she swallowed. She really must think before speaking, like she hadn't been telling herself that all her life.

She cleared her throat. "I, um, that doesn't create a conflict of interest does it? That I know Millie?"

The attorney smiled and shook his head. "Not unless she's involved in any part of your business plan."

"No, she's not."

Jim smiled. "If knowing a client of mine constituted a conflict of interest, I'd soon be out of a job. I've been in this community so long most everyone knows me."

The attorney placed both palms on his desk. "Well then, shall we put our heads together and see what we can come up with?"

Wordlessly, she nodded, gripped her purse and leaned forward on the edge of her chair.

An hour later, the two men, with Risky's input, laid out a plan for the best way to form the legal structure in preparation for her plan to build an animal rescue and adoption center on the land her father willed to her.

Jim Fowler stood. "I'll get right to work on the permitting processes. No use going any further until we know the path ahead is clear for this project. I should have some information for you in about a week." He shook her hand and excused himself.

The attorney nodded. "The process of drawing up the incorporation papers is quite simple, Ms. Williston. I don't think there's any hurry to do that before Jim gets back to us." He stood, signaling the end of the meeting.

A sense of anticipation filled her. "I'm so excited. It seems like this is really possible. Do you think it's possible?"

"Oh, indeed I do. Your facility would be a nice addition to the community. I envision many different activities and educational programs you could incorporate into the main mission of rescue. The possibilities are endless."

During her drive home, she noticed that her spirits had lifted. A sense of hope, direction and determination marked the opportunity for her to get her life on track. To take control of events, not just follow whims. She wanted to share her feelings with Edgar Pauley.

After changing into running clothes and shoes, she leashed up all six dogs, except for Harley and Shep, they didn't need leashes, and took off on Box Canyon Road. There was little traffic this time of day. The air was clear and crisp. She had new energy. Her babies picked up on it. For the first quarter mile, she had trouble keeping up with them.

Edgar, in his usual chair, waved when she passed his house.

She yelled, "I'll be back, Ed. Don't go anywhere."

"Ed-gar, hippie! You autta know that by now."

She grinned and kept running.

On the return loop, she opened Edgar's gate and let the dogs off leash. They scampered and chased each other around his front yard. Edgar motioned her to the porch.

She bounded up the few steps and flopped, breathless, into the chair next to him. "What a great run. My babies gave me a real workout."

He pointed to the tray on the small table between them. "I made some fresh coffee. Have a cup." He winked. "It's about time I saw a smile on that face o' yours."

"I have so much to tell you." She sipped at the coffee. "Hey, this is the best coffee you ever made. You go to cooking school or something?"

"You gotta be one of the biggest smart alecks I ever had the bad luck to encounter, little gal." His smile gave the lie to his words.

"That's why you love me, Ed." She reached across the space between them and squeezed his arm.

He grumbled and shook her off. "That's what you think."

After some more teasing small talk, they lapsed into a comfortable silence and sipped coffee. Finally, Risky opened up and told him what had happened with Chet and Terry. She'd also lost her job and nearly lost her best friend, too.

"Sounds to me like you done threw away two good men. They don't grow on trees ya know."

"I do know. Chet Jensen doesn't want anything to do with me, and Terry Redmond left town. What I did to poor Terry was unforgivable." She gazed at Edgar. "I loved both of them. I really did. But I also knew, deep inside, I was *in* love with Chet and his kid. I was too chicken to stay with him."

Edgar shook his head. "You done bollixed it up, all right."

"Yeah." She shuddered. "But I have to get on with my life and find some way to ask Chet and Terry to forgive me. I have to forgive myself first though, but I don't think I've suffered enough."

"That's a helluva waste of time, if you ask me."

She laughed. "You're good for me, Edgar. You don't beat around the bush and baby me like Daddy always did."

"Sometimes parents do more harm than good. Always tryin' to rescue their kids. We all gotta take a few knocks, get hurt in life. That's how ya learn to live in this world."

The sun lowered below the big trees on the opposite side of the road. "I better get going or you'll have to drive us home." She stood then leaned down and kissed his cheek.

"Get on outta here." He flapped his hand. "Don't leave any of them damn dogs behind."

She laughed and summoned her babies. "I have some plans to tell you about, Ed. Why not come over for dinner tomorrow. I need you to tell me what's wrong with them."

"That ain't for me to figger out, but I'll come and eat with ya anyways."

* * * *

The next morning she forced herself to sit down at the kitchen table and write the long overdue letters of apology to Terry and Chet. Terry's letter was addressed to the personnel department at Simi Valley Hospital with a request to forward. She sent Chet's letter to Millie's address, with a separate note to his mother included in the envelope. It took two hours to compose, write then discard and re-write the pages until they struck the honest phrasing those she'd hurt deserved to hear. The words remained inadequate to explain her callous behavior. When she finished, she punished herself with a long, grueling run all the way down Box Canyon road to Chatsworth Lake and back.

Chapter Forty-Three

Risky's Rescue Center, one Year Later.

The mayor presided over the ribbon-cutting ceremony. Ventura County Star and the local cable TV station covered the festive event. Their congressman attended, not wanting to miss the chance to deliver a speech. Ribbons and balloons waved and bounced in the breeze.

Risky smiled to see Dr. Larry and a couple of his staff from the veterinary hospital in attendance. She was amazed at the big turnout. Pony rides, a cotton candy machine and a petting zoo for kids took up most of the parking lot.

A local food truck, affectionately known as The Gaggin' Wagon, served fast food and drinks. Brad Tucker brought a fire department ambulance and a fire truck for kid's tours. Still, she couldn't believe all these people showed up.

In the middle of the crowd, a tall man lifted a little boy and set him on his shoulders. The boy waved.

She gasped and grabbed her throat.

His handsome dad quirked a smile, and nodded. Chet. Chet was here.

Oh, God.

The End

About the Author
Patricia Campbell

I wrote my first novel at the age of six. It was titled "The Mouse," and was two pages long—including illustrations! My mother saved that *first edition* and every now and then, I take it out and smile over it.

When my beloved husband of many years suddenly died, I'd come home after a long day of work and write. Writing allowed me to pour out all my sadness. Then, the more I wrote, the more I realized I would go on. I would be happy, I had a lot of living to do, and love stories to tell.

I'm published now in Romance novels and an anthology of short stories. But my first two manuscripts still reside on a CD somewhere in my house. I can't bear to erase them because they're mine, they're loved, and like a crazy relative one hides in the attic, they reside in a quiet, safe place.

https://www.facebook.com/pages/Patty-Campbell-Author/536855299661241
https://www.goodreads.com/author/show/6560120.Patty_Campbell
http://www.amazon.com/Patty-Campbell/e/B0092FJY7Y
http://pattycampbellauthor.blogspot.com
http://www.pattycampbell.com

www.ingramcontent.com/pod-product-compliance
Lightning Source LLC
Chambersburg PA
CBHW050515260626
47157CB00004B/1339